André Caroff's
MADAME ATOMOS

The Mark of
Madame Atomos

André Caroff's
MADAME ATOMOS

The Mark of
Madame Atomos

Translated by
Michael Shreve

A Black Coat Press Book

Acknowledgements: Thanks to Françoise Carpouzis & Catherine Losserand.

L'Empreinte deMadame Atomos and *Madame Atomos Jette Un Froid* Copyright © 1969 by The Estate of André Caroff; English adaptation Copyright © 2013 by Michael Shreve.
Introduction, Copyright © 2013 by Jean-Marc Lofficier.
The Woman in the High Castle Copyright © 2012 by Michel Stéphan and The Estate of André Caroff; English adaptation Copyright © 2013 by Jean-Marc & Randy Lofficier.
Before the War, Five Dragons Roar Copyright © 2011 by Pete Rawlik and The Estate of André Caroff.
Cover illustration Copyright © 2013 by Jean-Michel Ponzio.

Visit our website at www.blackcoatpress.com

Table of Contents

Introduction

This volume collects the fifteenth and sixteenth installments of the saga of Madame Atomos, a series of 18 novels published between 1964 and 1970 in the *Angoisse* horror imprint of French publisher Fleuve Noir. Our introduction to Volume 1 contains a biography of its author, André Carpouzis, a.k.a. André Caroff (1924-2009). More information about Fleuve Noir and its popular brands of science fiction and horror can be found in the introductions to the other volumes translated from their imprints and published by Black Coat Press: Richard Bessière's *The Gardens of the Apocalypse*, Gérard Klein's *The More in Time's Eye* and Kurt Steiner's *Ortog*.

The saga of Madame Atomos (her real name is Kanoto Yoshimuta) is about a brilliant but twisted middle-aged female Japanese scientist who is out for revenge against the United States for the bombings of Hiroshima and Nagasaki—where she was born, and where her family died in the nuclear holocaust.

Madame Atomos seeks to repay the United States by unleashing deadly new threats, such as radioactive zombies, giant spiders, a madness-inducing ray, flaming tornadoes, etc. The heroes opposing her are Smith Beffort of the FBI and Yosho Akamatsu of the Japanese Secret Police.

Volume 2 introduced the character of Mie Azusa, a.k.a. Miss Atomos, a younger version of Madame

Atomos, groomed to continue the fight in the event of her death.

In Volume 3, after Mie fell in love with Smith Beffort, she joined the fight against the deadly Madame Atomos who, in the meantime, had returned from the dead.

In Volume 4, Madame Atomos overreaches and the US Army finally destroys her powerful flying fortress. With her organization in shambles, she is forced to re-group, while increasingly devoting all her energies to achieve revenge on Smith Beffort and Mie.

In Volume 5 Madame Atomos continues waging war on the United States, first by turning the hapless residents of Baltimore into blood-thirsty monsters, then by unleashing uncontrollable wild fires over Nevada.

In Volume 6, Madame Atomos exacts a terrible revenge upon her enemies by killing both Dr. Soblen and Bob Beffort, the baby son of Smith Beffort and Mie Azusa. The latter swears revenge upon her once-mistress, while the deadly Japanese mastermind attempts to re-build her evil empire.

In Volume 7, Madame Atomos discovers that her frequent use of teleportation has rejuvenated her body, and she now looks like a very attractive young woman, Not only does this help her evade the FBI, but she uses her charms to seduce Yosho Akamatsu who is, of course, unaware that the beautiful Miss Icho Fuji is, in reality, her deadliest enemy…

Now read on…

Jean-Marc Lofficier

André Caroff

L'EMPREINTE de Mme ATOMOS

ANGOISSE

FLEUVE NOIR

THE MARK OF MADAME ATOMOS

Chapter I

In a foul mood, Smith Beffort tore himself away from watching the street being scoured by blasts of rain, swung around and said, "It's not possible, Evans! Miss Icho Fuji can't be Madame Atomos!"

James Edward Evans just shrugged and tapped the file in front of him. "Icho Fuji's left thumb print is an exact match with the left thumb print of Kanoto Yoshimuta, aka Madame Atomos. You saw so yourself, right?"

"She's 30 years old," Beffort insisted, "and the latter's over 50!"

"I know, but that doesn't change the facts."

"There must be an error!"

Evans slowly shook his head. "No way, Smith. We've had Kanoto Yoshimuta's fingerprints for years and Icho Fuji's were just lifted from the room at the Lobatos Hospital where she stayed before escaping with Miss Ida Brown… I'm as flabbergasted as you, but we can't deny the evidence: Icho Fuji and Madame Atomos are one and the same person!"

Beffort's stomach turned as he flopped into an armchair and lit a cigarette. Since he said nothing, Evans continued, "Moreover, don't forget that Madame Atomos vanished at the exact moment when Icho Fuji showed up in Padanaram."

Beffort waved him off wearily. "I remember every-thing, Evans, everything... Still, how do you expect me to just sit here and accept such an extraordinary trans-formation? Who would believe that Madame Atomos could have succeeded in growing 20 years younger? Look, it's insane!"

Evans spread his hands out as a sign of helpless-ness. "I don't have a goddamn clue, but it's a fact! Be-fore, she had flying saucers, a magnetic wall, a disinte-grator ray, and she wasn't real, she was right out of a science fiction story. Now she's lost her formidable power, but she's become a young woman again, very pretty, very attractive. Okay, got it!"

"Coming from her, nothing surprises you any-more?"

"Exactly, I have to admit it. And to be perfectly honest, I have to say that I wouldn't be surprised if she's already managed to build a new laboratory. Speaking of which, still nothing in your search?"

Beffort shot him a sidelong glance. "If I had any news," he stated dryly, "you'd have heard. The San Francisco region has been gone through with a fine-toothed comb by hundreds of men over the last three months..."

"With no results."

"We can't dig underground for thousands of square miles! Now, given Madame Atomos' habits, it's obvious that her laboratory is subterranean. Under such circum-stances, what can we do?"

"One fine day," J. Edward Evans. grumbled, "she's going to bring out a new weapon as terrifying as before and it's going to start all over again."

Beffort stubbed out his cigarette, even though it was only half-smoked, stood up and as he picked up his raincoat and hat, said, "We're wasting time in pointless discussions, Evans."

"It's to take stock of the situation," the FBI director defended.

The G-man stared at him coldly. "I don't need to go over this again and again to remember that Icho Fuji disappeared three months ago and during all that time she's certainly been dedicated to finishing her laboratory. Truthfully, I'm expecting a heavy blow any day now, Evans. It's the end of September and we haven't found a trace of Icho Fuji or Ida Brown. In San Francisco with the A.O.F.M.A.[1] Ritter's hit a brick wall so hard it looks like the secret society was dissolved after the death of Arthur Trigg. But I know it's not true, that our enemies have been working in the shadows while we're running around doing nothing and that the start of a new Atomos operation is right around the corner. Therefore, I can assure you that all our forces are ready to go. Whatever happens, we won't be caught off guard. In the meantime, you should inform the press that Miss Icho Fuji is enemy number one from now on. Tell them also that Madame Atomos is dead…"

"That's a lie," J.E.E. protested, "since her fingerprints…"

"Don't get all worked up! It's all just hoping that it'll wound her pride. As far as I know Madame Atomos, she will never accept playing dead. Her pride will force her to come out of hiding because in her desire for vengeance she'll only be satisfied if the United States knows unequivocally that Madame Atomos is behind the tragedy that strikes it."

---

[1] American Organization of the Friends of Madame Atomos.

Evans grinned. "I do believe you know her well," he said without the slightest hint of irony.

Beffort backed up toward the door, raised a finger and smiled. "Above all, mum's the word about that fingerprint. Make up a story. For example, tell the journalists that Icho Fuji is a lunatic, a fanatic who got the crazy idea of continuing the depraved work of her dead boss…"

"But she doesn't have her genius?" Evans offered.

"Okay! We're on the same wavelength! Get that out today and I'll take 50 to 1 that Madame Atomos/Icho Fuji will react before the end of the week."

"Agreed," Evans assured him. "The news will be out before noon."

Beffort winked, walked through the door, close it behind him and strode down the hallway.

At 12:45 Smith and Mie were in a restaurant on Rhode Island Avenue. They did not go there out of habit, but for an intimate celebration of their wedding anniversary. The young lady had finally regained her balance and a certain joie de vivre. She no longer obsessed over the death of her son. Time had done its job…

"Evans kept his word," Smith said. "If Yosho read the news, he ought to be wondering what we're cooking up. By the way, when was the last time you heard from him?"

Mie furrowed her brow and said, "Two weeks ago. He left the hospital when he called us. Say, Smith, don't you think we should be talking about something else? This is a special day, after all."

"That's true," Smith smiled, searching through his pockets. "Hold on, Mie, I've got a little present for you."

The box held a brooch. A beauty. At first blushing, Mie suddenly turned pale when she held it. "It looks like..."

"Yes," Smith confirmed, "the jeweler reproduced the model, but I can swear to you that this brooch is not radioactive."[2]

Mie got her color back and leaned over to kiss her husband. "Thank you," she whispered, "nothing could have made me happier."

Beffort hugged her, gave her a passionate kiss and then sat up straight when he saw that several customers were watching them.

Mie nibbled his ear. "Does it bother you to look like newlyweds, Mr. Beffort?"

"Out of practice. These last few years we haven't had much time to pay attention to each other, have we?"

Mie sighed, sat back and closed her eyes. "I dream of a cozy apartment without a single suitcase and without a phone, where we could live forever..."

"It's only a dream," Smith interrupted her. "If Madame Atomos showed up tomorrow in the North Pole..."

"We'd leave for the North Pole," Mie finished. "I know. Didn't you promise to talk about something else? If you've got no ideas, tell me what's on the menu. I'm starving!"

Beffort grabbed the menu and listed the dishes. Mie was only half listening. She was really just trying to distract him, to make him forget for a little while about his usual preoccupations. She thought that the atmosphere was perfect for it and the French wine would manage to

---

[2] See *The Seduction of Madame Atomos* in *The Resurrection of Madame Atomos*.

plunge Smith into euphoria. It did not matter if the euphoria was artificial.

"Bordeaux?" Smith proposed.

"Bordeaux," Mie accepted, casually watching a man enter the restaurant. He was well dressed, tall and looked like a businessman. His briefcase seemed full and heavy; behind his tortoise-shell framed glasses his eyes shined with a feverish glare. Mie took in all these details without thinking and would no doubt have forgotten the man right away if he did not end up staring at Smith.

"In the old days," Beffort reckoned, "it would have called for a Cutty Sark."

"Naturally," Mie approved.

She was watching the man weave through the tables and head straight for them. He switched his briefcase to his other hand, yanked open the zipper, stepped closer, leaned over and asked, "Mr. and Mrs. Beffort?"

Surprised, Smith looked up at him. "That's us. What do you want?"

The man dug his hand into his briefcase and smiled very kindly. "I have a message to give you from…" He pulled out a Colt, pointed it at Smith and shouted, "Madame Atomos!"

Instantly a series of shots broke the silence that the killer's announcement had instilled. Mie screamed and started to jump to her feet, but was pushed to the floor by Smith, who leaped over the table. The man shot again before doubling over when Smith punched him hard in the stomach. Then he collapsed under the G-man as the glasses and plates shattered on the tile floor.

Coming out of the kitchen, a waiter hit by a stray bullet grabbed his belly and dropped slowly to his knees, stunned. In the rest of the place everyone sat petrified.

They still did not understand, but the name of Madame Atomos had struck them with terror.

"Call the police," Beffort barked.

One of his ears was bleeding and the left shoulder pad of his jacket was torn off. He stood up, picked up the Colt and waved his hand around.

"Stay seated everyone and finish your lunch. The show's over!"

With shaky legs, Mie flopped onto the seat. She would remember this wedding anniversary…

The man woke up from his KO in a room next to James Edward Evans' office. His identification said that his name was Louis Radetich, a manager, living in Oakland. His briefcase contained a business contract typed in triplicate for the purchase of 50 tons of sheet metal for the Glenmont Company, whose headquarters were in Bethesda, northwest of Washington D.C.

Radetich snapped out of it and massaged his jaw. Beffort had hit him hard and the man was still feeling it. He looked around, confused, and murmured, "I've surely got a broken tooth…" Then he spoke more loudly, "Who are you and why am I here?"

One phone call had informed Smith that Louis Radetich had landed in Washington D.C. around 11:55. He had left his home at five in the morning and his plane had taken off fifteen minutes later from the San Francisco airport. He was in Washington on business. According to the FBI office on San Francisco, Radetich was an orderly man, a good father (of six children), a good husband and a tireless worker.

"You had an accident, Mr. Radetich," Evans said.

"An accident? Where's that?"

"What's the last thing you remember?" Smith asked.

The man wrinkled his brow. "Hard to say," he admitted, totally confused.

All of a sudden he looked completely out of it. Smith held out his pack of cigarettes, gave him a light, took one himself and sat across from him. "Mr. Radetich, your job obviously requires you to be clear-headed. You should have a good memory?"

"In general, yes."

"Do you remember taking a plane?"

"Of course. I was in the back, on the right in an aisle seat…"

"Was anybody sitting next to you?"

Radetich's face flushed slightly. "Uh, a woman."

Beffort tensed up. "Pretty?"

Radetich smiled and shook his head. "It's not what you're thinking. The woman was over 60 and a real chatterbox. When I lit my first cigarette she told me she worked in a cancer research institute and she painted a startling picture of what was going to happen to me if I kept smoking…"

He paused, touched his broken tooth and with a touch of humor added, "I don't know if it's important, but I can assure you that the lady had nothing to do with my 'accident'. Now, maybe you can tell me who you are?"

Beffort got straight to the point. "I work for the FBI and was calmly having lunch in a restaurant with my wife here."

Mie waved. Beffort continued, "Around 1 pm you headed straight for our table, pulled a Colt out of your briefcase and then shot at me seven times, *on behalf of Madame Atomos!* That's why you're here."

Radetich shrugged. "Ridiculous! This is some kind of joke…"

Beffort showed him his ear and jacket. "The first bullet grazed me, the second hit my earlobe, the third got buried in the belly of a waiter and the fourth tore off my shoulder pad. The others caused only material damage. Naturally I was forced to knock you out. There were still two bullets in your gun…"

Not saying a word, Radetich looked first at Beffort and then at Mie and Evans. The latter said, "It's all true, Radetich. The customers in the restaurant can bear witness. If it's any consolation, I can tell you that the waiter won't die and that we're sure that you weren't acting of your own free will."

"It's unbelievable," Radetich mumbled. "I've never held a gun in my life."

"Luckily," Evans said. "Otherwise Smith Beffort would probably not be sitting here right now. You shot at him from three feet away!"

The man wiped his forehead. It was all so disconcerting that he felt like he was living some unreal existence.

Beffort patted his shoulder. "I understand how you feel, Mr. Radetich."

"Thanks, but in my place…"

"In your place," Beffort interrupted, "I would try to figure out exactly when my memories stopped. In the plane did you eat or drink anything?"

"No. I just had a scotch at the airport bar."

"Which airport?"

"Washington-Virginia."

"Did you drink alone?"

Radetich shook his head. "I don't usually drink. I was invited by another passenger who had very kindly and skillfully got rid of the cancer researcher for me."

"And then what did you do?"

Radetich took a long pause and spread his arms in ignorance. "Sorry," he said in dismay, "I can't remember what I did after that drink."

Beffort and Mie exchanged a knowing glance. Not to be outdone, Evans said, "According to all evidence, Madame Atomos chose Mr. Radetich to answer the article published by the press. Since he came from California where we're looking in vain for the new Atomos laboratory, there's no doubt about the identity of the instigators of the attack... Now we just have to find out who drugged Mr. Radetich and how the drug can completely destroy his willpower..."

Chapter II

With Radetich's description, they made an Identikit portrait of the man he had had a drink with at the airport bar. It showed a young man, surely still in his twenties, with slightly slanted eyes and thick eyebrows. His nose was rather flat, this lips thick. His weak chin contrasted strangely with his square jaw and jutting cheekbones.

"Funny-looking guy," Beffort said. "He must be the product of a fascinating mix of races. His upper face is Asian, the lower negroid, but the eyebrows and chin are from a white."

Just then Eddy Witter entered the room. He was coming back from the airport where he had checked the list of passengers coming from San Francisco. "His name's Robert Costello," he said, nodding at the portrait. "But we shouldn't be too sure of it because his San Francisco address is false."

"And the old lady?" Beffort asked.

"Nothing against her. She really does work for a re-search lab. On the other hand, a waiter at the airport bar remembered a detail that might be important: after drink-ing with Mr. Radetich, Costello met up with a very pret-ty, young woman. It was because she was so pretty that the waiter has such a good memory. Here's exactly what he told me about her: 'She was built like a beaut. One of those birds you see on a magazine cover, you know?'"

"There are hundreds of women like that," Evans said.

"Sure," Witter agreed, "except most of them don't go riding around in a van riddled with antennas."

"Interesting," Beffort commented, "but you look like you're keeping something back, Eddy."

"Yes. The description that the waiter gave of the young woman reminded me strongly of Charles Hyde's description of Ida Brown."

Beffort whistled in surprise. "Damn! Aren't going a little fast, Eddy?"

"Mr. Radetich drugged, Costello on the plane, a van full of antennas with Ida Brown at the wheel," Witter enumerated, "I think it's a completely logical chain of events."

"Well said, but badly reasoned, Eddy. You're completely forgetting that the papers hadn't published the famous shock-statement when the plane with Radetich and Costello took off from San Francisco. Under such conditions how could Madame Atomos have prepared her retaliation when Evans and I hadn't even decided to provoke her yet?"

His words chilled everyone present.

"So," Evans proposed, "we have to conclude that Madame Atomos decided to attack during the flight? Knowing that Costello was on the plane, she contacted him by radio…"

"What radio?" Mie asked. "If that's the case, we should be able to check it. And more easily since the message must have come after the papers came out at 11:30."

"Good thinking," Evans declared. "Since the plane touched down at 11:55 and Costello had already buddied up with Radetich by getting rid of his chatterbox, we can deduce that the message was sent around 11:40 or 11:45."

"You're little geniuses," Smith congratulated them as he picked the phone. He quickly got in touch with the office he wanted at the Washington-Virginia airport, identified himself, and asked for any personal messages received by the Boeing flying out of San Francisco during the appropriate time period. He had purposefully not mentioned Costello by name, but it was precisely his name that he was given as the recipient of a radio-telegram coming from the San Francisco office.

"Okay," Beffort said, "the text, please."

"I'm quoting it here: *Father gravely ill. Stop. Take immediate action. Stop. Sister waiting in Washington with car 4. Stop. Signed, Aunt May.* Got it?"

"Got it. Thanks."

Beffort hung up and swung around to Witter. "Excuse me, Eddy. Now the presence of Ida Brown in Washington henceforth can no longer be doubted. Car 4 was brought in to remote-control Radetich to the restaurant. I don't know how Costello and Ida Brown influenced you, Mr. Radetich, but the result was remarkable!"

The manager nodded his head. "It was more than just influence," he said, troubled. "For almost an hour I was turned into a robot! Say, Beffort, do you think that this Costello could have made a mistake by talking to me before the plane landed?"

Smith furrowed his brow. "Why? What are suggesting?"

"He told me that he didn't like traveling by plane and that he planned to go back to San Francisco by train at 8:30 pm..."

"Today?"

"Yes, this evening," Radetich said calmly.

Beffort was speechless. It was stunning information and Radetich had been a hair's breadth away from not mentioning it.

The train station was flooded with people and even though the main nerve centers were being watched by a bunch of G-men, Beffort was not at all sure of being able to locate Costello in the human tide.

"He won't come," Mie prophesized. "To get to the West Coast by train takes three days. When you work for Madame Atomos, you're not allowed to waste time."

Beffort took a drag off his cigarette without taking his eyes off the traveling suspects marching by before him. "This is certainly part of a carefully prepared plan," he said. "Madame Atomos intended to kill me, but she also expected Evans to identify Costello and go looking for him. Though we have to admit that without Radetich we'd never have thought of coming here?"

"That's true, but no one can convince me that Costello didn't voluntarily confess his travel plans to Radetich."

Beffort stared at his wife. "Tell me, Mie, if Radetich took me out, what would have happened to him?"

"I certainly would have killed him," Mie said calmly. "My automatic was in my handbag and I can assure you that your murderer would never have got out of that restaurant alive."

"And if you missed?"

"A manhunt would have been organized…"

"Until Radetich would have been shot down," Smith finished. "So in the plane Costello was confessing to a would-be corpse. Since dead men don't talk…"

Mie cut him off by grabbing his arm. "Look, there, to the left. Costello and Ida Brown!"

"Unbelievable, but true, isn't it? We're going to kill two birds with one stone. As long as they lead us to the front door of the new laboratory…"

Mie shot him an incredulous glance. "You're not going to arrest them?"

Beffort smiled. "I'm being careful not to. As planned with Evans, I've given orders to leave Costello alone. How would you like to take a little trip, Mie?"

"With no luggage?"

Smith raised his arm. A few seconds later Eddy Witter appeared. He put two suitcases next to Beffort and said, "I hope I didn't forget anything. Here are your tickets. If you need me, I'll be in car 6, compartment 14. Goodbye."

"One minute. Where's Charles Hyde?"

"At the end of the platform. He's watching our marks get on board. What a stroke of luck, eh? Goodbye again."

"Did you think of packing my nightie?" Mie asked maliciously.

Witter blushed.

Smith intervened. "Don't bother him. Eddy didn't forget anything. I made a list. See you, Eddy."

"See you," Witter grumbled as he turned and left.

Smith picked up the suitcases and dragged Mie toward platform 5 which Costello and Ida Brown had just reached. In spite of his height, Beffort quickly lost sight of them in the crowd, but it did not worry him. He knew that Charles Hyde was waiting for the couple on the platform and that Eddy Witter was tailing them.

The tickets that were bought an instant beforehand gave them car number 27, which because of the last minute rush put them at the back of the train. There was only the baggage car behind them, the last car, which seemed a perfect position to the Befforts. As a lookout post and for any possible action, they could not have asked for better.

Mie and Smith climbed onto the train and into the "cross-country" compartment. It was equipped with two bunks, a movable table and a very comfortable little bathroom on the side. Mie was starting to take inventory of the suitcases when Charles Hyde showed up in the still open doorway.

"Costello and Ida Brown are in car 12, compartment 3," he announced. "They didn't talk to anyone and look totally relaxed."

"Keep an eye on them," Beffort advised. "After all, they might get off before the end of the line."

Hyde puckered is lips, took out a timetable and after consulting it said, "That would surprise me. This is an express train. Between Washington and San Francisco via Chicago, Denver and Salt Lake City, there are seven stops. The first stop isn't before six in the morning. So until then we're safe."

"Who's watching them right now?"

"Witter's in position in their corridor and the guys from headquarters are watching the other track. Basically I came to tell you not to go to the dining car without warning us. If you meet up with our marks…"

"Don't worry," Beffort jumped in. "We don't plan to sound any alarms." He looked at his watch. "We leave in ten minutes. Go and see what's happening up there, Charley, I won't be able to relax until this train gets rolling at full speed."

Costello and Ida Brown went to the dining car for the first call. The Befforts went later and ate with Witter, who gave them his report.

"Everything's okay. If they were ***ing on their honeymoon, they'd be acting no different… They locked themselves up in their compartment and immediately turned out the lights. The Atomos Organization must be going soft, eh?"

The train was rolling at full speed through the cold night. The hands of the electric clock read 10:30 pm and people were starting to clear out of the dining car. In the observation car fifty or so passengers were watching television, but everywhere else the hallways were empty. Apparently, the night would be quiet.

Smith looked hard at Witter. "Watch out, Eddy, it might be the calm before the storm. The people who work for Madame Atomos are generally shrewd. Anyway, they always act as planned. Since this train left the station in Washington, I've been wondering whether Costello and Ida Brown haven't been sent to lure us into a trap."

Witter looked up. "What makes you say that?"

"It's been too easy, Eddy. Radetich gave us the exact time and place to find Costello and he arrived right on time, dragging along some extra bait named Ida Brown. Both of them, without a hint of suspicion, without watching their backs, as if they already knew that they were in no danger…"

"I told you in Washington," Mie interrupted, "that it all seemed weird. You said that Radetich was a would-be corpse and that Costello had confessed to him without any fear because dead men don't talk. Why did you change your mind, Smith?"

"I repeat: it's been too easy. Look, logically, if Costello and Ida Brown could radio-control Radetich into our restaurant on Rhode Island Avenue, it would be silly to think that they didn't witness the spoiled attack."

"In that case," Mie declared, "they saw us walking out on our own two feet while Radetich was lying unconscious on a stretcher. Conclusion: the attack failed and Radetich was dead!"

Witter could not help laughing. "At the rate you're going, you could talk about it the whole trip! Personally I'd rather stick to the facts: Costello and the girl can't leave the train before 6 am. They're locked in their compartment and can't hurt us in any case. That's what you should be talking about! Excuse me, I have to take the watch."

He got up, winked at them and headed for the exit.

"Just another way of reminding us that we're sentenced to death by Madame Atomos," Mie sighed. "Don't you think we're making the FBI worry an awful lot about us?"

"All Americans are sentenced to death by Madame Atomos," Beffort corrected her gravely, "and every one of them can worry about the others."

Mie straightened up a little and said with some satisfaction, "Don't forget that we're a priority. We're alive and our enemy's actions are limited, apparently just leading us into a trap."

"You can say that again!" Smith confirmed. "We've captured Madame Atomos' complete attention. If she kills us, she'll get back to the United States. Therefore, we have to stay in good health. Let's start by getting a good night's sleep."

They got up from the table, left the dining car and walked through half the train to reach their compartment. The door was closed and a man appeared at the end of the hallway leaning against the wall. For an unaware observer, he was just a passenger like any other, going to smoke a last cigarette before heading back to his compartment. And the man, indeed, lit a filtered cigarette and watched the dark countryside flying by the thick window. In fact, there was nothing to see and the man pricked up his ears to know if the Befforts might not come back out.

A long moment passed before the man stubbed out the cigarette under his shoe and strode down the hallway. He stopped in car 25 and rapped the signal knock on the door of compartment 6. They opened up immediately and he slid in like a lizard.

"It's okay," he said, "they've gone to bed."

The other, a well-built man of mixed black and yellow races, just nodded and grabbed a railway map of Charleston, West Virginia. He put his finger on a point marked in red and said, "Is this the postal car here?"

"It's a baggage car," the man corrected, "but it's the same thing. The main point is to keep to this point, otherwise the whole thing'll fall to pieces. Do you have my guard's uniform?"

The black man opened a suitcase and pulled out a uniform and cap. "Everything's ready. What's going to happen with the car?"

"It'll be shunted onto an unused track and will smash into a dead end at full speed. After the crash it's unlikely that any of the employees will be able to say what happened. As long as you unhitch the car at this exact place…"

"When'll we get there?"

"Around 1 am. Don't doze off, okay? If you miss it, I won't be able to do anything."

The black smiled. "Don't sweat it, Downing. My job's a picnic compared to yours. How are you going to get car 27 evacuated without waking up the Befforts?"

It was Downing's turn to smile. "Don't worry about that, sonny, and never say my name aloud, nor the Befforts, without first checking under your bunk. This damn train is crawling with G-men. I hope Costello will be up to getting them all in the head car during the operation."

He wiped the sweat that was beading on his forehead and added, "Damn! It's all hanging by a thread! Who but Madame Atomos would have the gall to pull off such a thing?"

Chapter III

At 1 am Eddy Witter saw the door of compartment 3 open and Costello appear in the hallway. The G-man stepped back, slowly squeezing between the accordion pleats as Costello advanced in his direction, that is toward the front of the train.

The man had crossed half the distance separating him from Witter, who was getting ready to dive into the toilettes, when Ida Brown materialized in the hallway. She closed the door, turned around and headed straight for the dining car where the bar stayed open all night, but in the opposite direction that Costello had just taken!

For Witter the problem was suddenly insolvable in the meaning that he could not follow the man and the young woman at the same time. And the situation required exactly that—that they both be closely watched—because unexpectedly and therefore extremely suspiciously, they were both fully dressed! At such a late hour it was not normal.

Witter was in a panic when Costello seemed to realize that he was walking in the wrong direction. He turned around, walked faster and caught up to Ida Brown, who had already disappeared into car 13. Witter breathed a sigh of relief. Since the dining car was number 16, the couple was stuck between the car where Charles Hyde was sleeping and the one occupied by the Befforts. In case of an emergency, it might prove decisive.

Witter strode down the hallway and entered car 13 exactly when Costello and Ida Brown stepped into car 14. Through the window Witter could see no light, just an undulating, far-off line of hills cut out of the less dark background of the nocturnal horizon. This meant that the train was in the middle of the countryside, heading towards Cincinnati, Indianapolis and Chicago, somewhere to the east of Charleston, which they would not pass before 2 am if they kept to the timetable. Therefore, for the moment, the Brown-Costello team did not have the slightest chance of sneaking away if they caused the train to stop by pulling the alarm.

But, and this probability disturbed Witter, their behavior indicated that they were prepared to leave the train at any minute. You don't get dressed in the middle of the night to have a drink when simply ringing the buzzer could bring the steward running. And then why had Costello come out before Ida Brown?

Very intrigued, Witter followed the couple up to the dining car and stopped behind the glass door. From this vantage point he saw Costello escort his companion to the bar. They sat on the stools, ordered coffee and Costello pulled out his cigarettes.

At 1:35 they were in the same place. Behind the glass door Witter was feeling more and more intrigued. He liked situations to be clear. This one was bursting with uncertainty. Five more minutes ticked off in dead calm. Costello and Ida Brown were smoking and drinking tranquilly. On the other side of the counter, the bartender was daydreaming while drying the same glass over and over again.

Witter wearily shifted his feet and leaned back against the wall. He took a cigarette from his pocket and was about to light up when a group of passengers in pajamas appeared at the other end of the dining car. Their eyes were still puffy from sleep and their hair was a mess, but Witter noticed that the women were wearing their jewelry and the men were carrying luggage.

"Where's the conductor?" one of them asked.

Costello and Ida Brown turned around. The bartender approached the group, his eyes wide with wonder. In his whole career this was clearly the first time he had seen such a sight. "What's going on?" he asked.

His question silenced the group. Finally the man who had asked for the conductor spoke in disbelief. "Don't tell me you don't know about the wild madman threatening to blow up car 27, pal! He's holed up in compartment 8 with a load of dynamite and the railway guard evacuated us double-time! The conductor who's getting us new compartments is supposed to be waiting for us here. Where is he?"

Witter jumped. The compartment of the wild madman was occupied by Smith and Mie!

"Not to panic the other passengers is one thing," the man in pajamas said, "but to spend the night in a hallway in something else! If we aren't immediately…"

Witter did not hear the rest of the sentence. He ran as fast as he could to the back of the train losing all interest in the Brown-Costello team. The deserted hallways proved that the evacuation of passengers from car 27 had been a masterpiece of discretion. Apparently, except for the group in pajamas and the guard, no one seemed to know about the drama playing out.

Witter crossed car 25, sprinted through 26 and came to screeching halt in front of the communicating door, not believing his eyes. Through the window he could see nothing but the long gleam of rails being swallowed up by the night. Unbelievably car 27 and the baggage car were no longer hitched to the train!

Without a second thought, Witter pulled the alarm.

The train had been stopped for 15 minutes. Witter had made a hasty investigation with a real railway guard and very quickly learned that the false guard had been accompanied by a man of color calling himself a police officer and that the two of them had quietly evacuated car 27.

"When your neighbor is a lunatic loaded with dynamite," one of the passengers of car 27 stated, "you skedaddle on tiptoes!"

Witter understood perfectly well. They had prepared the affair masterfully. While the false guard was getting rid of the passengers, his accomplice was unhitching the car and with it the baggage car, then when Witter pulled the emergency cord, the whole Atomos team vanished into the countryside.

By radio-telephone the Charleston station gave orders to clear the track so a locomotive could go in search of the two cars inevitably stuck somewhere between mile 35 and the old switching yard.

While the train headed slowly for Charleston, Witter's fears were confirmed: Costello and Ida Brown were nowhere to be found. But he was even more surprised to hear that Charles Hyde had also disappeared! After the Befforts being expertly sidelined, the sudden elimination of Hyde struck a hard blow to Witter's morale.

Thus, in spite of the precautions taken by the FBI, Madame Atomos had triumphed once again! Evidently, Hyde had been kidnapped to be used eventually as a bargaining chip. But why did they unhitch the Befforts' car? A diversion to allow the Atomos commando to clear out quietly was a viable answer since it was the final result. Nevertheless, Witter doubted that Madame Atomos would be satisfied with such a paltry prize.

In Charleston Witter called Washington, got James Edward Evans on the phone and told him briefly what was still just an incident.

"Let's hope that it doesn't turn into a tragedy," Evans said, unable to hide his worry. "Naturally you're going to get Smith and Mie back?"

"When I hang up, I'll get on board the train," Witter reassured him. "But likewise, don't you think it's high time we let loose Owen Bernitz and his Green Dragon Force? Costello and Ida Brown might still be stopped."

"If they're holding Charles Hyde prisoner, we'll have to negotiate."

"That'd be better than finding his corpse on the side of the road," Witter remarked dryly.

Evans recognized that he was in a foul mood because he was worried and figured it was no good to talk strategy at the moment. The first thing they had to do was to find the Befforts. He said that he would contact the Green Dragon Force right away and that the Charleston G-men, therefore all of West Virginia, would be put on the trail of the Brown-Costello couple as soon as possible.

Witter hung up, went back to the platform and climbed onto the electric engine that was waiting only for him to get underway. Besides the driver, because of the importance of the event, an inspector from the railroad administration had also come on board.

"If we don't get on the line right away," he told Witter, "the traffic will be screwed up for hours."

The G-man nodded without saying a word. He knew that the next train had stopped well beyond the old switching station and therefore car 27 and the baggage car ran no risk of crashing into a train rushing down the track at full speed, but this was not enough to quiet his anxieties.

With all its lights on the engine rolled eastward for an hour, then the driver reduced the speed when he reached the switches of the abandoned post. Starting from now car 27 and the baggage car could appear at any moment in the yellow glare of the train lights.

The engine slowly crossed the half-mile marking off the center, continued on the uphill track and started a sweeping, steep-sided curve. Witter and the inspector exchanged glances. From here on in, considering the time that the passengers had been evacuated from car 27, it was physically impossible for the cars to reach this portion of the track.

"Let's go back," Witter said. "The solution to this problem must be at the switching station."

"You think the two cars were shunted onto a secondary track?"

"They couldn't just vanish, could they?"

They inspector shrugged. He had not for a second thought of this eventuality. On his order the driver backed up and stopped in front of the charging crane dating back to the time of steam locomotives. Farther on, around a loading platform, stood a rundown workshop and the cylindrical outline of a water tank. To the left was the old, one-story switching station with broken windows, but no trains were in sight in the whole place.

It was now 4:30. Dawn was pushing back the night and though visibility was not yet very good, it was more than enough for the three men to see the entire network of the station, the catenary system overlooking the main track and the uninterrupted line of telegraph poles standing like skeletons along the roadbeds.

Witter looked at the inspector and said, "Maybe you've got some idea of what happened to the cars?" He shook his head. Witter asked, "And this famous secondary track you were just talking about?"

"Just a shot in the dark. In fact, there is no secondary track in this sector. We can see everything right here, from the signal gantry to the turntable."

Witter examined one last time the deserted view of the old switching station and said, "If the two cars aren't in this area or on the track going into Charleston, that means that they're somewhere farther east and they weren't unhitched when we thought. All in all, the time indicated by the passengers only makes sense with respect to the speed of the train."

His reasoning helped the inspector regain his composure. What Witter was saying was concrete: speed, time—they were hard facts.

The engine set off again toward the east, reached the wide curve and continued at a good pace because the visibility was good enough now to spot any obstacles. Then the curve ended and the three men saw an endless straight line.

"Nothing," Witter muttered in disappointment. "Now the mystery deepens."

Troubled, the inspector rifled through a box on the control panel and took out a map of the rail system. The web of the switching station was faithfully reproduced. To the west stretched the line to Charleston. To the east it ran straight to Clifton Forge before heading back to Charlottesville.

"We're here," the inspector said. "Look. There's a secondary track farther east. Obviously it hasn't been used in a long time and I doubt it's still functional."

The driver peeked at the map and corrected him. "I know it. It's not a secondary track, but a siding. When there was only one line, the freight trains parked there to let the express through. It's really steep and used to have a bad reputation. A train with a heavy load always had trouble getting out of it. If I remember well, it starts about five minutes from the next signal."

He was not wrong. The old track did indeed begin after the signal, that is to say around 15 minutes from the switching station, and disappeared into the woods.

Witter and the inspector got off. The latter moved the old switch by hand was astonished to find it working smoothly, in perfect condition.

Witter bent down. "It's been cleaned and greased recently."

The inspector pointed out fresh traces on the rails. "I think we've reached our goal. One or more cars have recently taken this track."

His remark brought G-man to attention. Pale now, the inspector continued, "A siding track always ends in a steel bumper in front of a thick embankment... you understand?"

Witter stood up slowly. "Let's go," he said, walking to the engine.

"This old track isn't electrified," the inspector reminded him. "We have to walk."

Witter nodded, waved to the driver to come down and the three men headed into the woods. It was 5 am and the sun was gently rising over the horizon. However, it did not light up the rails, which were roofed with thick vegetation. In some places there were broken branches, snapped off. As he shuffled down the slope, Witter thought that car 27 and the baggage car must have barreled through this very place at 60 miles an hour.

The three men walked the 300 yards or so under the low branches and heard the groans well before seeing the wreckage of the baggage car. It had literally shattered to pieces when it crashed into the bumper. Its crumpled metal was splattered with blood and the ground around was scattered with burst suitcases and crates.

Of the five escorts, four had lost their lives. Thrown out at impact, the fifth was moaning in the grass. He had been there for four hours and lost a huge amount of blood, but he realized that his saviors had finally reached him against all odds.

"Can you talk?" Witter asked.

The driver had just gone back to the engine to call for an emergency lift by helicopter. Until it arrived Witter and the inspector could do nothing for the wounded man except keep him still in order not to worsen his injuries.

"What happened?" Witter pressed.

The wounded man grimaced, stopped moaning and murmured, "We were unhitched... The bastards even sabotaged the emergency brake. It was going too fast anyway..." He stared hard at Witter and added, "Hey, you're gonna take me to a hospital, aren't you?"

"Don't worry, a helicopter's on the way."

"I must have a bunch of broken bones."

Witter smiled and spoke in s soothing voice. "No problem, pal, since we can replace people's hearts nowadays, broken bones are a piece of cake. When did you realize that your car was coasting?"

"At the switches... We almost derailed we were going so fast... After we tried to pull the safety brake, then there was the explosion... The others are dead, aren't they?"

Witter nodded silently. The wounded man closed his eyes in exhaustion and clasped his hand around his arm torn up by a metal shard. It had been the longest day of his life.

Witter stood up and took the inspector aside, whispering, "He'll live for sure, but he won't be able to tell us what became of car 27."

The inspector furrowed his brow. "We don't know where it is right now, but since the baggage car must have been unhitched before it, it's clear that it can only be somewhere between here and the old switching station."

Witter scowled. "We checked the area foot by foot."

"What can I say? The car couldn't have flown away!"

Witter did not answer. When it came to Madame Atomos, anything could fly...

Chapter IV

Smith woke up abruptly and knew instantly that the train was at a standstill. When his eyes snapped open he saw that the nightlight was working. In truth, it was as dark as an oven and the heat was unbearable. He got up and lifted the shade, but his dilated eyes failed to see anything in the darkness.

"What are doing Smith?" Feeling him stirring, Mie had also woken up.

Beffort looked at the luminous dial of his watch. "Strange," he said. "It's 6 am and the sun still hasn't risen."

"We're stopped in a tunnel," Mie declared quite logically.

Beffort moved, found a box of matches and lit one close to the window. The flame danced, stood still and revealed a concrete wall. It could have been a tunnel if it was not sitting four inches from the window.

Struck by the anomaly, Beffort opened his suitcase and took out a flashlight. He unlatched the door and slid it open, pointing the beam of light at the hallway window. There, too, he saw a concrete wall almost touching the outside of the car.

When he went into the hallway he found all the compartment doors wide open, revealing the messed up bunks and bare luggage racks. Beffort stiffened up and visited all the compartments until he reached the rear of the car where, expecting to find the baggage car, he saw another concrete wall.

Sweating now, he went back the other way, said something to Mie who was speechless at seeing his face, and found the fourth concrete wall where car 26 used to be.

"Is it serious, Smith?" Mie, who had followed him, asked.

"Our car is literally encased in a kind of concrete box," he answered softly. "Looks like we're stuck in here."

"The roof?"

"He shook his head. "There's no air. That means that the car is closed inside a coffin that's probably located underground."

"The other passengers?"

"We're alone, Mie."

A long silence followed. An extraordinary silence already smelling of death. Like a broken-down submarine on the ocean floor…

"How did they manage to get our car into this box?" Mie finally asked.

Her question was important. Beffort thought about it for an instant before saying, "In my opinion, there's only two ways. First: the car was put horizontally into a hole dug out of the side of a hill or maybe a quarry that has a movable closure system. Second: it was lowered into a ditch."

"In the first case," Mie reasoned, "the movable wall must be less solid than the others. In the second case, we have to be in a kind of elevator that opens in some way above. Whatever the case, we can't be far from the railroad."

"Exactly. The car was brought here on the track. Otherwise we would have woken up."

"Conclusion?"

Smith shrugged. "We have no tools to get through the roof or the presumably weaker wall. We don't know where we are and we've got no way of communicating with the outside world. Therefore, all we can do is hope for help to come."

Mie took a deep breath and asked, "Smith, how long do you think it'll take us to die of suffocation?"

Beffort swept the flashlight around the car. "12 hours," he estimated, "give or take. Maybe we can save some oxygen by moving as little as possible. Come on, Mie, let's try to sleep since we can't do anything else."

They went back to their compartment, lay down, and Beffort turned off his flashlight. Neither of them spoke, but they were both thinking of Sam Forbes and Lucky Simms, dead in the exact same situation.

While the FBI, helped by troops of the local police and the first contingent of the Green Dragon Force, were trying to find traces of Ida Brown, Robert Costello and the false railroad guard and no less false policeman, Eddy Witter was setting up a systematic search between mile 35 and the track from the station. For, and this was really an encouraging certainty, it was impossible for car 27 to have been unhitched outside these two points. This had been mathematically proven after examining all the probabilities that, fortunately, were quite limited. A train has to stay on schedule. This fact eliminated a lot of guesswork.

Witter already knew that the baggage car had been separated from the train around one in the morning. Almost at the same time the passengers in car 27, informed of the presence of the "madman with a bomb", evacuated the car in less than ten minutes and went to the dining car where they did not arrive until 1:35 because of the bags they had to carry on their way.

"In any case," Witter concluded, "car 27 must have been unhitched between 1:10, which is before the old switching station, and 1:35..."

"No," the inspector intervened, "1:35 is no good."

Witter looked at him and asked, "Because there's no secondary track beyond the switching station?"

"That's right. I'm absolutely certain that car 27 is still on the line! You know, it's practically insane to imagine a car weighing 40 tons can get off the tracks without leaving a trace."

"Even using heavy machinery?"

"How could they get it near the line? Between mile 35 and the siding where the baggage car was tossed, there's no drivable road."

Witter bit his lip. He was standing on the platform in the middle of the switching station and looking out into nowhere. Except for the main track and the network of switches, there was, indeed, no road big enough to carry such a heavy car.

"Can you see a crane and platform with 30 double-wheels coming near this track?" the inspector asked.

Witter shook his head. In truth, he could not even believe in any underground possibilities. The roadbeds were undisturbed, the crossties solid and the rails whole. Unless car 27 was lifted by a giant helicopter...

Contrary to what Witter and Evans were thinking, Charles Hyde could move freely and was in perfect health. He had been in a deep sleep when the train stopped. The sudden halt immediately shook the G-man awake. His first reaction, very natural in such a case, was to open the window and take a look outside.

Hyde had seen lights bobbing along the train, heard shouts and then the beam of a flashlight fleeting crossed the face of Ida Brown. The young woman was running toward the dark forest and three vague shadows were in front of her.

Hyde had jumped into his shoes, snatched up his clothes and paralyzing pistol and then set off after the group. Thanks to the sound of broken branches, he easily followed the fugitives' trail and slowly closed the distance between them by keeping an eye on the flashlight that one of the four was using. Farther along, while Costello was looking at a map, Hyde got dressed and threw his pajamas to the nettles. He was surprised to see that the couple was now in the company of a colored man and a uniformed railway guard. By Costello's behavior, taking a long time with the map, Hyde knew that the train was not stopped at a point expected by the Atomos team.

So true was it that when dawn broke the group was still wandering in the forest. The early morning made Charles Hyde's task extraordinarily complicated. But he was sure now of his mission: he was the only one after them and had to follow Costello and Ida Brown at any cost because in his opinion the colored man and the guard were just bit players who probably did not know the location of the new Atomos laboratory or maybe even of its existence.

At 5 am the asphalt ribbon of road appeared through the branches. Hyde looked around, saw a road sign and read that it was highway 60 and the city of Charleston was only 20 miles west.

Hyde hid in the bushes and saw that Costello and his cronies were also hiding in the bushes on the side of the interstate. No one moved for 15 minutes and then Ida Brown walked up to the road sign and stood next to it, looking in the direction opposite to Charleston. Over the next few minutes a dozen cars passed without the young woman making the slightest gesture to stop them. Hyde figured that she was waiting for a car and the road sign was obviously the meeting point. It was high time he started thinking ahead.

Without a car he was taking the chance of being left behind by the Atomos team, thus losing any chance of following their trail, which, he hoped, would lead to the new laboratory or if worse came to worst one of the many shelters of the demoniacal Japanese woman.

Silently Hyde snuck away from where Ida Brown was waiting patiently. He went around 300 yards down the highway and spotted an emergency telephone that was used to call the nearest aid station in case of an accident or breakdown. Most of these stations on the interstates were controlled by the highway patrol whose service was marked by the double sign of a red cross and a monkey wrench.

Hyde hopped over the ditch, picked up the phone and pushed the button to sound the signal. He was immediately put in touch with an invisible speaker.

"Highway Patrol. Please give me the number of the post first."

"27," Hyde said. "Now, listen to me. I'm an FBI agent and I need a car as soon as possible."

"Okay. And I'm the president of the United States. Go fly a kite, pal. And hit the road before the next patrol car nabs you."

Hyde clenched his teeth. "My name is Charles Hyde," he said with menacing calm. "I don't know yours, but considering the duty hours you're keeping, I can assure you that you'll be surveying the New York back roads if you keep messing around. Now, send me an unmarked car. I'm following Costello and Ida Brown who work for Madame Atomos. Got it?"

"I got it, Sir," the man said worriedly. "Sorry but people call us a lot to…"

"Shut up!" Hyde yelled, "And send that car! Every minute counts!"

"Okay, Sir! Post 27. You'll have your car in 10 to 12 minutes."

Hyde hung up and went back under the cover of the trees. He did not believe much in the tricks of fortune, but the fact that the Befforts' car and the telephone post had the same number seemed a good omen to him.

From the top of a low hill, he checked to make sure that Ida Brown was still next to the road sign and then looked east. He did not know which direction his promised car would come from, which made signaling complicated since it would be unmarked and inevitably driven by a plainclothes officer.

Hyde felt worried all of a sudden. If he stayed at the top of hill he might not be able to signal his car. To avoid missing it, he had to stay near post 27 where it would be impossible for him to watch Ida Brown.

Four cars passed by at the speed limit and then a big Rambler station wagon at the lowest acceptable speed. The guy driving twisted a smile at Ida Brown standing next to the road sign. He flashed his headlights and stopped on the shoulder right in front of the young woman. She raised her hand, which brought out Costello and the two other men who climbed into the back of the car without further ado. Ida Brown sat up front and the station wagon sped off toward Charleston.

Hyde looked at his watch. It was now 5:40. The Atomos team had made their rendezvous with the Rambler, but it apparently did not go like clockwork. A delay of 40 minutes in an Atomos performance! That had never been seen before!

Hyde headed for post 27. If the officer on the phone had estimated correctly, the police car should be here in 3 to 4 minutes. Hyde smoked nervously while pacing around the post before he finally threw away his cigarette. To feel better, he told himself that the Rambler could not get very far if it kept under the speed limit. But there was no guaranteeing that it would or that it would not turn off before reaching Charleston. If Highway 60 were like any other highway, it would have a whole network of secondary routes pointing in all directions. Knowing that they were being looked for, the Atomos group would certainly veer off somewhere.

Chomping at the bit, Hyde watched the second hand of his watch. Less than 30 seconds… He looked up and saw a gray Chrysler barreling down the road in the middle of the highway, straddling the line divider without paying any attention whatsoever to the speed limit. Only a cop would do such a thing!

The Chrysler honked its horn, crossed the highway and skid to a stop in front of Hyde. As the smell of burnt rubber rose in the air, a young man leaned out the window. "Mr. Hyde?"

"That's me, cowboy! We're going to start this little rodeo together. The cattle's disguised as a Rambler station wagon and is trotting off to Charleston. Go!"

The young cop grinned and floored the accelerator. While glued to his seat for a second, Hyde asked, "Did you stick a rocket under the hood?"

"I like speed, Sir. Does the cattle have a big head start?"

"Five minutes, no more. Your name?"

"Stone… Dan Stone, Sir."

The Chrysler took a turn before climbing up a hill at full speed, then flew down the other side.

Hyde sighed, "Ever had an accident, Stone?"

"Just a fender bender, Sir. My car was a wreck and I was in the hospital for six months… But the train was coming on full throttle and the railroad crossing was clear."

Hyde lit a cigarette, glanced at the speedometer and sighed again. Before climbing into this car, he had thought that he drove well. "Are you part of the highway patrol, Stone?"

The man smiled, dug into his pocket and showed his card, saying, "FBI, Charleston office. I just happened to be at the station when you called. The car with the Befforts has disappeared and Witter still thinks you've been kidnapped by the Costello-Brown team."

Charles Hyde whistled. "You've got to be kidding! Well, do you know who we're chasing after?"

"Hell yes, Sir."

"Drop the Sir, Stone. My name's Charles Hyde. Tell me more about the car vanishing. I left the train in my pajamas without even grabbing my toothbrush."

Stone brought him up-to-date, telling how Witter had found the baggage car at the end of the siding and concluding with, "Right now there's roadblocks up just about everywhere. They're hoping to arrest Costello and the girl because they have to know where the Befforts are."

Hyde jumped. "Damn! We can't arrest them! Get on your radio, man! Urgent orders on my command: Don't arrest the Costello team for any reason!"

"The Befforts?"

"I'm on it, Stone! Send the message!"

Chapter V

In order to save oxygen, they avoided talking, but the silence that fell over them was heavier than a vault and in the end became intolerable. Mie turned over, opened her eyes in the darkness and felt for her husband's hand, whispering, "How long have we been here, Smith?"

He raised his arm to look at his watch. "8 am," he said. "We woke up two hours ago, which doesn't mean that the car hasn't been sitting here for a lot longer. I wonder what happened to the baggage car…"

Mie had also asked herself the same question.

Beffort thought hard and continued, "It was un-hitched before us. Then they cleared out car 27 of all the passengers before unhitching us. The trap was set up beautifully."

"No doubt," Mie agreed, "but no one could have foreseen that we'd be traveling in this car. What would've happened if by chance we ended up in car 3 or 6?"

"Nothing would've changed. Wherever we were in the train, they could have isolated us at any given moment by doing the same thing. All they had to do were two things: unhitch the cars behind us and then the ones in front. The main thing was to do it at the right time so that our car could be brought here and boxed up."

All of a sudden he stopped talking. In the next compartment he could hear a voice.

"Mr. Beffort, listen to me! Mie Azusa, come here!"

Smith lit his flashlight, jumped to the floor and rushed into the other compartment. The beam of light swept over the bunks and froze on the luggage rack where a small tape recorder was softly humming.

"Mr. Beffort? Mie Azusa?"

The machine was hooked up to a kind of timer to start it playing after being programmed by whoever had left it there. Behind Smith, Mie whispered, "It's the voice of Miss Icho Fuji, isn't it?"

Smith did not answer. There was no point. From the first second, he had recognized the voice of Madame Atomos.

There was a moment of silence, then the tape recorder started talking again. "Madame Atomos here. It's 8 am and you only have a few hours to live. You can be sure that I am sorry not to be able to witness your painful death!"

The voice of the sinister woman spoke in pure hatred. Mie could not help shuddering. She would have sworn that no one would ever be able to save them in time.

"Your car," Madame Atomos resumed, "is sitting 20 feet below ground in a tunnel dug inside a vertical well. The well holds machinery that my technicians transformed into a hoist and a movable plug to obstruct your tunnel so tightly that air can't get in. I'm telling you this so that you know that it's hopeless for you. From now on nothing can save you from the certain death that I have in store."

There was another silence. Beffort turned off his flashlight and told Mie quietly to sit down before he did the same. The tape recorder was mute for a long minute, then Madame Atomos continued her monologue.

"I could have killed you in another way, in a more spectacular way, but I firmly believe that the United States will be dumbfounded in learning that Madame

Atomos made the train carrying the Befforts disappear. It will be like a magic trick, inexplicable, and when I launch a new attack against your fellow countrymen, my forces will have to face only a pathetic resistance. In fact, Smith Beffort, my laboratory is finished! In a few days it will begin producing a terrible bacteriological weapon that will reduce your country to dust. Tomorrow morning, at sunrise, you will have met your death. And your death will free me from my torments!"

Madame Atomos laughed. Smith knew all too well that the recording had been made the day before, but he still felt like his enemy was in the compartment with them. It was crazy!

In a softer voice Madame Atomos added, "You have been dangerous, courageous and intelligent adversaries. Your disappearance will be the symbol of my triumph because there will be nobody else to foil my projects so skillfully. Goodbye, Smith Beffort! Goodbye, Mie Azusa! Hiroshima! Nagasaki! Compliments of Madame Atomos!"

The recorder spun a few inches of blank tape before they heard a click. The machine was off for good.

Mie hugged her husband, but they did not say a word to each other. They were both thinking of the bacteriological weapon that would destroy the USA if no one stopped it quickly.

Two hours had passed since the start of the chase. Highway 60 was far behind them, as well as the city of Charleston and Dan Stone's Chrysler was no longer following the Rambler station wagon, but rather a huge moving truck with the name of a San Francisco company. It had happened very simply, just before Charleston, on a little side road snaking through the woods. The truck was parked right after a curve, its back door was wide open and the station wagon just had to drive up the two rails before disappearing into the big truck.

Since then the truck calmly took the road heading southwest. Costello, Ida Brown and their accomplices remained totally invisible, which made Charles Hyde nervous and worried.

Stone shot him a sidelong glance and said, "Its eight o'clock. If this truck is going to San Francisco, it won't get there for three days... By then the Befforts might not be with us anymore."

Clenching his jaws, Hyde was like a statue.

"What do you want to do?" Stone asked.

Hyde pointed at the truck. "Four out seven people in that vehicle probably know where Smith and Mie are. The problem is to capture one of them without making the others suspicious since they're no doubt leading us to Madame Atomos' laboratory."

Stone winced. "If they don't split up, your plan's no good."

"So," Hyde assured him, "we'll wait and see. I can't ruin our chances when Witter and Akamatsu might find where the Befforts' car is hiding out. After all, a train sticks out like sore thumb, doesn't it?"

Standing on the platform of the old switching station, Witter and Akamatsu were once again, and just as uselessly, examining the miles of track where car 27 had been unhitched.

"What do you think, Yosho?" Witter asked anxiously.

After being dropped off by an FBI helicopter, Akamatsu felt the full force of the frightening enigma. Even though he was used to the Machiavellian plots of

Madame Atomos, he was nowhere near measuring up to this event. Nevertheless, he was keeping a level head and to prove it said, "first of all it seems that Madame Atomos only had three ways of getting the Befforts' car off the tracks: by air, by disintegration or by burying it."

The latter solution rang dismally in Witter's ears. Still, he agreed and said, "We agree. Except that the first two are contradicted by reality. First of all, Madame Atomos doesn't have her famous disintegrator ray anymore. Secondly, no unidentified flying object was spotted in the sector by the radar."

"So, we're left with underground?"

Witter bared his teeth. "Okay! But who's going to discover it? Between mile 35 and the siding dozens of men have already gone over the ground without finding anything out of the ordinary." He pointed to the switches and the main track running into the hills to the east and said, "If car 27 is buried, it has to be within this perimeter—it's a mathematical fact. Just like it's a mathematical fact that Smith and Mie can't survive more than 24 hours if their car is somewhere without air circulating."

Akamatsu looked hard at him. "You've thought of everything, haven't you?"

"I think so. We studied all the possibilities before us, but it's obvious that nothing very effective can be done in less than 24 hours!"

"Couldn't we use a metal detector to…"

"No," Witter cut him off. "The area's full of tracks and pieces of metal. The search gave us nothing and we can't dig up so much land. Not in less than 24 hours anyway."

"Listening to you," Akamatsu reproached him, "it sounds like all hope is lost!"

"If there is any," Witter admitted frankly, not concealing the gravity of the situation, "it lies in Charles Hyde. We can't do anything here."

Yosho Akamatsu glanced at his watch. It was now 9 am.

James Edward Evans knew that he would soon have to make a crucial decision. Even though he was stuck in his office, he was keeping up-to-date on the operations and knew that Charles Hyde was holding the key to the mystery. However, and this was the sticky point, Evans had to solve alone a daunting moral dilemma. Leaving Hyde to follow the trail to the Atomos laboratory would inevitably be signing the death sentence of Smith and Mie. Choosing to neutralize the Costello-Brown team would save the Befforts lives but sever their contact with the A.O.F.M.A. for who knew how long.

Now, according to the specialists, the United States should be preparing for the next Atomos offensive because in their estimation, even though there was no confirmation, Madame Atomos had had plenty of time to finish building her laboratory. Therefore, put simply, the Befforts' lives were on the scales against hundreds and maybe thousands of Americans!

A grim scenario... which Evans forced himself to forget in the hope that some unexpected event might take the terrible weight off his shoulders. Then, around 9:10, he was informed that the press and the radio were talking about nothing but the Befforts' disappearance and Evans knew that the situation was slipping away from him. He felt a kind of relief. Someone would finally take responsibility for his burden.

He was not wrong. At 9:20 a bigwig from the White House asked for him on the telephone. A little stiff, he picked up, identified himself and was put through to one of the President's personal collaborators.

"Hello, Evans," he said rather aggressively, "we feel like you're not very enthusiastic about keeping us up-to-date."

The man did not specify what he was talking about, but there was no doubt about it. Only Madame Atomos could cause such a stir so early in the day.

"I have nothing new to tell you," Evans answered. "The papers…"

"The papers," the Secretary of State intervened, "don't say that agent Hyde is on the trail of a team working for Madame Atomos!"

"That's right," Evans agreed, "but you have to admit that it's not the kind of information you want to shout from the rooftops."

"We entirely agree. Still, we would like to tell you that we consider the discovery the new Atomos laboratory essential. Our position is clear: Charles Hyde does nothing to alert the enemy. Is that understood?"

Evans pursed his lips.

"Understood?" the other pressed him.

"Yes," Evans grumbled, "but I hope you're aware of the sacrifice that entails?"

"If you're alluding to the Befforts, don't blow it out of proportion, please. Dozens of men are searching for them in the limited area."

"Six miles of land," Evans reminded him, "can't be considered a limited area. Especially since car 27 is certainly buried." He licked his lips and added. "Do you know that Smith and Mie Beffort will be dead at this time tomorrow morning?"

"Do you know how many American citizens will die if Madame Atomos uses her laboratory?"

Evans did not answer. The Secretary of State's reply was exactly what he expected.

The White House man spoke again. "Plus, Evans, you can't deny that Smith Beffort would probably tell us to do exactly that if he could talk to us."

"Probably so," Evans said.

The conversation was taking a more humane turn. At the White House they must have understood the cruel position in which Evans was wallowing.

"Listen, Evans, do whatever you can to get the Befforts out of this predicament alive. You have carte blanche and unlimited resources. But, on the other hand, find and destroy that laboratory! You've been searching around San Francisco for a month and even though no one says anything, everyone in the government has been watching you! The United States can't be thrown into a panic again! We're counting on you."

"You can," J.E.E. murmured. "I'll do what I have to, Sir."

He hung up, switched on the interphone and asked to talk with Charles Hyde. It took them a moment to establish contact and then a red light blinked on the radio-telephone installed in his office. Evans went over and picked up the earphone.

"Hyde?"

"Go ahead," the distant voice of the G-man answered.

"Keep trailing them," J.E.E. said dryly, "but forget about the idea of grabbing a team member."

"Even if Witter draws a blank?"

"The laboratory above all else!" Evans growled. "Priority coming from the White House."

"Don't tell me you're going to sacrifice Smith and Mie!"

"We're not sacrificing anyone!" Evans exploded. "I'll use up millions of dollars and half a million men, but we're going to get the Befforts out of this scrape! As for you, Hyde, stick to them like a leech! If you lose them, I can tell you right now that there's a bunch of us who'll be looking for new jobs!"

He cut off communication angrily, threw on his coat and dashed out of his office. For peace of mind, he needed to get to the old switching station.

When Evans got off the helicopter, he went straight to Witter and Akamatsu, who were craning over the rails.

"Any news?" he asked as he approached.

The two men looked up. "Nothing. Nada." Witter said. "The fate of Smith and Mie now depend on Charles Hyde."

Evans shook his head. "We have to make do without him. The White House just formally vetoed our project. The Costello-Brown team has to be given a long leash all the way to the Atomos laboratory."

Akamatsu was jolted. "Sounds like they're condemning our friends to death, Evans! There's no recent trace of a train here. Look, the tracks have been rusted for years."

"What do you know about it," Evans shot back. "There are acids that produce rust in less than three hours! Listen, if your investigation shows that the car could only have been unhitched on this section of tracks, then it has to be here. And if it's here, we'll find it. How many men will it take to dig up these six miles of land before the middle of the afternoon?"

"Put one guy for every ten or twelve square feet," Witter answered coldly, "and the job will be finished by noon."

Evans did not blink. He turned around and said over his shoulder, "Get me to the nearest telephone. We're going to bring in a regiment of engineers and dig up the rails, the crossties, the roadbeds and the whole shebang!"

He sneered and concluded, "With the blessings of the White House!"

Chapter VI

While all the people were busy under the flood-lights, two men from the Green Dragon Force were working secretly in the wings. They had been in Oakland for a little while and were getting out of taxi across from 303 Santa Rosa Ave. Their names were Ben Brady and Art Baxter.

Baxter looked at the house standing across the street and furrowed his brow. "The shutters are closed and the lawn could use a good mow," he said out of the corner of his mouth. "That's unexpected, isn't it, Brady?"

"Wait and see," Brady murmured.

They crossed the street and headed toward the house next door where a man was smoking a pipe in his yard. Over the fence Baxter asked, "Say, do you know when the owners of that house will come back?"

The man took the pipe out of his mouth. "I don't know, but if you need to know, go ask the dairyman who's got a shop down the street."

"He's family?"

"No, but he should know since he hasn't been de-livering there."

Baxter smiled. "That's a good idea, but we don't want the whole neighborhood to know." He leaned over the fence and said softly, "See, we're here about an in-heritance."

This time the man stood up and came closer. Baxter had just piqued his curiosity while at the same time giving him the impression that he had earned a certain amount of trust. People like to feel important.

"Talking to you," Baxter added, "is already taking a big chance, but I'll have to admit that we don't have much choice."

Since he looked worried, the man reassured him, "I won't tell anyone, don't worry."

"Thanks. How long have your neighbors been away?"

"Around two months, except that the husband only left the other day. Well, yesterday morning to be exact. I guess he went to meet his wife and kids somewhere on the coast."

"Vacation?"

"That would be logical this time of the year, wouldn't it?"

"Of course," Baxter admitted. "Say, do they take two months vacation every year?"

"No. Usually they're only gone for two or three weeks." He winked and added, "But maybe they're expecting an inheritance? I noticed that my neighbor was kind of nervous lately. Money can trouble a man, can't it? A big load?"

Baxter stared at him coldly. "That's none of your business. Goodbye and thanks again."

Followed by Brady, he walked away. Farther down the street they entered a post office and Baxter asked to get in touch with Saint Louis, Missouri, where the secret base of the Green Dragon Force was located. His first contact was fast and clean. They exchanged small talk before a system of private relays rang the phone in the office of Owen Bernitz, the head of the Green Dragon Force and their only boss with Smith Beffort missing.

"G.D. here in Oakland," Baxter said.

"Okay, Art," Bernitz grumbled, "you can talk."

Now Baxter knew that nothing he said would be recorded. "As agreed," he started, "we followed up on Louis Radetich and his family. From the get go, something doesn't click, Owen."

"Keep going."

"Radetich's wife and kids have been on vacation for two months and the house looks abandoned."

"Doesn't cut it, Art."

"Every other year," Baxter continued, "the family only took two or three weeks. And the neighbor claims that Radetich looked worried for a while. Then there's the grass—growing like wild in the yard... Okay, it doesn't prove anything, but my hunch is there's trouble brewing."

"Hunches," Bernitz snapped, "are zilch!"

"Again according to the neighbor, Radetich didn't leave his house until yesterday morning. We know he went to Washington to hit the boss, but what was keeping him from going to visit his wife and kids?"

"Now that's better," Bernitz approved. "Except that before giving 'em hell I need specifics, Art. You're going to get information and fast. We gotta know if Radetich got any mail during the last two months, if he went off to the coast on the weekends, and if the weapon he used against Smith belonged to him. Show your Green Dragon card to the FBI local director. He's the one who gave the info to the boss right after the attack. Now, if Radetich's house was empty, who told the FBI the our bird flew the coop at 5 am?"

"The neighbor?" Art Baxter proposed. "My guess is that he spends his time spying on the neighborhood."

"We'll have to see, Art!" Bernitz snapped. "Get some tips together and call me back asap! GO!" He hung up.

Baxter did the same and dragged Brady to the nearest taxi stand. He did not need a ribbon around his finger to remind him that at the bottom of some hole in the ground Mie and Smith Beffort were slowly but surely dying...

A thousand men armed with pickaxes and jackhammers, three bulldozers and some explosives had transformed the switching station into a lunar landscape without revealing a trace of an underground passage.

At noon everyone took a break, including J.E.E. who was tired of pacing around the land for nothing. They had torn apart the loading platforms, the old switching post and the water tank. They had ripped up the tracks and crossties, and carried away tons of rocks from the roadbed. For miles around the land was barren, as if it had been plowed for sowing. A crane had lifted away the scales and the turntable, which were glistening in the sunshine.

The huge engine shed was a pile of ruins far from its foundation, which had been dug up by the bulldozers and lay with gaping holes like a toothless mouth.

"Unbelievable!" Evans said downheartedly. "All this demolition with no result!" He took a deep breath and turned to Witter and Akamatsu. "So what do we do now?"

Admitting his helplessness, Witter shrugged. "We've dug three feet deep. Let's go five or ten."

Akamatsu stared at the horizon mutely. When he heard Witter's suggestion, he stirred, saying, "In my opinion, it's no use. The entrance to an underground passage would have to be at surface level and I'm not talking about a little hole in the ground, but a real tunnel 15 feet high! In our desperate search, we've lost sight of how big it is what we're looking for. Come on, it would take a huge hole to bury car 27 in!"

Evans nodded. "The hole was there and was specially modified to hold car 27. Madame Atomos waited patiently for the right time to put Smith on the trail of Costello by means of Radetich acting under hypnosis or a drug or some other means of persuasion. In that case, Yosho, after such considerable preparations, do you think that Madame Atomos didn't anticipate our every move?"

"Let's say she did. It doesn't change a thing."

"Sorry! Let's do the opposite of what Madame Atomos anticipated and maybe we'll get some results!"

Witter closed his eyes, putting his hands up to his head. "Slow down, would you? Talking in the abstract only starts when you don't understand a thing. We should have dug and we dug. Now, you're saying we shouldn't have dug!"

Evans forced a smile. "It's not very clear," he admitted, "but I expressed myself badly. I meant to say that in churning up the land, we've probably destroyed any clues that were there. Clues that would have made our search easier without digging."

"There were no clues," Witter retorted, "and you know it! Before turning into prospectors we examined everything: the tracks, the crossties, etc. In truth, as I've already said, we're paralyzed by the White House decision. The only way of saving the Befforts was to let Charles Hyde do something. There's nothing we can get out of here!"

He was getting worked up, forgetting that Evans was really not to blame, caught as he was between a rock and a hard place and he would have blamed him at the drop of a hat.

Akamatsu felt that their relations were about to deteriorate, which would break up the unity of the anti-Atomos forces and the Befforts would suffer the consequences. "Let's stop talking about it and start thinking," he proposed. "I think we have to put ourselves in Smith's shoes. He's underground and knows that we're searching for him. Right?"

"Right," Evans admitted.

"Okay," Witter said. "So?"

"So," Akamatsu said, "what's he going to do to try to give us a signal?"

Evans and Witter looked at each other. Akamatsu certainly gave them food for thought.

In the train car, it was still dark, but the temperature had risen several degrees. At the same time, the air was noticeably thinner. Smith and Mie were not yet feeling the first signs of suffocation, but their ears were ringing and their blood was pumping faster.

"They stopped," Mie said softly.

For a long time the ground shook under the blows of the pickaxes, the jackhammers and the bulldozers. Then everything fell inexplicably silent, heavy, dismal like a shroud.

Smith wiped off his sweat, forgot about his thirst and said, "Anyway, they're not far from us. Madame Atomos said that our car was 20 feet underground, but I think she was talking about the bottom of the tunnel."

"What does it matter?"

"Look, Mie," Smith explained quietly, "that means that the upper part of the tunnel is only six feet from the open air. Otherwise we wouldn't have heard any noise."

"To me it's the same thing," she sighed in resignation. "I don't see the difference between dying 20 feet underground or only six."

"Don't get discouraged," Smith advised her. "You know that our saviors are close. They're going to continued digging, find the concrete slab that's the ceiling of this tunnel and…"

"Before that," Mie cut him off, "they have to dig right above us. You haven't said anything, but it sounds like they're searching everywhere except where we are."

Smith remained silent. Heavy vehicles had driven overhead and there were crashes, shocks and explosions, but no jackhammer had gone at their immediate surroundings. He could not understand it.

"Apparently," Mie resumed, "they're searching at random in a wide area where our car's buried, but they haven't found any precise indication of where we are. It could take them weeks. Plus, they've stopped working, haven't they?" She stopped talking and listened hard, in vain. Then she asked, "What time is it, Smith?"

"Half past noon."

She said nothing, but he knew that she was thinking of how long they had left to live. 15 to 16 hours, no more.

At 3:05 the telephone rang again in Bernitz' underground office. The big man picked it up, took the ever-present cigar stub out of his mouth and said, "Owen here. Let's hear it."

"Art," Baxter said curtly, calling as agreed from the Oakland FBI office. "I've got a bunch of tips on Louis Radetich."

Bernitz started the tape recorder that was connected directly to the phone. "Go on, Art, I'm getting it."

"First of all," Baxter started, "I got proof that Radetich didn't make any trips over the last two months. Next, but this isn't sure, they think the Glenmont Company, which is headquartered in Bethesda, made no price inquiry for a possible purchase of 50 tons of sheet metal. Then it looks like the contract typed in triplicate that Radetich had in his briefcase was only made up to justify his trip to Washington."

"Okay! Mrs. Radetich and the kids?"

"A mystery. No one knows where they are. More: no one saw them leave. But around the neighborhood and especially on Santa Rosa Avenue they have a tight community. That's how I learned that Radetich is an ace marksman!"

"No kidding?"

"And how, Owen! He's even the champion of his shooting club. Funny that he missed Smith at less than six feet away, isn't it?"

"The Colt?"

"It could belong to him. We dug up a box of bullets in his office, 11 mm. Besides that his secretary assured us that he'd changed a lot lately. Even though business was good and he had no reason to be troubled. According to the secretary, Radetich must have been fighting with his wife."

"Yeah," Bernitz growled, "but I think instead that the guy went nuts because of the A.O.F.M.A.! Good husband, good father, tireless worker. Without your investigation he would've come through with flying colors. The bastard."

"You've kept an eye on him, right, Owen?"

"Come on! Stutton hasn't lost sight of him since Evans kindly cleared him. He'll be nabbed in ten minutes."

"What do I do now?"

"Stay in Oakland with Brady and make like a shadow. No need for Mama Atomos to spot you. When the Costello-Brown team gets there, you'll be ready to give Hyde a hand. Meantime, get in touch with Ritter. He's the one who's on the A.O.F.M.A. in San Francisco across the bay. He'll be interested in the Radetich case."

"Okay. Next check in?"

"Tonight, 8 pm. Later, Art."

Bernitz hung up and immediately dialed a number in Washington D.C. A few seconds ticked off before Bernitz was on the line with one of his men in touch with Ralph Stutton. He identified himself and asked, "Still got a handle on Stutton, Sammy?"

"Sure," the other confirmed. "Last heard the Radetich guy was buying a plane ticket. He's most likely going back to Oakland."

Bernitz snickered silently. "He's not going back home, Sammy. You and Stutton are going to shanghai him nice and quiet. Nice and quiet means no witnesses."

"At the airport in the middle of the day?"

"The element of surprise and I know just the way to make him do exactly what we want. We just have to get him a note with the A.O.F.M.A. sign and give him an emergency meet in a remote corner of the airport. Then you can nab him."

"We'll give it s shot. And what do we do after?"

"You keep him warm for me until 5 pm. I'll leave here in ten minutes. Be careful! If any A.O.F.M.A. people witness the move, Radetich's hide won't be worth a plug nickel. And we need him alive! The guy ought to know where the boss and his wife are! Got it?"

"Got it. We'll put on our kid gloves."

Bernitz hung up and rang for a car to take him to the station. He left with no luggage, not even an extra shirt, but he did not care in the least. He was too worried about the Befforts to be thinking about himself.

Chapter VII

Sitting still in his chair, Radetich, suddenly grown old, was drifting off listening to Owen Bernitz. Everything had happened too fast for him since the fake message at the airport. In the first place, he had really believed that he was among men belonging to the A.O.F.M.A. Then this guy's behavior made him think he was facing G-men. Now, without any warning, Bernitz was telling him straight out that it was a pure and simple kidnapping and that the Green Dragon Force was behind it.

Radetich quickly found himself between the devil and the deep blue sea. All the more so since Bernitz had taken the gloves off and was accusing him of working voluntarily for the new Atomos Organization.

"You're wrong," Radetich finally reacted. "If Madame Atomos hadn't kidnapped my wife and kids, I wouldn't be here!"

This did not surprise Bernitz.

"I shot at Smith Beffort," Radetich continued, "but I got the order directly from Costello! Luckily Costello also ordered me not to hit Beffort. If the waiter hadn't moved, my actions would have done completely harmless!"

Bernitz bared his teeth. "You steered Beffort onto Costello's trail! You got him to take a train that was sure to be heading into a trap! Don't tell me you didn't know that!"

Radetich smiled wearily. "I didn't know," he said.

"You played the game," Bernitz attacked. "They thought you were drugged or radio-controlled but you were acting of your own free will!"

"That's true," Radetich admitted, staring him straight in the eyes, "but you would've done the same if you got your wife's left hand in the mail!"

Bernitz' fury evaporated instantly. Ralph Stutton and Sammy fidgeted around. Radetich scowled and put a finger over the nervous tic in his eye.

"The package came around two months ago when I was about to inform the police. After I opened it, Costello called me. He told me to stay calm. If I didn't obey, my wife's right hand would arrive within 24 hours… As you said, I acted of my own free will!"

Bernitz did not reply. Even without proof, he was still sure that Radetich was telling the truth. The hand in the mail was exactly the horrible kind of detail that the twisted brain of Madame Atomos would concoct.

He looked at Radetich. "You're a brave man."

"No, I'm a panicking man. For two months I haven't had the slightest idea of what's become of my wife and children. I'm scared that some unconscious action of mine might be misinterpreted by Madame Atomos and whenever the mailman rings my bell, I can't rest until I see he's not carrying a package. For example, right now, I wonder what decision Madame Atomos will make regarding my family when she learns that I'm in the hands of the Green Dragon Force."

"You can be sure that no one saw you taken away."

"Maybe, but did you know that I have orders to get back to San Francisco on the 3:17 plane?"

Bernitz clenched his jaws. By holding Radetich, he would certainly cause his wife and six kids to be executed! "Do you think you're being watched by the Atomos Organization?"

"Why should they? Who would imagine that I'd be crazy enough to disobey? Still, if I'm not at home tonight, they'll know something went wrong."

He said this without losing his head, a man expecting the worst for too long to overreact now. Obviously Radetich reached and passed the depths of despair. If Bernitz asked him about his family, he would probably answer that he had only a slim hope in their chance of survival. However, in spite of this, he kept fighting in his way, unthinkingly, without worrying about the fate reserved for his own, personal future.

"You'll be home tonight," Bernitz stated. "Ralph, call the FBI headquarters. We need a jet fighter ready in 30 minutes." Stutton dashed off into the next room where the telephone was.

Bernitz turned back around to Radetich. "Like that, you'll be in Oakland before the regular plane. With a little cunning you can mix in with the passengers and any would-be observer from the A.O.F.M.A. will see nothing amiss. From now on you're under our protection. What are you supposed to do when you get home?"

"Nothing much. I guess Costello will contact me when Madame Atomos needs me again…" He shrugged and added, "Unless they don't need me anymore and want to kill me to keep me quiet forever."

"Won't fly," Bernitz grumbled. "The life of your family is a sure guarantee. Plus, you didn't tell us much. You don't know anything, do you? I was hoping for more from you, but Costello only told you what he had to."

"So you kidnapped me for nothing."

"Not really," Bernitz replied. "Now we know that you aren't working voluntarily for the Atomos Organization. Though it doesn't give us an edge, it does give us some satisfaction. In case of an emergency, as long as your family doesn't pay the price, I think you'll fight on our side?"

"I'm already on your side. But it's obvious that Madame Atomos has got me on a leash. It would take some really extraordinary circumstances to make me get off the fence I have to straddle."

Bernitz leaned over to him. "Listen, Radetich, this fight is nothing like a regular war. There are no front lines, no uniforms, no flags. And there are no holds barred. In the ring it's Madame Atomos against humanity. We don't need your formal declaration of support. We're only asking you to alert us if Costello or another member of the A.O.F.M.A. calls you."

"I hear you," Radetich assured. "Say, what's the deal between the Atomos Organization and the A.O.F.M.A.?"

"The first provides the men, the second the money, but sometimes it happens that the 'backers' of the new Atomos power become actors when the situation gets rough for their safety. This makes them very dangerous because even though Costello is obviously a member of the Atomos Organization, no one can say whether your bank manager is one of the chiefs of the A.O.F.M.A."

In a corner, standing agape, Sammy was listening to Owen, who usually spoke more crudely and used a lot of slang in order to spice up his conversation. Today he was talking like Evans or Beffort with perfect seriousness.

Eyes narrowed, Radetich was thinking. "You know," he said, "I often wondered why Madame Atomos chose me out of all the people in Oakland…"

"What's for sure," Bernitz stated, "is that she didn't choose you at random. It would take a very good marksman to miss Smith Beffort and you're the champion of your club."

"That's true, but how did she know? There are other good marksmen in Oakland. If my bank manager might be a member of the A.O.F.M.A., why can't one of my colleagues…"

"Or a friend or family member?" Owen slipped in, being on the same wavelength.

Radetich looked a little dazed. So far he had no idea where Madame Atomos' informant came from. From now on this informant could be located, if they could identify him…

Bernitz said, "It won't be easy, but if you can, you'll be hitting two birds with one stone. First this person will likely have a lot to say about the kidnapping of your wife and kids and where they're being held prisoner. Second he'll give us a new trail to the laboratory."

Radetich's face betrayed his emotion. Frozen for two months in a demoralizing waiting game, he was finally glimpsing the possibility of direct action against Madame Atomos and her criminal organization.

Bernitz watched him and knew that he was about to jump into the battle fray. He said, "Don't do anything stupid, Radetich. Getting yourself killed won't do any good. Got a heater on you?" Owen had suddenly find his old tongue again.

"No," Radetich said, "but at home…"

"At home," Bernitz cut him off, "is not right next door!" He slipped his hand into his pocket and brought out a skinny weapon with a kind of antenna for a barrel, a button trigger and a reservoir instead of a cylinder. "Take this. It's a paralyzing pistol. The guy you baste with this ray will be petrified for 60 minutes."

Radetich weighed the weapon carefully and a thin smile lit up his face.

Just then Ralph Stutton appeared in the doorway and said, "Headquarters is okay for the jet."

Bernitz looked at his watch and got up. "Let's go, Radetich. It's time to leave if you want to get there before the 3:17 plane. When we're on the road I'll tell you how to contact us fast in case of an emergency.

There were only four men standing at center of the switching station and its six miles of track. A gag order had been given and on this piece of American soil you could hear a pin drop. Evans, Akamatsu and Witter were watching the operator with his headphones carefully tuning his sound sensor. He swept over a 30 square foot area from his boom, looked up at Evans and shook his head before moving on a few feet.

It had been going on for hours and the sun was now setting. Starting from the wide curve to the east, the operation was carried out methodically but with aggravating slowness. It was almost 6 pm and they still had not hit the vast open space of the switching station. At this rate, they would not reach the end of the quadrangle before noon tomorrow.

"We're gambling with the lives of our friends," Akamatsu said suddenly. "If luck has it that their car is buried in the sector we can check before dawn, we'll win. But if that's not the case?"

Witter winced. "You're the one who came up with this system, Yosho. I'll say it again that this thing is useless if Smith is sitting still and quiet at the bottom of his hole. And I believe that's exactly what he'll do to save oxygen."

Evans sighed, "I don't think we'll find them. Sam Forbes and Lucky Simms died under almost identical conditions when the search parties knew approximately where they were."

The operator took off his headphones. His name was Morton, he belonged to the FBI and he had his fair share of ingenuity. "We've got to make Beffort show himself."

"How?" Evans asked.

Morton lit a cigarette and said, "Send him a message by Morse code."

"Yeah!" Witter mocked. "That's easy! And at 20 of 30 feet underground, he'll receive it, right?"

Morton was not flustered. "Even at 50 feet he'll hear a message pounded out on the ground by a thousand senders. Orchestrated by a leader and with a pickaxe handle in every hand, they can beat in rhythm a Morse like, *Beffort answer... Beffort answer...* or something. Between the calls a hundred sensors together with mine will wait for an answer. Of course, Beffort will have to strike a couple of metal objects together without stopping. Right now, he's obviously not thinking of it because we're silent. Logically he must be thinking that we've given up."

He bent down, picked up two big rocks and spoke to illustrate his action.

"One single blow will equal a dot. Two blows together will be a dash. It's the prison telephone. Beffort should know, right? *Tap... tap, tap... Tap... tap, tap.*"

"Damn!" Evans shouted. "That's the solution! Witter, bring the men back with their pickaxes! Morton, you take care of the sensors! How long for everything to be set up?"

"An hour max," Morton replied. "But you've got to repeat to the boys, if they don't strike in perfect unison, the message will be incomprehensible. Hey, you know, it won't be a picnic."

The heat was getting unbearable and the air harder to breathe, taking on a weird consistency, transforming slowly into a kind of syrup that their lungs had trouble absorbing. Contractions, wheezing, dizzy spells…

A slow death, gruesome, that they awaited in full consciousness. The Atomos death!

Bathed in sweat, Mie turned over on her bunk, felt for Smith's hand and squeezed it. "We won't hold out until morning," she panted. "What time is it?"

"6:30"

"Have they really given up?"

"No. I'm sure they're fixing up something, trying to figure out how to spot us. It can't be easy."

"When they're found us, it'll still take hours for them to get us out of here."

"Sure, but they'll send us down some oxygen before that."

Smith did not believe a word of what he was saying. In truth, he figured that the search had stopped in this area and moved elsewhere. It was logical. They would start up again later, but when?

"We really can't do anything, Smith?"

He had thought about it too long to delude himself. "Our car is literally stuck on five sides. With some tools maybe I could pry off a plank and slip between the wheels and crawl to the plug that's obstructing the tunnel…"

"Except," Mie intervened, "you have no tools."

Smith lit up the compartment with the flashlight and shined it on the paralyzing pistol and a pocketknife. "That's everything we've got. In a pinch I could unscrew one of the metal luggage racks, but what use would that be? So?"

Mie sat up on an elbow. "If we open the back door, we can't get to the plug?"

"Yes," Smith admitted. "But to open a solid concrete slab would take an explosion or at the very least a crowbar."

When he saw the desperation in his wife's eyes he decided to do the good deed and play the optimist. "I'll unscrew the luggage rack anyway. Hold the flashlight and shine it on me, Mie."

"You just said that it would be no use."

"I changed my mind. After all, the rack is steel and we can test how solid the concrete is."

"Concrete," Mie mumbled, "is not a brick wall."

"That depends on how thick it is. If it sounds hollow, I'll certainly be able to break it. Can you aim the light over here, Mie?"

He knew that all his efforts were in vain and was surprised to loosen the first screw with the flimsy blade of the pocketknife. Then he worked slowly, pretending to hit a stubborn screw.

While watching him work, Mie thought of nothing but death.

Chapter VIII

Ready on site 20 minutes before the plane from Washington landed, Louis Radetich had no problem mixing in with the group of passengers heading toward the main terminal. His move had no doubt been made easier by the darkness that now bothered Radetich who wanted to detect any would-be surveillance. He found his car in the parking lot and sat behind the wheel, keeping an eye on the rear-view mirror.

During the drive home, he saw no suspicious cars following him. When he pulled up to 303 Santa Rosa Avenue, his heart felt terribly empty. He had been vaguely prepared for some immediate action but now he felt that the physical encounter he was hoping for would not happen tonight.

After parking his car in the garage, he went straight to the entrance hall of the deserted house and right away felt the crushing weight of his solitude. Unthinkingly, he opened his briefcase and put away the documents, but he slipped the paralyzing pistol into his belt. He silently went through the house from the basement to the attic and made sure that all the doors and windows were locked, just as Owen Bernitz had advised him.

Then he picked up the phone, dialed a number and only had to wait for one ring before he said, "Radetich here."

"Are you home?" Art Baxter asked.

"Yes, everything's fine since I got to the airport, so I have nothing special to report."

Baxter sensed his disappointment. "Don't get impatient," he advised. "The Atomos Organization doesn't usually throw in the towel and we can't forget that most of its people are heading for Oakland right now behind Costello and Ida Brown. Theoretically they shouldn't need you for two or three days. Act normal."

"It'd be hard for me to do otherwise!" Radetich raged.

"It's better that way, believe me, because there's nine chances out of ten that they're watching you. The fact that you're still alive proves that Madame Atomos doesn't know about your meeting with the Green Dragon."

Radetich sank back in his chair and murmured. "Doing nothing will end up driving me crazy. While I'm sitting here, what's happening to my wife and children?"

"No one, me least of all, can answer your question right now," Baxter said softly, "but you have to understand how important you are in the coming events. At the moment the whole Atomos Organization is waiting for only one thing: the announcement of the Befforts' death. From now on, I mean until tomorrow morning, nothing serious will happen. If you can't sleep, do like everyone else, Radetich: sit down and turn on your television. They're broadcasting live from the switching station because every American is interested in the situation."

"I understand, but my family…"

"If the Befforts die," Art Baxter cut in, "we can all start preparing for the same fate! Madame Atomos will go hog wild celebrating her victory and the country will suffer the most dreadful disaster in its history. Turn on your TV, pal, and forget about your personal troubles. Smith and Mie Beffort have disappeared—it's like 100 H bombs are exploding over the USA! Good night."

Radetich heard a click, hung up in turn, and turned on his TV.

If Madame Atomos had chosen to kill the Befforts like this, it was to satisfy her need for vengeance and at the same time get some self-advertising. People were not talking enough about her; and a little too much about Miss Icho Fuji.

Even though she was both these women in one, she was aware that her new appearance was no longer enough for her. Unbelievably rejuvenated, transformed into a ravishing young woman by the miracle of self-disintegration, she had lived through an extraordinary adventure when she became the mistress of Yosho Akamatsu.

It could have lasted a long time if Icho Fuji had not been literally controlled by Madame Atomos. The latter was the mind, the former the body and this reversal of personality had prevented the total mutation caused—God knows how!—by computers.

Finally, Madame Atomos remained Madame Atomos in the skin of another, which, all things considered, became bothersome. For, the mind was disturbed by the body. A body with nagging feelings that had to be satisfied if she did not want to sink into a pernicious, mental repression. But then the mind was working better, even though it fell short of its old performance. To the extent that the construction of the new laboratory had expanded, dragged on for months and the whole Atomos Organization, like its boss, was lacking punch and imagination.

In short, Madame Atomos was almost regretting her rejuvenation and its carnal needs that prevented her from

81

dedicating herself fully to her vengeance, the supreme goal of her life.

Thus, she figured that she had not taken enough precautions concerning the Befforts. Lacking moderation, carried away by unusual passion, she had responded spontaneously to the article published in the press. They said she was dead. They were putting Icho Fuji in her place.

Hiroshima! Nagasaki!

Madame Atomos had let loose a war cry and a few hours later Smith and Mie were rotting away at the bottom of their hole with her compliments, the prospect of a long and painful death, and only one out of ten chances to see the light of day again. It was one chance too many!

Formerly, Madame Atomos would have delved deeper into the problem and fixed it so that the baggage car would have been unhitched an hour or two before the Befforts'. This would have made the search zone huge and the entire Unites States army could not have covered it! Instead of this, Madame Atomos must have been watching the thousands of men walking around on top of the Befforts. Because, like all the Americans, she was also sitting in front of her television screen that was sending direct images from the switching station. But with the landscape churned up by bulldozers the terrible woman could not have said definitively where the well that led to the tunnel was. She no longer recognized anything and she sweated every time a shovel hit the ground. She was drowning in suspense! She almost died of a heart attack.

One man and a pickaxe for every 30 square feet. A sound sensor working over every 300 square feet. A throng of floodlights shining through the night and lighting up Morton who was standing on a hastily built observation tower, holding a microphone wired to 20 loudspeakers and getting ready to play the delicate role of maestro.

Motionless, filled with emotion, almost petrified, Evans , Akamatsu and Witter.

Farther away waited the HF cameras with telephoto lens, their technicians frozen and the reporters whispering to respect the orders of silence. An endlessly dramatic air extended over everything all the way into every house.

The direct broadcast had emptied the streets, the countryside, the theaters and restaurants, the train stations and airports. America and the rest of the world sat before their televisions or in front of their radios. Madame Atomos' name was on everyone's lips, pronounced in every language.

"Attention!" Morton shouted.

His voice, loudly amplified, rolled through the valley, then over the entire Earth, with an infernal force. At the same time, the pickaxe handles rose up.

"5, 4, 3, 2, 1, 0!"

A pause and then, "Dot... Dot... Dot." In rhythm, the picks typed, "*Tap... Tap... Tap...*, composing the S of Morse Code, the first letter of Smith that they had chosen over Beffort, thereby saving two letters to simplify the message. Nevertheless, to send out "Smith, answer," with the double taps for the dash, it took them 60 seconds.

"Stop!" Morton ordered.

Instant silence and the sensors swept over the ground trying to pick up an answer for another minute.

Every operator had a whistle to blow in case of response, but the first try was fruitless. They started again.

Twenty minutes later, they still had no answer, but there was obviously no question of stopping. They were playing their final card and had no other options.

Smith had completely unscrewed the luggage rack before Mie was exhausted by the lack of oxygen and had to lie down on the bunk. She had fought against it for an instant before her eyes closed and she dropped off to sleep.

Smith knew that she would never wake up again. The air had become more and more unbreathable over the hours and he was already feeling the lethal effects of anoxemia that inevitably followed anoxia.

He put the metal rack on the ground, left the flashlight on and lay down on the bunk. Now Smith was sinking into an unconsciousness that would probably have been eternal if nothing had disturbed the silence around him. It came from very far away and had a definite rhythm, persistently piercing the wall that separated Beffort from reality. But, tedious because of its monotony, the call almost changed into a lullaby, becoming in Smith's sleepy mind the dull and syncopated sound of a moving train.

Things were going against the goal desired by Morton and the pickaxe men, completely unaware, who continued, unfazed, their weird concert. Then Smith's brain finally sent out a hazy signal that was like a train approaching a switch. Lying down in the car, the body answered the brain. Smith opened his eyes, saw a glass door reflecting the pale halo of the flashlight and tried to figure out where the sounds were coming from. Faraway, the sounds became louder as he focused his attention until they were nearby, finally raining down in a still meaningless, pitter-pattering barrage. With extraordinary effort Beffort sat up, mouth hanging open, desperately pumping the scarce oxygen, listening with all his strength.

Tap, tap, tap... Tap-tap. Tap-tap... tap, tap... Tap-tap...

Automatically, by reflex, his mind translated: 3 dots, S; 2 dashes, M; 2 dots, I; 1 dash, T...

Beffort fell backward, not sure that he was not dreaming, but still recording the whole message: *Smith, answer.*

Then there was silence, the call repeated, another silence. Time enough to listen. Beffort tried to scream, but only produced a ridiculous groan that popped inside his skull. He lay back down, worn out.

Half-asleep, instinctively getting some strength back, he listened again to the shocks echoing through the ground. They were calling him from the surface, but maybe he could not answer!

Mie brought her hands up to her throat and then started scratching at her chest. She was suffocating. Smith's arm fell off the bunk and his fingers touched the metal rack, gripping it furiously...

They were on the 42nd call and everyone had lost hope when a whistle sounded during the listening break. No one moved, as the order had been given and Morton turned off his mic while Evans, Akamatsu and Witter ran silently to the operator who was waving his arms excitedly.

He was standing around a ditch containing the dismantled machinery from the turntable and had clearly heard the blows that Beffort was making with the fortuitously unscrewed rack. Metal against metal. Loud cracks echoing in the headphones like a howitzer going off, deafening, in the direct line of fire. It lasted 15 seconds and then abruptly stopped.

"Where is it?" Evans asked, white as a sheet.

The guy tapped his foot. "Right under here, very close… Anyway, no more than 20 or 30 feet."

Evans raised his arms. From the end of the platform a truck raced forth carrying an oxygen pump and towing a drill mounted on a twenty-foot trailer. One inch diameter and a bit that could shatter the rock…

Akamatsu and Witter leaned over the well. "A light!" Akamatsu yelled.

The engineering officer aimed his flashlight at the hole and was immediately astonished. "Takes some heavy machinery to move a turntable!"

While hauling out the turntable, the bulldozer had destroyed the mechanism inside the well. At the time, because of the wreckage, no one had noticed the two motors or the guide tubes or even the huge counterweights.

Now, in spite of the twisted scrap metal, Akamatsu saw the installation clearly. He said, "Hydraulic system. The turntable wasn't turning round, but going up and down! Nice work!"

The light shined by the officer traced the clear circle of concrete, revealing the dozen, massive, steel hinges of the plug.

"A huge waterproof chamber door!" he said.

Ten feet away the drill started up, whining, biting, piercing the ground like it was paper.

Evans arrived, all worked up. They'll have air in ten minutes," he babbled.

"That'll be fine if they can breathe," Akamatsu responded. "Why do you think Beffort stopped answering?"

Suddenly Evans went pale. "That'd be too stupid!"

Akamatsu nodded at the well. "We should work faster. Plus, the two jobs won't get in each other's way. The drilling can continue, keep sending down air, but we can also blow out the plug as soon as possible!"

Evans turned to the engineer. "Is that up your alley?"

The officer smiled, nodded and rushed off to the military truck. 60 seconds later he came back leading a team with a ladder, a portable Hugh drill and a pack of explosives. "Back off," he said, "this well's gonna blow in a minute and shrapnel will fly."

The portable drill whined in unison with the whirring drilling machine with an irritating noise. Evans stepped away, pulling Witter and Akamatsu with him, looked at his watch and bit his thumbnail impatiently.

All of a sudden, the pyrotechnicians jumped out of the well, yanked up the ladder and dove. There was a Boom!, ridiculously faint, but a spray of debris sprang out of the hole, scattered in the air and rained down. The men were already replacing the ladder and flying down while an ambulance sped up with its siren screaming for no good reason.

Just like in a well-directed movie, men jumped out carrying stretchers, followed by the intensive care unit connecting the masks to oxygen bottles. Then, on the backs of the men, Smith and Mie appeared, unconscious.

Evans ran up. A major stopped him, understood his unasked question, winked and gently pushed him back. "Okay, they're alive. Come to see them in the hospital in Charleston. In the meantime, stay back, please."

Evans stepped back obediently, his eyes moist, as happy as he was on the day his son was born.

Madame Atomos screamed out in rage and threw her television on the floor. Then she ran to the telephone inside her laboratory. She was shaking with anger and was forced to dial the number twice before getting it right, which upset her even more as she listened to the endless ringing.

When someone picked up, she exploded, "Summer, contact Radetich immediately! Get him to Charleston right now! This time, he has to kill Mie and Smith Beffort at the hospital! As a backup, get Downing on the same mission!"

"Downing is heading for Oakland right now, Madame."

"Change of plans! I want him to backup Radetich!"

She slammed the phone down, and stood under the ceiling fan. For the first time, Madame Atomos was feeling a lack of nerves.

Chapter IX

Louis Radetich had ended up falling asleep in front of his television screen without seeing the latest news update, but feeling confident about the Befforts' fate. The ringing telephone woke him up around 1 am. Radetich reached out, picked up and identified himself.

"Summer here," said an unfamiliar voice. "I'm a friend of Robert Costello."

Radetich was jolted awake. "Watch what you say," he murmured, "I'm not sure my telephone…"

This was part of the plan cooked up by Owen Bernitz to force the other end to tip his hand. Summer only had to give an outline. He knew very well that Radetich's line might be bugged. He was already afraid that he had said too much.

Not to panic him, Radetich added, "Just a precaution, but twice as careful, twice as safe, right?"

Summer felt a little better. "I have an important message for you," he whispered instinctively. "How soon can you meet me on the main road in Lakeside Park?"

"15 minutes," Radetich said.

"Bring a suitcase. You're taking trip… But we'll talk about that soon. Hurry up. At Lakeside Park, park by the sidewalk on the lake and wait. I'll be meeting you myself. See you soon, Radetich."

Summer hung up. Radetich did the same, then feverishly dialed a number, waited, biting his lip and frowning when he heard a voice he did not recognize.

"Louis Radetich here," he said warily. "Who are you?"

"Ben Brady. Why are you anxious?"

"The man who's supposed to answer is named Baxter."

"He's sleeping. But I know all about your situation so go on."

Radetich gulped and hesitated. Owen Bernitz had warned him to be extremely cautious and now he was seeing traps in the smallest unexpected event. He said, "Baxter never mentioned your name."

"Okay! Hold the line, I'll get him out of bed!"

There were four minutes of silence before Baxter's voice came over the line. "What's happening, Radetich?"

"I just got a call from a guy named Summer," Radetich answered with relief. "He's a friend of Costello and wants me to meet him right away on the main road in Lakeside Park near Lake Merritt."

"He didn't say anything else?"

"Yes. I'm going to take a trip, but he didn't say where. What are you going to do?"

"Nothing much. Go to your meeting and don't worry about anything. Someone will trail Summer after he's given you instructions and I hope he'll lead us back to the laboratory. Before you get the train or plane, call back on this number to give us your destination."

"That's all?"

Baxter laughed softly. "You don't realize it, Radetich, but thanks to you we've finally got some fresh leads!"

"If you arrested Summer," Radetich retorted, "you could find out right away where my wife and children are. Since Smith and Mie Beffort are out of danger, I figure you should be worrying about my family from now on. If you don't do anything, I'll take care of Summer myself!"

He was suddenly becoming worked up. Baxter brought him down. "If you do, pal, Madame Atomos will know all about it in no time. And if Summer doesn't know what's become of your family, you'll be responsible for a monumental mistake." Radetich did not respond. Baxter went on, "You've got your experience in your field and we've got ours in the fight against Madame Atomos and her organization. Get to Lakeside Park, call us afterward, and let us do our job. Okay?"

"Okay, Radetich accepted."

He hung up and took a deep breath to calm down. At this rate his nerves would not hold out for long. When he went into the next room, he avoided looking at the family photo on the dresser. He opened the closet and took out a suitcase that he hastily stuffed with indispensable underwear and toiletries. He threw in two shirts and a pair of shoes, snapped it shut and went out through the side door to the garage.

Five minutes later his car pulled up along the sidewalk of the main road facing Lake Merritt. The place was quite dark and deserted. All on edge, Louis Radetich lit a cigarette. He had seen no one was and wondered if the Green Dragon Force had really had time to set up a team to follow Summer.

A minute passed, then Radetich thought he saw a shadow move around one of the bushes bordering the lake. He felt like he was being watched and this made him even more nervous.

Unconsciously, his hand dropped to his belt to feel the warm butt of the paralyzing pistol. At the same time he threw his cigarette out, which arched through the air before rolling on the sidewalk, leaving a trail of sparks, then going black. Radetich slumped down in his seat and waited. This rendezvous might only be a pretext for Summer to hide in the shadows and get him in his sights…

"Radetich?"

The man leaned through the window. A round face, very anonymous and a little flabby. Nothing like the killer Radetich had imagined.

"Here's a plane ticket. In the package, there's a gun…" Summer spoke rapid-fire, scrutinizing the night suspiciously. His anxiety made Radetich calm. Madame Atomos' people were human and vulnerable.

Summer stood up straight, listened hard, and then leaned in again. "In 20 minutes a jet's taking off for New York with a layover in Charleston. There you'll go to General Hospital where Smith and Mie Beffort are under observation…"

Radetich picked up the package. By its size and weight he knew that Summer was giving him a serious weapon.

"The package also has a silencer," Summer said, sounding more confident. "With a little luck you might have time to escape after killing them…"

Radetich was petrified. From the start he knew that they would order him to do something like this. His lack of reaction surprised Summer.

"You understand?" he asked.

"I understand," Radetich answered, "but what do I do if they don't let me into the hospital?"

"You'll figure it out. You have to accomplish this mission at any cost and…"

"If they arrest me before I can get a shot off, which is likely, neither you nor Madame Atomos can do anything."

Summer had a cruel smile on his face as he waved his finger. "Figure out how to get through the barriers, Radetich, otherwise it's your wife and kids who'll suffer the consequences." He snickered, his round head framed in the open window, and Radetich punched him in the face. He was glad to hear his nose break. Summer stumbled back.

"Get out of here!" Radetich said through clenched teeth, barely controlling a rising fury. "Get out of here before I take you down!"

Summer stopped the bleeding with his handkerchief and backed off, sneering. "I won't forget this, Radetich!" He went through the gates of the park, melded with the shadows and then disappeared completely.

Radetich wiped his forehead and turned the key with his shaky hand, but it was like in a dream when he heard the engine rumble. He was already sorry that he had not captured Summer and he regretted his angry outburst. Only breaking a murderer's nose was doing things halfway!

Radetich got on the road and was at the airport in six minutes. He left his car in the parking lot, grabbed his suitcase and went to find a telephone booth.

"Well?" Baxter asked. "You think you're clever? Punching a guy who can take it out on your kids?"

He was not reproaching him. His words were only meant to show Radetich the strength of the Green Dragon, invisible but present on the road in Lakeside Park.

"You socked him good!" Baxter added. "Now all we have to do is follow the trail of blood he leaves behind. So, you're going to Charleston?"

"How did you know?"

"Bah. They make mics now that can pick up a conversation more than 100 yards away."

"Right. What's going to happen in Charleston?"

"Exactly what Madame Atomos wants. You'll get in to see Smith and Mie, you'll kill them, and you'll be able to escape without too much trouble. A little later, the news will be broadcast across the country and Madame Atomos' whole body will start tingling. Except that in the meantime our friend Summer will certainly have led us to one of the Organization's refuges if not the laboratory itself."

"And if he gets away from you?"

"Don't worry, he won't get away from us," Baxter stately firmly. "Take your plane. You'll be in Charleston around 8 am and have a little free time before the 9 o'clock visiting hours at the hospital. You can take a walk around the city."

"Why?"

"Just to let us see if Madame Atomos is watching you. She always likes to supervise her work. In Washington Costello and Ida Brown played their roles. It would be unthinkable for them to let you go solo in Charleston. You see, Radetich, you haven't finished helping us!"

Radetich was speechless. Nothing was important unless his efforts could help get his family out of the clutches of Madame Atomos. In the meantime, he felt like he was a puppet in the terrible woman's hands and he was only doing what she wanted him to do. The only actions he could count as his own: breaking Summer's nose and agreeing to work with the Green Dragon. For a man dying for action, it was meager.

The damn truck had not stopped once since Charleston except to fill up with gas when absolutely necessary and Hyde was surprised when it stopped just outside of Wichita, Kansas.

Hyde slammed on the brakes, turned onto a side street and made a quick U-turn, which woke up Dan Stone.

"The truck's stopped and there's no gas station in sight," Hyde said, opening his door. "Take the wheel. I'm going to get a closer look."

He got out, walked down the sidewalk and peeked around the corner. Down the street the truck was already taking off. Hyde was back at the car when at the last minute he spotted the man hurrying toward the taxi stand. He no longer had on his uniform or his cap, but Hyde recognized him as the fake train guard thanks to his peculiar walk.

Stone answered his wave by bringing the car forward.

"We're splitting up," Hyde decided. "You keep after that heap. I'm going to follow that fellow you see on the other side of the street. Keep in permanent radio contact with 555-6289. Goodbye, Stone!"

"Goodbye," Stone said, peeling out as usual.

Charles Hyde sprinted across the street and hid in the shadows. At 2 am it was deserted, of course, and he had to avoid raising the suspicions of the man who might recognize him from the train a few hours earlier.

The man got in the first taxi. Hyde waited for it to leave before running to the next car. He flashed his FBI identification right away, knowing through experience that this made things easier, and ordered, "Follow your partner without being seen. His fare belongs to the Atomos Organization. You understand, don't you?"

"No kidding?"

"No kidding," Hyde assured him.

The cabbie started his engine and pulled away from the stand. Over his shoulder he asked, "To be totally invisible, you want to get to the destination before him?"

"You know where he's going?"

"Wichita Municipal Airport. That's what the guy said before climbing in. If we cut through Douglas Avenue and Southwest Boulevard, it's a cinch."

"Okay!" Hyde accepted. "Step on it!"

As the taxi sped down Douglas Avenue, Hyde knew he was taking a risk. In fact, if the fare gave the first taxi another address on the road, the tail would be cut before it had even begun. Very anxious, Hyde rubbed his chin with a nervous hand, heard his beard scratch and told himself that he must have looked pretty ordinary. If he changed his walk a little and his general appearance, he might just get by unrecognized.

He thought about this all the way to the airport. The driver did not say a word, preoccupied with handling the turns, miraculously hitting all the green lights, and performing so well that the taxi entered the Wichita Airport only eight minutes after leaving the stand.

"Sure we're here first?" Hyde asked.

The cabbie nodded vigorously. We're five minutes ahead of him. My partner gave his fare a little tour by taking the periphery roads. Bound to happen with a guy getting out of a truck with California plates."

Hyde did not comment. He paid the fare on the counter, left a reasonable tip and got out of the car.

From the terminal he could see the other taxi arrive. The fake train guard got out, balked an instant, then finally headed for the ticket counters. He bought a ticket, looked at a timetable, then walked slowly to the little cafeteria. He seemed in no hurry, so Hyde figured that his plane would not take off anytime soon. At the same counter, he confirmed his supposition: the Boeing (flight 312) for New York via Salt Lake City, Louisville and Charleston, flying out of San Francisco, would not land in Wichita until 5:18.

Hyde also learned that the man's name was Downing and he had reserved his seat only until Charleston. The G-man got a ticket for the Wichita-Charleston leg, made sure that Downing was still in the cafeteria and went to a phone booth to call Washington. Sammy got on the line and connected him with Ralph Stutton's dispatch at 555-6289, which handled all the information for the Green Dragon Force.

"Charlie Hyde here. I'm at the Wichita airport…"

"I know," Stutton interrupted. "Dan Stone already contacted me. He said you were on the trail of a guy from the Organization."

"Exactly. His name's Downing and he just bought a plane ticket for Charleston. Considering the fact that Smith and Mie…"

"Shh!" Stutton whistled. "Wait a minute!" Hyde heard papers rustling. Stutton asked, "Flight 312 out of San Francisco?"

Flabbergasted, Hyde confirmed. Stutton grumbled and explained.

"Louis Radetich is on that plane that's doing its little night train work by making a bunch of stops. Radetich got on around 1:40 in San Francisco. His destination is Charleston. More precisely, General Hospital where he's supposed to kill the Befforts. Art Baxter predicted that a member of the Organization would be watching over him."

"Okay, but what's going to happen in Charleston?"

"Radetich will accomplish his mission and manage to escape…"

"I don't get it!" Hyde jumped in. "If Radetich is being radio-controlled, how do you know that he will do what you want?"

Stutton understood that Hyde knew nothing about recent developments. He briefly brought him up-to-date on Radetich, concluding with, "His collaboration has already allowed us to identify a certain Summer, operating out of Oakland, and under surveillance by Baxter's men. As for Downing, I think you should keep a close eye on him, don't you?" Not in his power to give orders, it was a suggestion.

"Very close," Hyde agreed. "Who knows if he isn't supposed to kill Radetich after the hospital attack?"

Both of them were on the right track, but it did not matter. From now on Downing would not be able to move his little finger.

Chapter X

In Oakland Ben Brady and his team had followed Summer since he left Lakeside Park. A tough tail. The guy was terribly suspicious and had made an extraordinary slalom course through the city before heading for a small house in a southern suburb. Without the three radio cars at his disposal, Brady would never have managed it. Now the house was being watched and the telephone had quickly been tapped thanks to the FBI.

For the moment, the FBI, staying within the bounds of the collaboration established by Beffort, left the operation to the Green Dragon. In the fight against Madame Atomos, it was better to avoid rocking the boat, causing waves and stirring anything up, so that soon the area around the house was as bare as a stage during intermission. But the actors were ready in the wings for the next scene.

A light filtered through the vertical slit between the curtains, proving that Summer was awake, undoubtedly waiting for a call from his boss to get back in the saddle.

"Maybe he's patching up his nose," Hank Seurer said.

Brady shrugged his shoulders. "It doesn't take two hours to plug your nostrils…"

He was not calm. He had a vague fear that Summer was putting one over on him. And it was not necessary for the guy to know he was being watched to pull it off. The rules of the Atomos Organization envisaged all kinds of things, their so-called "security", meant to foil any would-be pursuers. In the present case, for example, it could be that Summer had already left the house with the light on in order to make it look like he was home.

"If this dump's got a basement," Brady replied, knowing his Atomos traditions, "we're screwed."

He was sagging under the weight of his responsibility, so he felt a sense of relief when Art Baxter arrived with Yosho Akamatsu, come directly from Charleston. On learning that Summer had not used the telephone since his meeting with Radetich, Akamatsu frowned. "Not likely."

"The wiretap…"

"Set-up too late," the Japanese said curtly. "Summer must have called his boss right after walking through the door. I wonder…"

He did not finish his sentence. He fished some night-vision binoculars out of the car, adjusted the settings and trained them on the house. Close-up on the slit revealing the corner of a table, the back of a chair, part of a lampshade and, farther back, hidden in the shadows, the face of a woman.

Akamatsu stared at the face until his eyes hurt, but he could not determine if it was a picture or a real woman standing absolutely still. With the help of his imagination, he thought the face bore some resemblance to Icho Fuji. He gave the binoculars to Baxter, who screwed up his face.

"You've got good eyes. I think the thing looks like anything but the head of a woman."

Akamatsu laughed to himself. Baxter was smart, in the practical sense, but not an ounce of creativity flowed in his blood. In fact, he could never see a laboratory where there was only a mid-sized house. And maybe he was right, but they had known for a long time that the new Atomos laboratory was in the Oakland suburbs and in spite of their painstaking searches, they could not find it.

"Well?"

Akamatsu took back the binoculars. Again he saw the corner of a table, the back of a chair, the lampshade, but he searched in vain for the blurry white smear that Baxter had called "the thing". All he could see was a big dark zone. Worried now, Akamatsu was about to give up when a thin outline cut across the ray of light, turned around and disappeared behind the curtains.

"What's Summer look like," he asked.

"Tall, fat, flabby," Brady said. "You see him?"

Suddenly excited, Akamatsu did not answer. If what he was timidly thinking turned out to be true, Louis Radetich will have done the United States a great service by forcing Summer to show his true colors.

Thirty seconds ticked off, then the outline passed by again, slipped out of view, came back, turned around the table and went to sit in the back of the room where Akamatsu had seen the face hidden in the dark.

Akamatsu felt sweat beading on his forehead. With the binoculars still glued to his eyes he asked, "Do you know why Summer didn't call anyone?"

"You just said that he called before we got the wire-tap set up."

Akamatsu shook his head. "I said that was probable. After seeing Louis Radetich, Summer should have reported to Madame Atomos. Except he didn't need to call because Madame Atomos is in the house!"

Baxter, Seurer and Brady all jumped together as if they were jolted by an electric shock.

Akamatsu voiced his thoughts, "None of this is really surprising. Of course, Madame Atomos knows that the Befforts are under observation at General Hospital in

Charleston since she ordered Radetich to murder them. This is the only important thing in her eyes. She paces around, sits down, gets up, but stays near the phone to wait for the news of the Befforts' death. But it's only 5 am and Radetich won't get to Charleston until 8. Then another hour until the hospital opens for visiting hours at 9 am..."

He spoke like a man thinking aloud without knowing it. He kept watching through the binoculars and felt like he was only a few feet away from the pale face of Icho Fuji. He was sure that if he had a rifle, he could lodge a bullet right between her eyes.

"Baxter," he whispered, "find me a rifle with a scope right away."

Baxter swung around to go. "And if it's not Madaame Atomos?"

"It's her, Baxter!"

"You can't be sure. Through a crack in the curtains 50 yards away in the dark. Even with binoculars no one could be sure of anything." Since Akamatsu hesitated, he added, "After sleeping with her, you've been seeing her everywhere, Yosho!"

"I've had the feeling from the start," the Japanese retorted. "This woman is a rabid beast. We have to take her out!"

Art Baxter did not move. "I agree with that, but before shooting, we should make sure of her identity. In the house there's Summer and a woman. You can kill the woman pretty easily and it'd be a good thing because she obviously belongs to the Organization. Still, if she's not Icho Fuji, an alarm will go off, right?"

Akamatsu lowered the binoculars. Baxter was right, strictly logical. "What do you propose, Art?"

He tacitly admitted that he had not categorically recognized Madame Atomos as Icho Fuji. Baxter breathed more calmly. Yosho could have forced him to get a sniper rifle. In the hierarchy of the Green Dragon Force, he stood right under Smith and Mie Beffort.

"First of all I propose we circle the house. Then a commando team of two or three men enter the yard and get as close as possible to identify the woman."

"Okay! I'm one of them, of course, and I'll bring the rifle that you're going to get for me."

This time they were on the same wavelength, but by staying on the safe side and without in any way being to blame, Art Baxter had just saved the life of Madame Atomos...

In front of his boss, Summer felt uncomfortable. When he came back from his meeting with Louis Radetich, he could not hide his broken nose or his blood-soaked handkerchief.

Madame Atomos fixed her icy gaze on him. "An incident, Summer?"

He had told her, like talking to a brick wall, then Madame Atomos had completely forgotten it. He became a piece of furniture in the corner. Madame Atomos did not open her mouth, kept moving around, and when she sat down she did not bother to pull down her skirt. That was the problem. Sometimes she did not remember that she had turned young and desirable, especially when she was worried or troubled like now. As an older lady she could control her men without arousing any disturbing thoughts. Rejuvenated, she no longer carried the same weight; she exuded too many charms to foster the same obedience.

Summer sat there in turmoil. The more so since he had not known Madame Atomos as an older woman and he had a hard time imagining this pin-up doll killing so many people. However, the facts were the facts. This pretty girl was the greatest criminal of all time! Yes, Summer felt comfortable.

Behind her façade, Madame Atomos was eyeing him with all her experience, wondering if he was strong enough to back her up during the offensive she was preparing. Underneath them, 65 feet under the floor of the house, was the laboratory where there was waiting, all lined up in an armored room 10,000 vials of XBC-250, each containing 10 grams of a dreadful bacteriological substance.

She still did not have enough to kill all the inhabitants of the USA, but by releasing the vials from an airplane at 300 miles up, the result would be very satisfying. Madame Atomos had the plane, the bacteria and two or three million casualties in view… Nothing was missing except the telephone call from Charleston that she was hoping with all her dark soul would inform her of the deaths of Smith and Mie Beffort. As long as they were alive, she could think of nothing else and…

"Madame?"

She looked over, stared at Summer and saw that he was suddenly panicking. "What is it, Summer?"

He nodded to a board on the wall dotted with tiny lights. One of them had lit up. "Someone just entered the yard," he murmured, forcing himself not to jump up.

Despite her incredible cool-headedness, Madame Atomos felt herself literally turn pale. She bolted to her feet and stepped forward at the very moment when Akamatsu pulled the trigger of his rifle. The bullet put a hole in the window, whizzed through the room and lodged in the wall, kicking out enough dust to make Madame Atomos run into the hallway.

Summer was hot on her heels. She rushed down to the basement and turned the secret handle while Summer locked the heavy bolts to the door. Without a sound, the false wall slid open onto an elevator car. If the elevator were not on the floor, it would not open. It was simple, but particularly effective as a security measure.

Madame Atomos and Summer stepped into the elevator and the false wall hissed closed. After Madame Atomos pressed a button, the elevator descended into the bowels.

Akamatsu and the others could always search. Short of destroying the house and the basement, they had no chance of discovering the laboratory.

Yosho Akamatsu did not know, at the moment, that Madame Atomos had just escaped death. Jumping up at the very moment when Yosho pulled the trigger, the terrible woman looked like she had been hit by the bullet. Since the opening in the curtain was as thin as a castle arrow slit, they could see nothing through the cracked window.

In the growing confusion, Seurer shouted, "You killed her!"

Two minutes of hesitation, then they tried to break down the front door while Seurer shattered the window, all of it making a lot of noise. Finally, itching to get in, Akamatsu could climb through the window. He saw the empty room and the bloody handkerchief and thought for a minute that Madame Atomos was wounded before he realized that the handkerchief probably belonged to Summer.

"The bullet hit the wall," Brady said.

In a rage Akamatsu searched the house and came upon the heavy door fitted with locks that he had to blow off with a machine gun. When the door flew open revealing the stairway down to the basement, there was no more mystery. Following her long-established tradition Madame Atomos and her accomplice had escaped thanks to an underground passage!

They probed the basement in the hope of finding a hollow wall, but they searched in vain. Akamatsu was expecting as much because this kind of failure was also part of the tradition. He immediately took the usual, mandatory measures. "Art, contact the FBI and police. The house needs to be sealed off right away and they have to watch the roads, trains and airplanes.

Baxter nodded and dashed off to the radio car.

"Brady," Akamatsu continued, "get your explosives men together. We're going to demolish this house, clear off the rubble and go at the basement."

"That'll take some time!"

"You have a better idea?" Akamatsu asked sarcastically.

Brady turned around, frustrated, sure that his men would not finish their job before dawn broke. By that time, Madame Atomos could have reached Nevada, Arizona or Mexico!

Frozen on the front porch, Akamatsu was thinking the same thing.

Art Baxter tilted back his fedora nervously. "It's okay. Everything's in place."

"So fast?"

"The FBI and the police were already on alert since we spotted Summer. In San Francisco and Oakland they've been getting things ready for a long time. If you hadn't opened fire, Madame Atomos would be locked up tight in there right now!"

He was playing hardball. The two men stared coldly at each other before Akamatsu replied, "It's not my fault but yours, Art! By sneaking into the yard, you set off an alarm! If I'd shot from the street…"

"You shouldn't have shot!" Baxter lost his temper. "If we'd taken our time, we could have surrounded the house! It's not the first time that the Green Dragon Force tripped an alarm. Now Madame Atomos is buried like a mole and no one can say where she'll pop up!"

His silence suddenly calmed Baxter down, who stopped rubbing salt in the wound. He lit a cigarette and said, "Luckily Dan Stone hasn't lost the truck and Charles Hyde is still on the skirts of Downing. Sooner or later Madame Atomos has to give a sign to one of them."

Akamatsu pointed to the telephone line and said, "Madame Atomos was waiting for a phone call. Isn't it logical to think that someone, probably Downing, was reporting on Radetich's mission?"

"That's a thought…"

Akamatsu dragged him inside the house. "Look, Art, Madame Atomos was sitting next to a telephone. She was there for hours, couldn't get away, just walked around the living room and went to sit back down."

"I don't believe it," Baxter said. "You just told us your theory and I didn't agree. Knowing that Radetich couldn't do anything before 9 am, Madame Atomos didn't need to be…"

"It was stronger than her, Art!" Akamatsu cut in. "I saw Smith at the hospital in Charleston. He was shattered, but he could still talk. With his help we found the tape recorder in car 27. The machine had a message recorded by Madame Atomos announcing a bacteriological attack against the USA after the Befforts' death. When her first try failed, Madame Atomos was just waiting for the results of the second before sowing death!"

"Okay," Baxter capitulated wearily. "Let's admit it. What does it do for us?"

"Downing is going to call here first. If no one answers, he'll call another number. By mobilizing enough people, we should be able to locate Downing's call from Charleston pretty quickly and therefore the address of the number Downing calls."

Baxter did not give in. "Great! On the condition that Downing doesn't ask for a number from the Oakland operator from where a third party will call Madame Atomos."

Akamatsu furrowed his brow. The idea deserved some thought because with nothing better to go on, Downing was their only viable lead.

Chapter XI

Ralph Stutton, the dispatch operator of 555-6289, had kept Smith Beffort up-to-date on the development of the situation. Ten minutes after Akamatsu missed his target, he knew that Madame Atomos had fled with Summer. He climbed out of bed right away, got dressed and left the room where he had been moping around.

He had played the victim long enough.

In the corridor, he ran into Evans whose eyes popped open as wide as flying saucers. "Good God, Smith, what's got into you?"

Beffort stepped around him. "Let me go, would you? I'm in fine shape and this ridiculous little period of observation is useless. Do you know that Madame Atomos just escaped from Yosho?"

"Yes, but you're not the one who's going to collar her! All precautions have been taken. Oakland is sur-rounded, the roads, train stations, airports…"

"I know!" Beffort shouted. "Spare me your cata-logue and get me a jet! We have to be in Oakland before sunrise! Witter can stay here to protect Mie and when Radetich gets here…"

"Hold on," Mie spoke up from the doorway. "I need some fresh air and exercise, too. Who said that I had to stay in quarantine?"

"You're going to mess up all our plans, Mie!"

The young lady finished buttoning her dress and slipped her feet into her sport shoes. "Our plans don't wash anymore," she said coldly. "We're supposed to be declared dead in order to save Radetich's wife and kids, but Madame Atomos wasn't on the run when we made that decision and we were hoping to get her moving. Now do you know what will happen if she finds out we're dead?"

Evans nodded. "She'll unleash a bacteriological attack against the United States," he recited, "but if Radetich fails in his mission, I'm afraid his family won't be growing any older."

Smith looked at his watch. There was no joy in his smile when he said, "It's 4:30 am, which gives us time before Radetich gets in for visiting hours. And for medical reasons, the opening hours can be delayed. In short, we can prolong the suspense almost indefinitely."

"Madame Atomos won't play along for long," Evans said.

"All the reason to get to Oakland fast! Find me a supersonic jet, Evans! We have to be there by 7:30!"

Evans did not blink. Three thousand miles in three hours was nothing extraordinary. With the time difference it was really a piece of cake.

In Wichita Charles Hyde was playing cat and mouse with Downing, who, after making a telephone call, became extremely suspicious. Hyde would have given anything to know where he had called because it was obvious that Downing was on pins and needles now.

In fact, the man had called a number he made up, just to see if Hyde was really following him. The result was not affirmative, but not exactly negative either. There were few people at the airport and it was normal enough that this big guy was doing whatever he could to kill time, even if his entertainment seemed to be Downing himself... Nevertheless, the Atomos agent had memorized Hyde's face, which vaguely reminded him of someone. It could have just been a resemblance, but

Downing doubted it; he wracked his brain trying to re-member before he was finally sure that he had seen Hyde on the train carrying the Befforts.

For his part, Charles Hyde was thinking fast about what he should do. He knew that Downing had spotted him, but it was, unfortunately, inevitable in the forlorn and deserted airport. It would last until Charleston where a more serious tail would certainly alert him and he would not fail to react.

Hyde gave up looking for an immediate solution, sure that everything would play out in Charleston.

As expected the Boeing landed at 5:18 and Hyde boarded quickly without paying a any special attention to Downing. From the top of the platform he glanced behind him and saw the man coming on slowly. This gave him time to check out Louis Radetich, whom he did not know.

When he showed the stewardess his ticket, he also flashed his FBI badge and asked, "Don't looked sur-prised, my dear, but the next passenger who will get on this plane is a dangerous guy."

The girl tensed up, then smiled. "Got it, G-man," she murmured. "What can I do for you?"

"One of your passengers is named Louis Radetich. He boarded in San Francisco. Just tell me where he's sitting."

She must have had an extraordinary memory be-cause without looking at the passenger list she said, "Number 6, to the left toward the end of the aisle. Say, We're not going to be hijacked to Cuba, are we?"

She was joking, but Hyde was in no mood to play. He went directly to his seat without saying a word. He looked at Radetich as he passed by. He had his eyes closed, like he was sleeping, but the wrinkles slashed across his forehead betrayed his deep anxiety. Hyde sat down, watching for Downing, who entered the cabin, and to his great surprise headed for the seat next to him.

As a discreet tail, what a success! Where things stood now, the G-man's behavior was laid out for him. He stood up and without smiling said, "If my wife hired you to follow me, tell me right now, pal! It'll save you a lot of trouble."

The guy's jaw dropped.

Hyde snickered and counted on his fingers, "I arrived in a taxi, just like you. I bought a ticket and you did the same. I got on this plane to Charleston and here you are! You think I'm a chump? And the phone call you made without taking your eyes off me?"

He was switching roles beautifully, catching Downing off guard, rendering him speechless. "Are you a private eye?"

Barely recovered from his surprise, Downing shook his head and instinctively backed up when Hyde pointed a finger at his chest and stated, "Don't deny it! I'm sure I saw you somewhere yesterday or the day before!"

"You're mistaken," Downing finally babbled. "I thought you were the one following me. If you remember, I got my ticket before you did, right?"

"Sure, but I was at the airport first."

"A coincidence."

Hyde gave him a big smile and slapped him amiably on the back. "Tell you the truth, I like it better that way. But we've still seen each other somewhere."

"Could be," Downing said cautiously.

Squinting his eyes, Hyde stared him down, then after a minute he said slowly, "Were you on a train the other night?"

"No. I live in Wichita and I haven't traveled for a year. I repeat that it's a coincidence." His face had changed and his eyes hardened.

Hyde knew right away that the little man was a killer. He played the dummy, meaning that he completely ignored the threat growing in Downing's eyes and said, "But I would have sworn you were on that train... You gotta admit that if you haven't traveled in a year it's kind of strange that you're going to Charleston on the very same day as me, eh?"

He was being the cheerful nag, trying to nitpick and split hairs, succeeded in giving the impression of being drunk or with a screw loose. To himself he was wondering how Downing was going to recognize Radetich who looked like he had no idea who he was.

"Hold on," Downing said wearily, "here's a letter to me. You can see I'm not a cop, right, pal?" His suspicions were vanishing like mists in the sun because it was glaringly obvious that a man on someone's tail would never act like this.

Hyde only glanced at the envelope. It was addressed to B.L. Horner, broker, 206 South Ellis Street, Wichita, Kansas. A flimsy cover, cooked up right there on the truck, but with some papers in the name of Homer Downing did not have to give his real name when buying the plane ticket.

Hyde smiled, gave him back the envelope and held out his pack of cigarettes, which he never smoked. "Sorry, pal, I'm in a rough spot with my wife. If you smoke..." He dropped the pack in the man's hand. As good a way as any to get the guy's fingerprints to know, in the end, who he really was.

Even from the bottom floor of her hidden laboratory, Madame Atomos felt the explosions and falling rocks that spelled the destruction of the house. She could not believe it. She had figured that her enemies would search the house and then go elsewhere after seeing that she had vanished. In truth, this reaction of the Green Dragon Force was unimaginable.

Sitting across the table from her, Summer jumped at every explosion. His nerves were frayed and he panicked even more when he looked at the tragic mask of Madame Atomos. And her silence was becoming unbearable to him. Why was she waiting to order an evacuation?

A stronger shock than usual made Summer spring up like a jack-in-the-box. "They're in the basement," he wheezed like a hunted beast. "But I closed and bolted the door!"

The fool! He locked the door from the inside and he was astonished that the Green Dragon Force had found their trail so quickly. The snub-nosed 38 suddenly materialized in Madame Atomos' clenched hand. She was seeing red.

"I'm going to kill you, Summer!" She exploded. "Not only did you lead my enemies to the house, but you went and showed them how to get to my laboratory by locking the door that should have stayed open! It's your fault that what I worked on like crazy will amount to nothing! You don't deserve to live!"

She furiously emptied her gun into his belly and with great pleasure watched him drop to the ground. She had to force herself not to crush his skull in with her heels. Then all the consequences of her senseless action sprang up: she had just killed the pilot of the plane parked at the Oakland Airport! Now she would be forced to fly it herself and at the same time drop the vials of XBC-250 over California!

But before that, she had to trust her peons to load the boxes of vials onto a van, lead them to the airport and reveal her great secret to get them on the plane. Madame Atomos clenched her jaws. She was missing Robert Costello, Ida Brown, Downing and company. Here, except for the few scientists who had created XBC-250 she only had grunt workers at her disposal.

The time of the Great Brain organizing and controlling everything was gone. The wheel had turned. Madame Atomos had become a lone wolf whom the forces of the United States was tracking without mercy, whom they shot at on sight through open slits in the curtains... A wave of discouragement washed over her. She was certainly going to be killed before she could avenge the thousands of deaths of Hiroshima and Nagasaki...

Suddenly the buzzing interphone snapped the sinister woman out of her thoughts. She switched it on and leaned over the microphone. "Madame Atomos here."

"Willer here, Madame. I just got back and can give you the report you asked for: Oakland is surrounded by the police and I found out that the army is coming to reinforce the blockades. In an hour or two no one will be able to leave the city."

"The house?"

"It's already razed to the ground and 100 men are going at the basement. Yosho Akamatsu is in charge of everything!"

Madame Atomos stiffened up. She did not know how Akamatsu had managed to get to the house so quickly.

"Radetich must have been watched since Washington," Willer said, "and it's through him that Summer..."

"No!" Madame Atomos shouted. "I think Radetich betrayed us! Kill his wife and kids immediately! Then do what you have to get Downing out of the trap in Charleston!"

"But…"

"Follow my orders! It's obvious that the Befforts were informed by Radetich and have taken precautions!"

"So, Madame, it's the end. Akamatsu and the members of the Green Dragon Force will soon reach the elevator. 30 minutes later they'll invade the laboratory."

"We're going to evacuate," Madame Atomos said softly. "But before that, we have to finish the essential job. Grab a strong man, Willer, and go with him to unit 30. Get the boxes loaded onto the service van marked General Deliveries."

"And the evacuation order?"

"I'll take care of it. For the moment, kill the Radetiches, inform Downing through our contact in Charleston and meet me in unit 20. That's all."

She crossed the room and turned on her television screens so that she could supervise the work going on in the different rooms of the laboratory. Everyone was still in place, but a certain nervousness was starting to show in all their movements. They were obviously listening to the explosions coming from the surface and with no news they were troubled by it.

Madame Atomos giggled silently. She knew that her 25 collaborators would die in the rubble of the laboratory, but to avoid hell breaking loose in panic, she had ordered Willer to execute the Radetich family, which he would tell everyone. The logical conclusions, then, would follow: it was useless to kill the Radetiches, who would die anyway if Madame Atomos intended to blow up the lab. So, the Radetiches' death sentence meant that they really were going to evacuate.

Madame Atomos flipped a switch and a bell started ringing throughout the underground installation. This meant that everyone was supposed to listen intently to the boss. By watching her screens, Madame Atomos made sure that her call had been heard, then when everyone was grouped around the loudspeakers, she spoke gravely.

"My friends, you are aware that this is a particularly crucial time. The FBI and the Green Dragon Force are about to discover our refuge. Moreover, the city is going to be completely shut off. Before the situation turns hopeless, we're going to evacuate."

Madame Atomos let the rumble of approval run through the rooms before continuing.

"When I give the order, you will all walk to the lowest level where you will find a secret passage you don't know about yet. You can open it by pulling the emergency lever on freight elevator number 3, which, I remind you, has never been used. Nevertheless, to be absolutely safe, do not touch the lever before at least 45 minutes. The tunnel will lead you to our next gathering point. Over and out. Hiroshima! Nagasaki!"

She did not add her compliments, but everyone knew. Not one of the people she had just spoken to would live for long. By pulling the lever, one of them would set off the explosion of 1,500 pounds of TNT! The delay of 45 minutes was given in the hope of killing two birds with one stone. First she would, by then, be on the outskirts of the city and she figured that the explosion would draw the attention of the police. Second, it was likely that Yosho Akamatsu and the Green Dragon

Force would have reached the elevator and so would be blown to bits by the huge explosion.

At this last thought, Madame Atomos caught herself smiling.

The smile of a little girl who has just been given a new doll.

Truly, this woman was evil personified.

Chapter XII

At 6 am Willer, Monroe and Madame Atomos were in front of unit 30 to which only Madame Atomos had a key. Willer and Monroe had come in the van marked General Deliveries. The vehicle was stolen three months ago and was kept at a print shop that Ida Brown had bought on behalf of Madame Atomos. The print shop was a long way from the city, but connected to the laboratory by a freight elevator. To get to the surface would be child's play. The difficulties would come later when the van had to take its chances on the Oakland streets. But for now Madame Atomos had other things to worry about.

"The Radetiches?" she asked.

"It's done, Madame," Willer answered. "I also called our agent in Charleston. He'll alert Downing when the plane lands. Umm…"

"What?"

"Our agent is worried about Louis Radetich. He's hoping that you'll punish him."

Madame Atomos' black eye flashed. "This guy has to stay alive and know that his wife and children are dead because of him. After that, it will eat away at him for the rest of his life. This punishment is horrible, Willer."

She smiled icily as she opened the door of unit 30 and turned on the light. All around the walls, from floor to ceiling, stretched rows of metal shelves loaded with boxes. At first glance, ignorant of their contents, Witter and Monroe thought the boxes were holding Madame Atomos' treasure. They might be diamonds. Unit 30 was only a cellar but its walls and door were armored like a safe, not a crack to be found.

The two men looked at each other greedily. Madame Atomos said, "You have 30 minutes to get these 1,000 boxes into the van. They're not heavy and you can finish in 15 minutes, but be careful! If just one box is opened or falls, you're dead men!"

The glitter in the eyes of Willer and Monroe faded. Madame Atomos pushed them urgently into the small room and they began their task as gently as midwives.

Madame Atomos left without saying another word and went back to her office where she could better hear the erosive work of Yosho Akamatsu's team. At this stage, the use of explosives was too dangerous for fear of collapse and the men were picking away at the walls with jackhammers. It would not happen on its own, even when the elevator was discovered. Akamatsu had to stay down there, unaware that he was literally standing on 1,500 pounds of TNT! Madame Atomos would have liked to watch him die since she did not have him completely at her mercy. She had been his mistress and was having a hard time forgetting his embraces. She had dreamed of keeping him hostage, of making him disappear and become her pleasure toy that she could do with what she wanted, whenever she wanted, in the steamy warmth of a locked room...

Madame Atomos got hold of herself and cursed. Once again she loathed her new body that was plunging her into forbidden desires!

Hiroshima! Nagasaki!

Shuddering, Madame Atomos slammed the interphone button, got in touch with the radio room and asked to be put in direct contact with Spencer 17, the name for the truck carrying her commando team. It crackled for an instant, then the far-off voice of Costello, unrecognizable to a stranger, spluttered through the speaker.

Madame Atomos said, "Change your route, Spencer 17. The new meeting point is in sector 16, area B. Got it?"

"Sector 16, area B," Costello repeated, knowing that radio messages had to be brief to foil any would-be locating devices.

"Watch yourselves," Madame Atomos added. "Akamatsu is here and Radetich is no longer one of us. Use the emergency plan. Over and out."

She cut off communication and listened for a minute to the pounding of the jackhammers. Her situation had never been so precarious. If she wanted the odds in her favor, she had to leave nothing and no one behind her. Wipe the slate clean…

She reloaded her 45, slipped the gun into a big handbag already stuffed with money and left her office never to return. It was 6:30 when she got back to unit 30. Willer and Monroe were putting the last of the boxes on the van whose engine rumbled quietly. Madame Atomos moved a few piles of boxes, sat in the makeshift seat and pointed at the two men.

"We're going to the Oakland airport where there's a plane ready to take off. We'll have to load the boxes on board there before heading for a safe house. Everything is riding on you now. Avoid the cops and the roadblocks. If they try to stop us, open fire and break through the barriers. We have to get to the airport at all costs!"

Willer and Monroe nodded. They were wanted in five or six states and Madame Atomos was sure that nothing would stop them as long as they were alive.

They had said that Oakland was surrounded, but it was easier said than done and not exactly the truth. In fact, once the house was located, they took it as the center of a pretty wide zone, roughly circular, two and half miles in diameter, extending into the city as well as the southern suburbs.

They were fully aware that an Atomos refuge had long, tunnel-like, underground passages that stretched for up to a mile before coming to the surface, so the 2.5 miles gave them a good safety margin, in the hope that this time Madame Atomos would run into one of their impregnable walls. Plus, they could do little better on such short notice. Thousands of men were already involved in the operation. To accomplish a perfect lock down would take ten times more men. Therefore, they were hoping that Madame Atomos would not slip through, but no one was betting on it. Akamatsu least of all!

"We made it!" Baxter exclaimed. "The boys just found the shaft, a kind of elevator! I think we'll be in the lab in no time."

He was elated and raised an eyebrow on seeing Akamatsu's somber face. "Don't get all excited, Art. If we found something, it's because Madame Atomos is already long gone."

"Impossible! All the vehicles on the road around here have been checked and cleared!"

Akamatsu looked at his watch. 6:40. "People are going to leave for work soon. The streets will be full of people and cars and Madame Atomos will slip through our fingers like a slimy eel. She's always worked like this."

He seemed so sure of the fact that Baxter started feeling discouraged. "Damn! Then tell me what we have to do!"

Akamatsu shrugged. "Nothing in particular. All the usual measures have been taken, haven't they? Without a stroke of luck I think we're going to lose this round, Art. Let the men keep digging, but we're not doing any good here."

"Okay. And where will we do any good?"

"A patrol," Akamatsu said curtly. "Seurer, Brady, you and I are the most qualified to thwart Madame Atomos' plans. In less than an hour the Befforts and Evans will land in Oakland. I wouldn't want Smith to be staring at a blank slate first thing. Let's go, Art, we don't have a minute to lose."

They all climbed into the Baxter's car and started exploring the area while contacting the checkpoints by radio. The results were negative everywhere. All along the "front" line, no suspicious vehicles had been stopped.

At the same time, after evading several checkpoints, the General Deliveries van came in sight of the famous "front" line. On Madame Atomos' order, Willer, who was driving, parked in a dark alley and turned off the lights. Looking through a crack between the boxes, Madame Atomos had guided the van as she wanted through the southern suburb. Now she was staring at the luminous face of her watch, counting the seconds.

"We're wasting time, Madame," Willer ventured to remark, fear growing inside him. "If a police car…"

A huge explosion interrupted him. The windows of the nearby houses rattled, the boom echoed through the air and at the end of the alley the men at the roadblock jumped on top of their cars to get a better view of the dancing flame that lit up the sky.

Willer and Monroe swung around. They were close to panicking themselves. In a sharp voice Madame Atomos said, "The laboratory just blew up with Akamatsu and his partners."

"And ours?" Willer asked.

"I had to sacrifice them. In five minutes all the police will learn that Madame Atomos preferred death to prison. Then we'll be free to do as we please."

The two men glanced at each other. They were not choirboys, but their boss' cruelty scared them stiff. Terribly calm, Madame Atomos gave her instructions, then at 6:55 the van left the alley and headed for the road-block. To the east, in this rainy season, a dreary dawn was rising, dissolving the electric lights without substituting its own, making visibility extremely bad. A gloaming...

Willer obeyed the sign that an officer was holding that read "Stop!" He halted and saw that the other police were not very interested in the van. Suddenly, probably because of the explosion, they looked like innocent bystanders.

Willer lowered his window. "I'm coming from down there," he said excitedly.

"You know that Madame Atomos just blew herself up?"

"Of course! Don't you think the radio's good for something?"

"Go on, get out of here!" He was standing on his tiptoes, watching the fire spread, listening to the sirens blare. Ambulances, fire trucks, rescue services...

Willer put the van in gear, eased through the block-ade and headed down the now empty road. He could not get over it and mentally tipped his hat to Madame Atomos, who spoke behind him, "Not so fast, Willer. If we reach the airport at 7:30, that will give us plenty of time. No need to risk a stupid accident. We're too young to die, aren't we?"

Somewhere on Highway 54 between Liberal, Kansas and Dalhart, Texas, Dan Stone was still following the truck. A tedious, monotonous tail that plunged the G-man into a kind of sweet slumber. The truck seemed to be veering south instead of keeping its route to the west. Stone had asked for news from 6289 and knew that Charles Hyde was hanging onto the skirts of Downing, that the Befforts and Evans were going to Oakland where Akamatsu had a lead, but he was not yet up-to-date on the destruction of the Atomos laboratory.

So, when the truck stopped at a gas station, Stone did not react as he might have under other circumstances. In his view, the truck was just stopping to fill up again and nothing important could happen before reaching the final destination. He sped past the pumps for 200 yards before parking his car on a side road and waited. Watching from ahead. Classic.

In the meantime, in order to respond to Madame Atomos' order, Spencer 17 put the emergency plan into action. Quite simply, because Stone's tail had gone unnoticed, they opened the back of the truck and pulled out the ramp. Then the Rambler station wagon backed out, turned around and drove off toward Liberal before the wide eyes of the station attendant.

Liberal was to the north. Stone was to the south. In other words, Costello, Ida Brown and the colored man were sitting pretty. And Stone saw nothing but taillights, so he got back on the tail as if it were nothing when the truck passed him. His excuse: he had no way to check whether the car was still in the truck.

20 minutes later, the station wagon pulled into a parking lot in Liberal. It was 7 am and the streets were beginning their usual activity. The trio abandoned the car. Ida Brown left the lot first, hailed a cab and got driven to the airport. Her final goal was sector 16, area B, which Madame Atomos had indicated as the next meeting point.

Robert Costello took a bus to the train station and bought a ticket for the 7:23 train.

The young and muscular black man walked to the southern end of the city to get a bus ticket for Clinton, Mississippi. Before the end of the line, he would have to change transports several times, just like Ida Brown and Costello, to reach the mysterious sector 16.

At 7:06, the Boeing landed on runway 3 and taxied up to the gate before shutting off its jet engines. The ground team rolled out the luggage carts, the jet bridge connected to the cabin and the stewardess opened the door, inviting the passengers to walk directly into the terminal.

Charles Hyde pretended to be in a hurry so that he was one of the first to get into the terminal. He headed for a telephone booth without turning around. During the trip he had managed to reassure Downing completely, without, however, reassuring himself about what fate the Atomos Organization held in store for Radetich.

He called General Hospital and got Witter on the line right away. "I'm had, Eddy! I buddied up with him on the plane, so he'll spot me on a street corner or through a window in a flash."

Witter kept silent. Hyde saw Radetich walking in the middle of a bunch of passengers and figured that Downing would not be far behind. "If you don't make a decision, our man's gonna fly the coop!"

"Let him go," Witter said flatly. "It's clear that his mission is to watch Radetich and since he's coming to the hospital…"

Hyde breathed heavily. All this trouble he went through!

"Don't cry about it!" Witter joked. "A lot of things have changed since you left Wichita. Mie and Smith aren't in Charleston anymore, Madame Atomos blew up her laboratory and some people think she went up with the blast."

"My foot. There's no way!"

"In your opinion," Witter admitted, "but you never know."

"Who would fall for such a trap?"

"The Oakland police as well as the local FBI who are refusing to follow Akamatsu's orders. A bunch of guys are searching the ruins of the lab hoping to find the mortal remains of Madame Atomos. What a joke! As if they didn't know that this damned pretty woman is almost indestructible!"

Hyde shrugged for no good reason. "Will Smith get there in time?"

"I don't know," Witter admitted. "When the lab was blown to smithereens, his plane was still over Colorado. Come to the hospital, Charlie. If Madame Atomos managed to save her hide, we'll get stinking drunk as a consolation."

"That sounds good to me," Hyde accepted.

He hung up, stepped back into the teeming hall and quickly dove behind a pillar. 30 feet away from him a very pale Downing was talking with a stranger.

Chapter XIII

Where the house used to be there was nothing left but a huge crater full of wrested trees, jagged foundations, various wreckage and strange laboratory equipment that the blast had thrown to the sky. The searchers were finding bits of human flesh, an arm, a leg, a severed head.

Hoping to find the corpse of Madame Atomos, they had been generous with the workforce and in spite of the blaze burning two feet away dozens of men were picking away at the center of the ruins.

Firefighters were battling the flames all around. Several nearby houses had caught fire. They had to evacuate them and the occupants were standing on the sidewalk across the street, tired, haggard, wearing whatever they had had on.

Off at a distance, Art Baxter was shooting furiously at a tin can that had already been dented by the neighborhood boys. "Now," he said, "we're screwed!"

"Unless Madame Atomos is underneath," Brady hazarded.

Akamatsu let out a hollow laugh. "She's not there, you can bet on it. But just wait until they dig up the family of Louis Radetich... poor guy."

Baxter and Brady said nothing. If the Radetiches had really paid the price for the operation, Akamatsu could be held morally responsible. By shooting at and missing Madame Atomos, he had, without a doubt, compelled his enemy to destroy the laboratory.

"Radetich's wife and kids," Baxter said, "would have been killed anyway. Madame Atomos never left any of her prisoners alive."

Baxter looked at his watch. "7:20. If we say that Madame Atomos fled right before the explosion, she's had 35 minutes now to get to safety. She had to cross Oakland and the suburb and then she must have lost a little time getting through the barricades safe and sound. So in the end, she's not out of range. If these two numb-skulls will listen to you, Yosho, we still have a chance."

He was referring to the chief of police and the local FBI director who had refused to take Akamatsu suggestions. They had the right because Smith Beffort, or Evans in a pinch, held absolute authority in the anti-Atomos fight. Plus, the two men sincerely believed that the sinister woman was under the rubble—they were acting in good faith. It was tough to get angry with them.

Moreover, they had to admit that the hope of capturing Madame Atomos on the run was a just a fantasy. Oakland and its suburbs were teeming with men on the job, some from San Francisco on the other side of the Bay, and the usual traffic jams were forming around the city. How could they ever hope to effectively control such crowds?

At 7:25 a car driven by Hank Seurer appeared at the end of the street and was stopped by the police. Seurer showed his Green Dragon ID, went through and pulled up in front of Akamatsu, Baxter and Brady.

"There's news!" he shouted as he jumped out. "Smith Beffort and Evans just stopped all traffic in and out of Oakland. The trains aren't leaving and the planes have been grounded since 7:10."

"Where's Beffort?" Akamatsu asked.

Seurer pointed to the sky. "Up there! He got on the radio when he found out the police and local FBI were refusing your orders. The White House is fully behind him and the army's already in the game... Without being too optimistic, I'd say that Madame Atomos is trapped."

Akamatsu scowled. "Just a little while ago she looked trapped in the house. Then she was inside the police lines. Now she's somewhere within a huge zone... Her field of action is becoming wider and wider, Hank."

"Okay, but she can't get around on foot anymore. A dozen miles from here the army's forming a wall. Everyone's being forced back into Oakland, which will soon be declared a city under siege. Believe me, I heard Smith Beffort's orders and saw the White House communiqué. They're going whole hog again! If I were Mama Atomos, my hair would be turning white. No cars, no trains, no planes! Damn, what's left for her?"

"A nice hideout," Baxter said. "We're playing all our cards, but who's to say that she's not hiding in one of these buildings?"

They all raised their heads at the same time. With Madame Atomos, you could never be sure of anything.

In Charleston, although the problems were different, Charles Hyde was having a tough time. Downing had become his center of interest because, against all expectations, he did not seem to be sticking to Louis Radetich. Therefore, it stood to reason that the Atomos Organization was changing tracks. It must have got wind of the Befforts leaving the hospital and so knew that Radetich would kill nobody, which, after the destruction of the laboratory, would put it completely on the defensive.

Left to himself because he could not call Witter without losing sight of Downing, Charles Hyde found himself badly handicapped before the inevitable tail even began. At the end of the terminal Downing and the stranger were just parting. The latter headed for the parking lot and got in a car whose license plate Hyde could not make out because of the distance, and headed toward Charleston.

Downing stood there for a moment, hesitant, then he decided and slowly retraced his steps. He was so obviously suspicious that Hyde stayed hidden behind the pillar. He figured the man would detect the danger if he saw him, which would likely bring unexpected and surely harmful repercussions.

Downing walked toward the booking counter, bought a ticket, looked at the clock and started wandering across the terminal. He looked more relaxed as he watched the planes taking off and landing every three minutes on the runway. Hyde thought his mark would not sneak off so he left his pillar, slipped in with travelers and went back to the telephone booths. He instantly knew that he could not use one of them without been seen by Downing. They were out in the open for all to see and even with the glass door closed there was no way to remain incognito. But Hyde definitely had to call Witter. Downing was ready to take another trip. In an airplane the G-man would be recognized in a second.

Hyde looked around. For the moment Downing had his back to him, but in a few seconds, he would turn around and the danger would be there. Hyde rushed downstairs to find the bathrooms and another row of phone booths. He shut himself up in the first one, dropped a few coins in the slot and dialed the number of

General Hospital. Just like last time he was quickly in touch with Witter.

"Downing didn't follow Radetich," he said right off. "He was intercepted by a stranger, then bought a plane ticket. I can't keep on his tail, Eddy."

"I'll send a replacement since we have time. What happened to Radetich?"

Hyde glanced outside, but the hallway was deserted. "The last time I saw him," he said matter-of-factly, "he was getting in a taxi. That was around 15 minutes ago so you'll probably be seeing him very soon. The guy you're sending me, do I know him?"

"No. We have to agree on a meeting place because he doesn't know you either. Let's say you wait for him at the top of the escalator to the terraces. He'll be carrying a newspaper and start fanning himself with it going up. You contact him. His name's Hizer. Afterward you'll have to point out Downing. By the way, do you know where he's going?"

Hyde heard a faint noise. By some kind of premonition he swung around just when Downing was taking aim. Hyde dropped to the floor. The bullet shattered the window before crashing into the metal wall. Hyde pulled out his 38 and shot as he stood up. He felt his left arm burn, but he saw Downing stumble with a purple bud blossoming in the middle of his forehead before he dropped his gun and fell backward like a felled tree.

"Hello! Hello! Charlie?"

Worn out, Hyde picked up the receiver. "It's okay, Eddy, cancel the meeting. Downing just tried out his squirt gun on me and I had to take him down."

"You hurt?"

"A bullet grazed my arm. If you can send a car, I'd appreciate it."

They did not say it, but they both knew that Downing's death spelled a new victory, indirectly, for Madame Atomos. From now on they could only count on Dan Stone following the truck. The empty truck! Except no one knew that.

Dan Stone found out when he saw only two mangled corpses in the wreckage. The truck had been burned up three minutes earlier on the fortunately deserted road in the muffled roar of an infernal explosion. The flames had sprung out, all-consuming, then the vehicle blew open, spitting shrapnel in all directions.

It was stunning and stupefying. Stone only fully realized it a little later when he discovered that the Rambler station wagon and its passengers had left no trace. No witnesses, no danger. Dead men don't talk. The Atomos method...

Louis Radetich got out of the taxi in the downtown district, entered a diner and ordered coffee after sitting at the counter. He knew about nothing so when the latest news bulletin about the events in Riverside came over the radio he turned pale. He learned that the laboratory had blown up, that they were taking corpses out of the ruins, that Madame Atomos might be among the victims, but that Smith Beffort did not believe it and he was going to look for her personally.

Radetich paid, left the diner and got another taxi to take him to General Hospital. He was unable to analyze how he felt, but he had the feeling that Smith Beffort and the Green Dragon Force were not playing it straight with him. At the hospital he asked for authorization to see Beffort, in case the radio had given out false information, and found himself face to face with Eddy Witter.

"So, it's true. Beffort didn't wait!"

"Staying here was becoming useless, Radetich," Witter explained. "By destroying her laboratory Madame Atomos forced us to change our plans."

Radetich's face was gray and his skin looked coarse and taut; his bones were pushing through. "What's happened to my wife and children in all this?"

Witter tried to reassure him. "You know, we haven't had much time to deal with you. We're chasing Madame Atomos and…"

"Summer?" Radetich was in no condition to listen to or accept any murky justifications. He had been waiting a long time and now he had to know.

"Summer got away. He led Baxter's men to a house in the suburbs of Oakland where Madame Atomos was hiding. She was recognized by Akamatsu, who didn't hesitate to take a shot at her. Unfortunately…"

"I don't care about the details," Radetich cut in. "Baxter guaranteed me that they would follow Summer to know where my family was being held prisoner! I heard on the radio that the laboratory blew up and they were dragging corpses out of the ruins! Can you tell me that my wife and children haven't been killed?"

Witter lit a cigarette and offered his pack to Radetich who waved it off nervously. The G-man did not know what to say to the worry-ridden man.

"Answer me!" Radetich ordered.

Witter shook his head. "I can't tell you. Nevertheless, there are no signs that your family was in the laboratory. Given the two possibilities, don't choose the worst."

"When will you know?"

"I get regular updates on what's happening in Riverside. They'll be calling back in four or five minutes. Sit down and try to relax."

Radetich sat and said bitterly, "If Baxter had simply followed Summer..."

"He did and things would have turned out differently if Madame Atomos hadn't showed up. You know, Radetich, she was preparing to use a bacteriological weapon against our country. With that she became a woman to shoot on sight. I hope your wife and kids will get out alive. If they do, you'll have Akamatsu to thank for it. His action forced our enemy to call off a horrific attack that would have killed your family along with thousands of Americans."

Radetich stared at him stonily. "You mean that if my wife and children are dead, they'll receive posthumous medal of honors? You think that's a consolation!"

Witter walked to the window. "Certainly not, but what might happen to you has already happened to many others, including Mie and Smith Beffort who lost their only son. Before your family was kidnapped by the Atomos Organization, you can't deny that you didn't feel directly concerned with the battle we were waging against Madame Atomos."

"That's true," Radetich answered frankly.

"To such an extent that you never imagined you'd be fighting her yourself one day. However, if you had, maybe our enemy would have been defeated years ago. Thousands of people have fallen under the blows of Madame Atomos, but those who were spared remained indifferent. You were one of them."

All of a sudden Radetich was aware that Witter was skillfully anaesthetizing him, setting him up for the worst, by calling up general subjects. He stood up, but the sound of the telephone ringing stopped his rebellion clean in its track.

Witter reached for the phone, but before picking up he said, "It's Oakland. If you're ready for anything, you can listen in."

Radetich hesitated, but finally picked up the headphones. He spoke softly. "Let's go, Witter."

The G-man picked up the phone. "Witter here."

"Akamatsu. I've got bad news, Eddy. And worse because you'll have to tell Louis Radetich when he gets there."

Witter kept his eyes lowered. "It's about his wife and kids?"

"Yes. We just found them on the bottom floor of the laboratory in a room that was miraculously spared by the explosion. I don't know how you're going to tell Radetich, Eddy, but someone shot them dead in cold blood. I saw Mrs. Radetich with her hand cut off and the kids were so skinny that they must have been starved… It was dreadful."

Louis Radetich dropped the headphones and sat down slowly without saying a word.

Witter gritted his teeth while he listened to Akamatsu saying, "There are other casualties, people from the Organization, then we found out how Madame Atomos got away in a car that was parked for months probably behind a print shop. There were oil stains and tire tracks… Downing?"

"Dead. Hyde brought him down in self-defense. I'm going, Yosho, Radetich arrived."

"Go easy, okay? Such a blow could really traumatize him."

Witter hung up and when he turned to face Radetich he was struck by the expression in his eyes. Radetich did not move. He simply said, "I want to enter the Green Dragon Force."

He said no more. There was no need.

Madame Atomos just notched up one more enemy. A man who would fight to the death, savagely, without ever forgetting the martyrdom suffered by his wife and children.

Chapter XIV

In the fresh air of the early morning, despite the cloudy sky and faint light, Madame Atomos felt glad to be alive. Once again she had escaped the police, the FBI and the Green Dragon Force. She was feeling powerful and invulnerable. In a few minutes she would take off and spread death over California, then go and hole up in Texas, specifically in Dalhart (code: sector 16, area B) where another laboratory was being built. There she would meet up with Costello, Ida Brown, Armstrong and maybe a little later with Downing…

Madame Atomos took a few steps on the dewy grass and looked around. The private airfield was attached to Oakland's main airport, located right next to the San Francisco Bay. It was reached by a small, winding road that wound along the bay and that few people used because it was private. A small, private plane bought by the A.O.F.M.A. sat in the hangar: twin engines, four seats. Cruising speed of 350 miles/hr; fuel range of four hours. Before his sudden death Summer had taken loving care of it, knowing full well that it was the lifeline if their ship sank, so that Madame Atomos had no doubt that it was in perfect working condition.

The van had been parked near the hangar and the two men had just started loading the lethal boxes. It was 7:30. If all went well, Madame Atomos figured she could be off at 8 am, by herself… She was only sorry that her lack of information cut her off from knowing the movements of her adversaries. Being a pirate ship, the plane had no radio and the van had not been equipped with one to avoid attracting attention. And of course

Madame Atomos had been in a hurry to leave the lab and worried only about the most urgent business, completely forgetting to put a small transistor radio in her handbag. You can't think of everything when your life is at stake.

Madame Atomos pinched her pretty lips a little as she heard the sound of an engine, which had just struck her ears. It was coming from the sky. A US air force helicopter! Madame Atomos bolted and reached the hangar just when the aircraft appeared over the jagged fringe of trees bordering the airstrip. Four men on board, two machine guns, missiles...

The helicopter flew low over the field before shooting up like a rocket and disappearing over the bay. A patrol... Madame Atomos pinched her lips a little more. Willer and Monroe looked glued to the ground, holding their boxes, worry in the eyes. Their hunch was that even with the airplane it was not going to be a piece of cake.

"Hurry up, let's keep moving," Madame Atomos said. Despite the vamp that she had become, she still spoke like a mature woman. It was weird.

Willer got back to work and Monroe followed him. They made a few trips back and forth and then Willer asked, "What's going to happen when the plane takes off?"

In the Organization they did not usually ask the boss questions like this. Madame Atomos' eyes narrowed and inflamed. Eyes of napalm. "What did you say?"

If Willer were more veteran, he would have been more careful. But it was true that Madame Atomos' new skin diminished much of her authority. A very beautiful woman rarely succeeds in leading men.

Willer leaned back against the van. Off to the side, Monroe, wide-eyed, did not know what to expect. Willer added, "They're watching the skies but it's just you they're looking for, isn't it?"

Madame Atomos sighed. "Are you scared?"

Willer waved that off. "No, but we don't want to die like idiots." They must have discussed it while loading the plane. They were obviously not very eager and the helicopter cooled them down even more. Willer went on, "Staying on the ground, even though Madame Atomos staying silent keeps them going, we can still cross the bay and lay low in San Francisco for a while."

"Finish loading the plane," Madame Atomos ordered. "We'll talk about it afterward."

Willer turned to look at Monroe and then turned back. "We're going to need money, Madame."

For him, outside her laboratory and without her team, Madame Atomos was just a girl like any other, though more shapely than most, and he thought it would be pretty easy to impose his will. The crook was heading merrily down a deadly road, forgetting about the voluntary destruction of the laboratory and all the consequent casualties. But as the killer of the Radetich family, the man had too much blood on his hands to be impressed by the Japanese woman's record.

Madame Atomos sighed again. It was a challenge, if not a revolt. Strange times! She had to cut to the quick before it was too late… Trouble. Except that only half the boxes of XBC-250 were on the plane.

"In short," Madame Atomos said, "you want money to finish your work?"

Willer smiled and slowly nodded. Very casually Madame Atomos opened her purse, pulled out a wad of bills and threw it at Willer's feet. "Pick it up."

"Hey, that's not enough for two to live in Mexico. We'll need four times that much."

Madame Atomos nodded, pulled out her snub-nosed 38 and opened fire. Willer dropped with the first shot, but Monroe ran behind the hangar where he unholstered his 45. Madame Atomos agilely slipped behind the shelter of the van and ducked when she heard two bullets whizz by. Incredible! She, Madame Atomos, having to battle it out with a baboon not even worthy to shine her shoes!

Hiroshima! Nagasaki!

Bang! Bang!

Monroe watched his new hat go flying and he turned pale. Things were not turning out like he had wanted. Willer was lying in the grass with a bullet through his right eye, uglier dead than alive, and Madame Atomos seemed to handle a gun as deftly as a tube of lipstick.

Madame Atomos peaked out. Monroe shot again and again wildly.

"Stop!" she shouted. "I give up!"

"Throw out your gun!"

Madame Atomos tossed out Willer's gun, which she had swiped up on her way. Monroe went to pick it up and was shot down before he had taken three steps. Child's play!

Compliments of Madame Atomos!

Trains and planes were stopped, roads blocked, identities checked, cars searched. Patrols were in the air and on the ground. Radio silence, radar surveillance and the army advancing like a steamroller, pushing back everything in front of it. There were a lot of people in Oakland and the start of a panic.

They knew that Madame Atomos was there. They knew that she had a bacteriological weapon. They listened to their breathing, kept an eye out for weird symptoms. A kid was picked up on Telegraph Avenue with red spots on his skin and was given a battery of tests for a simple case of measles. Women with slanted eyes could not move an inch, especially if they were young and pretty, and even after taking their fingerprints they held them. A guy from Detroit had said that it was pretty easy to forge them by sticking another skin on the tips with prints just as natural…

"Since this morning," Baxter said, "Madame Atomos has been seen 500 times by convinced witnesses. Headquarters is getting dozens of calls, constantly, reporting Madame Atomos in ten different places at the same time. Unbelievable!"

The clock had not yet struck eight. By "this morning" Baxter meant the time that had passed since the explosion of the laboratory, but for him these miserable 65 minutes seemed like hours.

Sweating and excited Seurer ran into the office waving a paper. "It's finally here! At post 35, the license plate of a General Deliveries van was jotted down right after the lab exploded. We've checked and it's a fake!"

Akamatsu stood up and found the location of post 35 on the Oakland map. "Southwest. From there you can get on Highway 260, which goes into Alameda. But the van could have turned off and taken the bridge to San Francisco. If there…" He made a long face, not wanting to believe it.

"Hold on!" Baxter said. "All the roads into Oakland were already closed…"

"Not completely," Brady corrected. "The lab blew up around 7 am, or 20 minutes before Beffort gave or-

143

ders for the blockade. The roadblocks were still full of holes."

They were silent. Each of them was aware that time was on Madame Atomos' side. Unfortunately, they could do nothing more than they had already done.

"Look for the van?" Baxter proposed.

Akamatsu shrugged. "A pebble in the ocean."

He was heartsick since he had missed his shot. And Madame Atomos was capable of disappearing in 30 seconds if need be. As it was, she had had one full hour to sail off.

A pebble in the ocean... sail off? Akamatsu shuddered.

Instantly, he had an answer. Madame Atomos had always used water to make good her escapes. When surrounded, she always had a river, lake or ocean near her refuge.

"The San Francisco Bay!" he said.

Damn!" Brady barked, "Why didn't we think of that earlier?"

At the end of the rope, they were bound to come to this conclusion. Akamatsu jumped on the radiophone, asked for Smith Beffort, whose plane had landed to fuel up, and was quickly put through.

"Yellow Mask here," Beffort said. "Any news, Yosho?"

"Not exactly, Smith, but a suspicious van got through post 35 at 6:55."

"Oh? That's news, isn't it?"

"Sure, if you say so… Hey, Smith, do you know that the ocean is only 30 minutes away from the San Francisco Bay?"

"I know, but I don't think that Madame Atomos is headed that way. It's old hat now."

Akamatsu furrowed his brow. Beffort was certainly right. But knowing that the forces of law and order would think this very thing, Madame Atomos could have played her cards face up.

"Plus," Beffort added, "to reach the coast she'd first have to get through the barriers set up by the army. In my opinion, Yosho, she's still stuck inside our lines and is going to try to get away when she sees the net closing in on her. That's why I'm staying in the air."

"She'll leave through a tunnel, certainly not on a plane or helicopter."

"Be careful! Madame Atomos is 30 years old now! She's changed her habits without meaning to, unconsciously, and simply because it'll fit with her new personality. Nevertheless, nothing's stopping you from going to see what's happening on the beaches."

"You don't want to come?"

"No, I'm staying in the air. I can receive all the radio messages and intervene fast. At the first sign, I'll dive down, let loose the machine guns, drop the bombs... Got it?"

"Got it," Akamatsu confirmed with a touch of disappointment. He was in a slump, not feeling up to snuff, was almost sure that he would mess up anything he did. There was bad luck that one could do nothing about.

"But stay in touch with me," Smith requested.

"Understood. If I run into Madame Atomos, I'll ask you to dive down, shoot and bomb. Later, Smith."

He signed off, unhappy with himself, feeling like he had been inept and a little sarcastic.

The US air force helicopter landed at the Oakland airport and the Major went to report in while they prepared the aircraft for another round. His name was

Mitchell and he was a hard, blunt man. He pushed open the door of the coordination center and pulled out his flight log. Notes, verifications, suspicious objects, etc.

Without a word being said, the log passed to the leader who compared it with other reports:

A group of pedestrians heading east had been spotted by the pilot of GH-310. They were pushed back into Mitchell's sector and were now walking in Oakland. Normal behavior. They were six workers.

A beige Ford with a blue top was seen on Highway 61. Since it was parked for a long time, the highway patrol passed by. Out of gas...

Mitchell yawned on the sly. It was all routine. All of a sudden the leader asked, "And the private airstrip?"

Mitchell sneered. "Closed. No activity."

The other looked up. "But they could use it to take off..."

"Oh?" He had seen so many strips of land, roads, houses and cars that they were all mixed up. The centralization leader knew what it was like. He was questioning a Major who could not remember because he was dizzy from all the fleeting sights.

"You also noted a van," he reminded him patiently.

"Possible."

"True, Major, it's written right here."

"Okay, I believe you, Lieutenant."

"Make an effort, would you? I'd like to know if this vehicle had any markings."

Mitchell smiled and his hand sliced through the air. "I passed by like that... like a shot!"

The Lieutenant looked at a memo coming directly from the FBI. "This morning," he said amiably, "a General Deliveries van went through post 35. This post is located on the way to Alameda. Later, they checked the license plate and found that it was fake. Since then the G-men have been thinking that Madame Atomos was inside."

Mitchell suddenly woke up. "No kidding?"

"No kidding, Major. When you go back there, why don't you take a closer look at this van? We need to be at least half-certain before sending in the commando teams."

"Okay, I'll set her down."

The lieutenant shook his head. "Strictly forbidden! If you hit a bull's eye, call Yellow Mask who will decide what steps to take. Airstrip position, vehicle description, access roads. Be very careful. If Madame Atomos is hiding around there, she might shoot you down. We don't know what kinds of weapons she's using. Lastly, she promised to toss some bacteriological germs over the USA and she might want to try them out on you first."

Mitchell shifted his feet. "I'm taking off in eight minutes. Heading straight for the airstrip…"

"No, Major," the lieutenant intervened quietly. "No matter what, don't set off any alarms. Make your usual round and let off the gas when you're near the target. The Colonel just wants you not to shoot by!"

Mitchell smiled, picked up his log and went to drink a coffee in the cafeteria where he met up with his team. With a mysterious look, he leaned over and said, "Boys, we've got a top secret mission. Did you photograph that private airstrip?"

The three men nodded. Mitchell lowered his voice. "Looks like Mama Atomos might be there." Then all he did was laugh, loudly.

See, that was the problem: they did not believe in Madame Atomos until it was too late to escape her deadly clutches.

Chapter XV

Madame Atomos had never been so vulnerable. She only had traditional weapons at hand and so could be killed with ridiculous ease by the first comer, but she did not think about that for even a second. Her immediate goal was to spread the terrifying capsules of XNC-250 over California and it took her another fifteen minutes to finish loading the plane.

When all was ready, after loading a couple of parachutes as well, she sat in the pilot's seat, started the engines and let them warm up while watching the runway, which was just long enough to take off without making any mistakes. Madame Atomos bit her lip. She had not flown for years and was completely unfamiliar with the type of plane she had to get off the ground. Clearly, her chances were weak. 40-45 %, no more, was being optimistic.

She was thinking about this when Mitchell's helicopter appeared at the end of the runway. He was coming a lot more slowly than the first time and his heading would bring him directly over the airstrip. On such a close examination, nothing would be hidden.

Petrified, Madame Atomos felt her pulse race. The double doors of the hangar were wide open and she had no idea whether her plane was out of sight or not. And the van was sitting outside for everyone to see. Plus, there were the bodies of Willer lying with his arms outstretched and Monroe, less visible but…

A disaster!

Madame clenched her jaws and stared agape as the helicopter disappeared over the treetops. It was unthinkable!

In the helicopter, the radio was calling Beffort feverishly. "GH-310 to Yellow Mask... GH-310 to Yellow Mask..."

"Yellow Mask here," Beffort's cold voice came over. "Go ahead, GH-310."

"We just spotted the van marked General Deliveries, plus two corpses not seen on our first pass. And up close we saw the double doors of one of the hangars wide open..."

"Any movement?"

"Nothing. The position of the airstrip..."

"I know it," Beffort cut in. "Stay on alert while I get the commando teams out there and keep your radio on. Over and out."

Mitchell grumbled. He was going to get stuck with a surveillance job instead of getting in on the action. He got the helicopter to turn around and gain some altitude because the clouds were getting lower and lower, scattered with hazy strands that could be concealing a treetop.

"Airplane at three o'clock!" the engineer suddenly shouted.

Mitchell turned his head and saw a silvery arrow shoot into the clouds. A fleeting vision, almost unreal, but unmistakable. Heading up into the sky, the twin-engine could have come from nowhere but the private airstrip.

Mitchell estimated the speed of the pirate plane and said, "Too fast for us. Contact Yellow Mask!"

The radio operator winked and got in contact.

With the lever stuck to her belly, Madame Atomos climbed into a thick lump of dirty cotton. The engines were roaring and the plane responded perfectly. Summer had done a good job and his painless death was well deserved.

At 6,500 feet the twin engines suddenly sprang out of the clouds into a blue sky and dazzling sunlight. Madame Atomos squinted, pushed back the lever and set her heading. Now nothing could stop her from dumping the boxes of XBC-250, one by one, in an almost continuous line. Down below the result would be almost instantaneous and the people would drop like flies with their tongues swollen and their lungs burning. Madame Atomos was confident in the product's potency. She had experimented on three workmen snatched in Oakland.

She turned completely around because of the parachute, which was hampering her movements, and froze. Three quarters of the way behind, a supersonic fighter plane had just appeared out of nowhere and was already lit up with orange lights. Tracers slammed into Madame Atomos and then several missiles hit the twin engines tail, which rattled on impact. Motionless, Madame Atomos clearly saw the tense face of Smith Beffort as the fighter sped by, banked very far away and came back as fast as lightning.

Madame Atomos started a nosedive, but found the plane descending with frustrating slowness. She breathed a little sigh of relief when she hit the sea of clouds, but she knew it was only a temporary safeguard. Beffort would not give up. He would give it all he had to bring her down in flames.

A small, dry ball of spit formed in Madame Atomos' throat. She was caught in an indefensible position, almost hopeless. She could not hide in the clouds forever or evade all the radar. From the ground they were no doubt following with telescopes as well! She was going to jump but thought otherwise because she was still over the zone under army control. The problem had no solution! But if she waited too long, a squad would have plenty of time to intercept her. They would find her and…

The explosion shook the plane as other tracer shells popped through the thick fog. Madame Atomos changed her course drastically, headed west, as the air around her exploded. Marks of fire, flame and hell! They were battering her from the ground to force her to rise into the clear sky where Beffort was waiting for her.

Her muscles in pain, Madame Atomos dove again, surprised that her plane was not more severely damaged, and fell through the cotton like a rock, emerging suddenly into the dull light that was spreading over the land. In a flash she saw San Francisco sprawled out, the highways and then the anti-aircraft batteries firing away, volley after volley.

The plane reeled, lost a wing tip. The cabin was riddled with bullets while Madame Atomos pulled on the lever to hide in the clouds once again. Panting and out of breath, she suddenly realized that death was her co-pilot. If one single capsule of XBC-250 broke, she was a goner!

There was another impact, somewhere behind her, and Madame Atomos tried in vain not to head out toward sea, but with the steering broken, the plane was not responding to her commands. It continued its route straight ahead, at full speed, toward the Pacific Ocean, completely out of control now.

Totally exhausted, Madame Atomos slunk back in her seat. This time she was playing out her final act!

The twin-engine plane was sighted over San Francisco, then over San Mateo. During its whole course, the anti-aircraft defense kept up its barrage without success. The machine seemed to be invulnerable.

It was true that they were shooting very inaccurately, through an almost solid curtain of clouds using radar and sound locators. Moreover, the important thing was not to lose track of it. Sooner or later, it would be force to land, somewhere, anywhere... Higher up, in the fighter plane, Smith was starting to think it was taking too long. By their calculations Madame Atomos was heading for the Pacific, which made no sense.

"What's she thinking?" Evans asked, his forehead furrowed in concentration.

"Only she knows," Mie murmured.

Smith was anxious and did not hide it. "It all smells foul, Evans. In theory, knowing she's trapped, she should try to land in some remote spot, far from the forces gathered in this sector. Her plane can set down on a short runway, whereas ours can't. With some luck she might hide in a forest before a team can come to our rescue. By flying over the Pacific she's committing suicide. Not her style, is it?"

The radio operator of the fighter plane signaled that he was receiving a new positioning. He quickly marked the coordinates of the twin-engine on a notepad and handed it to Smith, whose face became a little tenser.

"Now," he said, "she's flying over an area not under the army's surveillance. In a few seconds her plane will fly straight out to the ocean."

He felt his stomach turn when he remembered that Atomos Island used to be in the same direction. Of course it was disintegrated by an atomic explosion and almost nothing remained of it, but still the worry was there, born out of the ashes, simply because Madame Atomos seemed set on heading for Hawaii.

It was ridiculous, impossible. Hawaii was almost 2,000 miles to the west, out of range for the twin-engine. But in the past Madame Atomos had proven her inventive genius. Smith would not have been surprised to see the plane change suddenly into a rocket ship!

"Weather!" the radio barked.

He listened and made notes. Smith looked and read that the wind was rising, blowing west-east, already pushing the clouds inland. He looked over at the pilot who was turning the fighter around to stay on top of the invisible twin-engine.

"Plane at eight o'clock!"

Smith leaned over, unbelieving, and did in fact see that the plane was coming out of the clouds that the wind was chasing away. Caught between the sky and the sea, Madame Atomos was becoming easy prey. The radio started crackling. 100 different spots were signaling the appearance of the plane.

"I can't believe it," Mie exclaimed.

The fighter banked and started its attack dive. In 30 seconds the twin-engine would be shot down. Beffort and Mie exchanged glances. None of this made any sense.

"Go!"

Weapons started firing.

"Stop!" Smith shouted.

The pilot repeated the order, without understanding, seeing immediately that the first round had hit the target.

One of the engines was on fire and the plane was tilting sideways, slowly.

"Get closer," Smith ordered.

The fighter sped by, grazing the target, turned around and came back. It all happened very quickly, but even a one-eyed man could have seen that the plane was empty!

"Good God!" Evans said in bitter disappointment.

The Madame Atomos' plane toppled over, for the last time, and plunged into the ocean where it made a huge splash. No one knew it yet, but the terrifying capsules of XBC-250 were rendered forever harmless.

A dizzying fall in the icy air, the snap of the parachute, shoulders feeling dislocated, then a slow descent into the fog. Feeling unreal and wicked cold. Hair floating in the wind, her skirt flying up to her chin, Madame Atomos was staking all she had.

It lasted an eternity and though she still thought she was in the clouds, Madame Atomos felt her legs crash into hard foliage. It cracked, broke, then disappeared and Madame Atomos hit the soft ground and rolled, while her parachute tore apart noisily, shredded by a pine suddenly turned into a Christmas tree.

No more sound. Pitch black. Madame Atomos patted herself, realized she was unharmed, barely even scratched on her thighs, with her 38 lodged between her full, firm breasts. She slipped out of the coarse harness and walked straight ahead, a survival instinct, but also to warm up.

She was on her feet, uninjured and deadlier than ever, frenzied by her extraordinary luck, certain that nothing could stop her now.

Hiroshima! Nagasaki!

A clearing, a field, a road. Madame Atomos ran her sharp nails through her hair, adjusted her skirt, hiked up her bra and then magically produced a wad of dollar bills from her panties. After that she grabbed her 38, hid it behind her skirt and stood on the side of the road, her breasts pushed out, one thigh revealed, sexy.

Samuel Casak, a traveling salesman, was breathless. He was coming from Los Angeles up the coast to San Francisco to try to sell beauty products, but he was in no hurry to get there. He stopped his Chevrolet in front of the girl, stuck his head out the window and asked, "Where you going, honey?"

The bullet shattered his skull and when Madame Atomos opened the car door, he dropped to the ground without any help. She dragged him into a deep ditch, got behind the wheel and set off. While driving she rifled through the contents of the suitcase on the seat. Lipstick, cream, makeup remover, perfume, pink, green, blue, black... Wigs, false eyelashes, false nails, false breasts!

Madame Atomos screeched to a stop on a narrow dirt road and choose a big pot of black cream. Wess & Wess, extra dry, no skin damage, used by actors in the National Theater. It took 30 minutes, including the undressing, but in the end she had become a very pretty little black woman with slanted eyes. After all, with all the mixed races, it could have been worse!

She got back on the road, turned on the radio and found out right away that her plane had crashed into the sea and that they were looking for her between Oakland, San Jose and San Francisco, a triangle inside of which she had probably jumped. Madame Atomos was not in the triangle, but would be soon if she kept on going. She stopped, whipped the car around and drove the other direction.

They were announcing her description over the radio, calling attention to the right index finger that was cut off at the first knuckle. Madame Atomos grimaced. That was her weak point. Even as a black, she would be suspect if a wary policeman made her raise her hands.

She drove for 20 minutes, entered Santa Cruz, and before realizing it she hit a line of cars inching through a police roadblock. 15 feet a minute... Madame Atomos leaned out and saw the policemen checking IDs and searching trunks. She knew she had no chance of getting through. How stupid!

She could think of nothing to do, so she stayed in line until her black eye spotted a gas station. The cars passed right by. Madame Atomos turned in and rolled up to the pump. Nothing was more normal. To get out of the station, the cars had to get back in line.

Madame Atomos asked the attendant to fill it up, check the tires, battery and oil before she headed for the bathrooms, making sure that no one was watching her when she skipped around the building. She crossed a yard, went down some stone stairs and came out on a lower street. Pretty soon the attendant would start wondering what happened to her, but he would not sound any alarms right away, maybe never at all. A black girl, right, they come and go.

Madame Atomos walked fast, came to an avenue at the end of which she could see the sea. A beach, a harbor, boats! The taxi stopped when she raised her hand and drove her to the harbor in less than five minutes. She paid the fare, got out and strode down the deserted pier. Her lazy attitude hid her fury. Although she looked meek, she was ready to kill, gash, destroy.

Boat rides, the sign read. Madame Atomos examined the boat. Two big engines… She stepped onto the gangplank, smiling and swishing her hips. Captivating!

"Can you take me to Monterey, young man?"

The guy had seen plenty of lookers, but nothing like this one. He did not like colored women very much, but some things are just too good to pass up.

"50 dollars for Monterey," he said.

Madame Atomos pulled a 100-dollar bill out of her bra. "I have money. Can we go?"

She was being a little ridiculous, but the guy could not know what the light gleaming in her eyes really meant.

"Okay, let's go, babe!"

He was sure he would get it on with her during the trip. Like a man on his way to a party, he was feeling good, whistling as he stepped off the deck, staring at the girl's chest.

Off the coast of Santa Cruz, Madame Atomos shot him in the neck and pushed his dead body into the water. Then she stood at the helm and opened the throttle. The boat bounced and went full speed ahead toward Monterey from where the terrible Japanese woman would be able to reach Los Angeles, San Diego… and Mexico.

Hiroshima! Nagasaki!

Madame Atomos started singing…

Michel Stéphan: *The Woman in the High Castle*

Hawthorne Abendsen's eyes followed the Japanese woman as she glided about the room. She had introduced herself as a devoted reader of his, but something about her did not ring true.

Abendsen was no fool. Since the Japanese conquest of the Western half of the United States, and the publication of his novel, *The Grasshopper Lies Heavy*, many had tried to kill him. Unlike the Nazi, whose assassination attempts had been brutal and unsubtle, the Japanese schemes had been refined and complicated—just like them. As for the woman in front of him, a mind less sharp than his own might have taken her at face value; but he was Hawthrorne Abendsen, whose book had changed the world. He could not be fooled by her, no matter how clever and fascinating she was.

She had introduced herself as Kanoto Yoshimuta. Her eager, hungry eyes had met his squarely, taking in as much as she could. Then, she had sat demurely in front of him in order to share tea in the best Japanese fashion. Looking into her eyes, Abendsen had had a glimpse of a strange, new world— one that both fascinated and disturbed him. He was not unaccustomed to that feeling, however. After all, he had written his own book transcribing what the *I Ching* had shown him. He saw himself as a faithful scribe, obeying the dictates of an unseen power whose existence he would never be allowed to question nor contradict.

The Grasshopper Lies Heavy told the tale of a world where the Allies had been victorious over the Axis powers. Even thought it had been couched in the guise of a clever fiction, Abendsen knew that it spoke of another, truer reality than his own. Now, the sudden apparition of this strange Japanese woman spoke of yet another.

He felt powerless before the intensity of her burning gaze, and understood with extraordinary clarity that this woman was far more dangerous than the Nazis or the Japanese spymasters who had previously tried to assassinate him. But the game she wished to play was fascinating, and Abendsen never tired of playing it

"I am always happy to meet one of my loyal readers," said Abendsen as his opening move. "I feel that you know much about me, but I nothing about you."

"Questions are a challenge to oneself," replied the Japanese woman.

"But answers must be shared if one is to arrive at the truth."

"Yet answers are also a prison, and questions must all too often remain unanswered. I feel that you are trying to cheat, Mr. Abendsen. Are you afraid of me?"

"In all candor, yes, I am, Kanoto. There is something about you that is beyond my understanding. You are both here—and not here. You are something that I cannot fathom..."

"Perhaps you are dreaming?"

"I thought so, once, but no longer. I feel entirely lucid. I know what you wish to know, what you need to know... But I cannot give it to you, Kanoto, because you are not part of my book."

The Japanese woman did not flinch, but Abendsen felt her profound disappointment.

"Here, your people won the war," the writer continued, "Everything would be perfection for you. You no longer would have any reason to blame the Americans, because they—we—were defeated."

"This is what I seek."

"I know. But embracing this world would remove your reason for existing."

"And yet, I am here, before you."

"But you are not in my book. And my book is the only truth. It was dictated to me, you know. It is not the answer for you."

"Your book may not be the absolute truth; there may be another way..."

"I do not have that knowledge, Kanoto. I only know that your life is governed by your hatred of the Americans. When that hatred disappears, you, too, will disappear."

"That is ridiculous!"

"Yet, that is why you came to me looking for answers; that is why you keep me locked up here against my will."

"What do you mean? You're Howard Abendsen; you're the Man in the High Castle; I visit you only as a devoted reader..."

"You lie. You are the director of this psychiatric hospital in which I have been an unwilling patient for months. I was briefly touched by the pink beam of a Vast Active Living Intelligence System which has made me aware of other realities. You have taken me prisoner and are keeping me here against my will because I know too much—and you need answers. You have come to doubt your life's purpose, and indeed the very reality of your world."

Kanoto Yoshimuta jumped up to her feet and headed for the door.

"We will resume this conversation later, Mr. Abendsen," she said. "For now, you need to rest."

Abendsen raised his voice, almost shouting.

"Your world is coming apart at the seams, Kanoto," he sneered. "Only I have the power to show you a new one. But for humanity's sake, I will not be including you in my next book."

Kanoto stopped listening. She closed the heavy reinforced door behind her, trapping the writer alone in his cell. After checking that the electronic lock was functioning properly, she walked towards the two orderlies who stood guard at the entrance of the hall.

"Take good care of him," she ordered. "If he has new flashes, call me at once. I may need to arrange for his transport elsewhere."

"I'm not looking forward to it; that guy really scares me," said one of the orderlies, immediately realizing that he may have said too much.

But Madame Atomos ignored the comment; she had just noticed, on a small television monitor placed on the orderlies' desk, several uniformed men moving into position around the hospital grounds.

"What's going on?" she barked into a microphone.

"It's the FBI," answered a voice on the intercom. "They've surrounded the hospital. There are cops everywhere."

"Everything is ready for immediate evacuation?" Madame Atomos asked one of the orderlies.

"Yes, Madame. The Western tunnel is clear and the explosives are in place. We only await your orders."

"Let's go then," said Madame Atomos.

The two orderlies opened the cell and grabbed the writer who screamed unceasingly.

Madame Atomos pressed the button that revealed the hatch leading to the secret escape tunnel beneath their feet. She gave a final glance to the monitor screen. She saw several G-men scramble near the entrance and thought she recognized Smith Beffort.

The writer was lying. Somewhere, there was a world where all would be right for her. She just had to find it.

For the first time that day, a smile appeared on her lips.

André Caroff

Mme ATOMOS JETTE un FROID

ANGOISSE

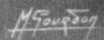

FLEUVE NOIR

THE COLD WAR OF MADAME ATOMOS

Chapter I

Madame Atomos had disappeared only a month ago and there was no sign that she would reappear anytime soon. Her laboratory in Oakland was destroyed, her scientists were dead and the better part of her gang was on the run[3]. In short, Madame Atomos had to start from scratch. It would not be easy because all the police in the USA were keeping their eyes out for her. Moreover, the face of the terrible Japanese woman was plastered on every wall, in all the newspapers and magazines, and for a month decorated the cover of *Life*.

It was mid-December. The cold was bitter but dry. Behind the window of his toy store Stephano was not smiling. Business was bad (around 3.4 % less than last year in the same period) and in spite of the coming holiday the inhabitants of Amarillo, Texas were not loosening their purse strings. 3.4%!

And taxes were not a penny lower!

Stephano was worried sick. He had started the business only 16 months ago, was still paying off a pile of loans, and was wondering gloomily what tomorrow would bring. He felt glum as he watched the street teeming with people getting off work and he thought that if only 2% of the crowd bought something from him the

---

[3] See *The Mark of Madame Atomos* in this volume.

end of his month would be taken care of. Then his gaze fell upon a magnificent brunette and he turned off his internal calculator.

She was really pretty, curvy; Stephano had never seen such perfect legs. She was walking fast, but stopped at the crosswalk and looked up, waiting for the traffic light to change. In the group of pedestrians there were other girls, but Stephano only had eyes for her.

The light turned green. The group poured between the cars and mixed with the group coming from the opposite sidewalk, which caused a little commotion before the light changed again. To his surprise Stephano saw the pretty girl standing in the same place, in the same position, as if she were glued to the spot. The crowd flowed around without bumping into her. She did not bother the pedestrians and nobody paid any attention to her, except for Stephano who was bored in his empty shop.

Ten minutes went by. The girl watched the traffic light without moving an inch and Stephano was starting to think that she must have been a little screwy. Just then a customer entered. She wanted a construction kit for her ten-year old son. Something not too simple but not too hard, not too expensive but good quality. She pestered Stephano for 20 minutes, made him bring out half his inventory, and finally left without buying a thing. Stephano could have strangled her!

He cleaned up his shop, lit a cigarette and went back to stand before the window. He could not believe his eyes: the little brunette was still on the sidewalk, watching the traffic light, ready to cross, but she had not budged. Not an inch!

Staying like that for 30 minutes was a real feat, even if you were meeting someone. Stephano thought that she might be watching a clock, but immediately realized that there was not one in the direction she was looking. No, she was only interested in the traffic light.

Stephano did not take his eyes off her for the next 15 minutes. He felt like he was staring at a statue. Then the face of Bill, the neighborhood policeman, popped up in his line of vision. Bill winked at him. Stephano waved him in.

"What do you need, buddy?"

Stephano pointed out the girl.

Bill whistled in admiration. "You've got front row seats here, eh?"

Stephano looked at his watch. "She's been like that for 50 minutes."

"Ah! And?"

"I mean she hasn't moved an inch in all that time! Take a good look at her. Her head's raised, one leg in front of the other, an arm bent… She's almost off balance. Strange, isn't it?"

The policeman watched the girl for five minutes until he finally became bewildered. "It's not possible. She's a mannequin."

"No, no, no, she's a living, breathing beauty. I watched her walking down the street, swishing her hips and she stopped there with the other people waiting for the light to change. She hasn't moved since then. That's all."

"Okay, I'm going to have a word with her. Something's not right here."

He did not know what was "not right" and felt a little uneasy, which Stephano made worse by asking, "Is it against the law, Bill?"

The policeman took off his hat, scratched his head and put his hat back on. He was annoyed. "No, it's not against the law. I can't even accuse her of working the streets, can I?"

Stephano mocked, "That would be a whole new method..."

Now that Bill was taking charge, he could joke about it. Of course, the girl's attitude and behavior was weird, but not seriously disturbing. At least she was standing up. As long as you are standing up, you are in good health. Everyone knows that.

He said, "You're not going to leave her like that, Bill!"

"No, I'm going to have a word with her. If she's been there for almost an hour... Okay, I'm going."

Stephano clapped his hands and said "Bravo", but Bill did not respond. He left, crossed the street without worrying about the cars and stepped onto the sidewalk. With a severe look in his eyes, he walked up to the young lady and stopped right behind her.

"Miss?"

He spoke loudly, like any self-respecting police-man, but she did not bother to turn around. Bill walked around her. Now he could see that something was wrong with the girl. Her eyes were like stone, she did not look like she was breathing and her face was covered with a thin film of frost.

"Miss, you have to move on."

A crowd was already gathering around Bill and the girl. However, as opposed to what usually happens, no one was speaking. The little brunette's immobility over-whelmed everyone. A statue!

Bill gulped. He did not know what to do.

"She's dead," an older woman said. "I'm sure she's dead."

A man started to laugh. "Have you seen the dead standing on tiptoes like this? I think the girl's joshing. Some kind of publicity stunt. Hey, I'm sure there's a hidden camera filming us right now."

His comment calmed everyone down. Enjoying the attention, he continued, "Look, she's got frost on her face. It's not cold here, is it? I wonder where her microphone's hiding?"

With his hands behind his back, wringing his nightstick, Bill was still hesitating, but starting to think about a television show. If it was live, he must have looked like a fool! By now, drawn by the crowd, cars were stopping to see what was happening and a traffic jam was forming in the intersection. Bill got to work.

"Move on! Move on! It's not a circus!"

People shifted, but only to walk in a circle so that nothing changed. Bill figured that the fun had lasted long enough. "You, actress girl, come here!"

He grabbed the girl by the arm and pulled. The arm snapped off and the girl, thrown off balance, fell to the side, stiff as a board. Bill's reflex was to catch her, but she slipped through his hands and crashed to the sidewalk, shattering to bits, like a window broken by a rock... Bill backed up and dropped the arm, which also exploded when it hit the ground. A woman screamed like an idiot and started a panic. Everyone ran while Bill stood at the intersection, alone, with a broken woman at his feet whom they would have to pick up with little shovels. Insanity!

Smith Beffort crossed his legs and held out his pack of cigarettes that Dr. Waugh waved off. He asked, "In short, Miss Lodge was refrigerated?"

"Literally. I don't know how it happened, but I do know that she was cooled down to around 300 degrees centigrade. If you figure that rock splits at -50 degrees, then it's no surprise that Miss Lodge shattered when she hit the ground. Right now she's starting to warm up, gradually, but it obviously won't change her condition. She'll be buried in bite-sized pieces, that's all…"

The doctor's black humor made Mie shudder. Beffort smiled curtly, thanked Dr. Waugh and took his wife outside.

"Where are we going, Smith?"

"To see John Stephano," Beffort said.

He hailed a passing cab and gave Stephano's address. When they arrived ten minutes later, Beffort introduced himself and asked, "You were the first one to notice Miss Lodge?"

"That's right. She was over there, near the traffic light."

"Tell me, Mr. Stephano, are you sure that no one put her there next to the light?"

Stephano smiled. "She was coming out of Morris' when I spotted her and I can assure you that she was alive. It's only when she got to the crosswalk that it happened. It was like someone touched her with a magic fairy wand."

Smith and Mie thanked him and left. The fairy was no doubt Madame Atomos and the magic wand a new refrigerating ray! The stunning death of Miss Lodge was probably just a trial run.

"Madame Atomos got a laboratory back together in spite of being hunted," Beffort said somberly. "And only 30 days after the Oakland affair!"

"It was to be expected, Smith. Madame Atomos never put all her eggs in one basket and she still has a bunch of co-conspirators around the USA. Nothing will change as long as she can count on the A.O.F.M.A. Plus, Ida Brown and Robert Costello are still on the run…"

Beffort examined the crosswalk. It was surrounded by buildings chock full of windows. The day before maybe Madame Atomos or one of her servants were standing at one of them.

"What are you going to do, Smith?"

"Nothing," Beffort answered. "We don't have enough witnesses, not the slightest clue. Miss Lodge was murdered by Madame Atomos, that's for sure. Except for that we don't know anything else. We have to wait, Mie."

"Wait for what?"

"More deaths, unfortunately! In Amarillo or some other town."

Two days later a line of 300 people was waiting for Texas Port to open where the latest western of Henry Hathaway was making its exclusive debut. Robert Mitchum and Catherine Justice were starring, which explained the big crowd. Cinema was not dead! It was bitter cold, but a prospective audience had never cooled their heels in such a good mood. The coming holiday also had something to do with their carefree attitude.

Across from the theater the Befforts and Akamatsu were sipping their last scotch before returning to their hotel. Mie had managed to clear Smith's mind of his worries by the arrival of the Japanese as an observer. They had eaten at the Ethery restaurant and had come to this bar purely by chance. Naturally, however, in spite of Mie's efforts, the two men ended up talking about the brutal and rather extraordinary death of Miss Lodge.

"What I don't understand," Akamatsu said, "is that the young lady kept standing after being 'refrigerated'."

Smith took a drag off his cigarette. "She stopped exactly when John Stephano saw her freeze for good. I guess if the ray had hit her while walking, she would have fallen right away and shattered in front of everyone."

"Why her?" Akamatsu wondered.

"Oh, it's likely that Madame Atomos didn't choose her in particular. The preliminary investigation showed that Miss Lodge led a very ordinary life, very quiet and with no mysteries."

Akamatsu swallowed the Cutty Sark. "Nothing really proves that Madame Atomos was responsible for Miss Lodge's death," he said without too much conviction.

Beffort smiled ironically. "If you have another explanation, I'm all ears."

"A natural phenomenon?"

"Come on, Yosho, stop dreaming. Miss Lodge could have been struck by lightning or suffered congestion from cold... in fact, anything could have happened to her. But not that. No natural phenomenon can produce such extraordinary cold. Dr. Waugh was positive: 300 degrees centigrade, not one degree less."

Mie leaned over between the two men. "What if we went to the movies? Look at all the people across the street."

Smith sneered. "As far as drama," he said, "our battle against Madame Atomos is quite enough for me. Isn't that right, Yosho?"

But Akamatsu was not listening. Stiff and alert, he was staring at a gray Ford parked across the street. Beffort and Mie followed his gaze. Akamatsu mumbled,

"I must be seeing things, Smith. The young lady behind the wheel looks like Ida Brown."

Beffort opened the curtain wider, but the Ford was parked between streetlights in the shadows and it was impossible to make out the features of the driver. However, he could see the man in the back seat.

"What car are you talking about?" Mie asked.

"The gray Ford," Akamatsu responded, "in front of the theater's service entrance. Hold on, it's starting up."

It was not much help to Mie because the Ford drove away from the bar, cruising along the sidewalk with the line of people, slowly, into the bright light coming from the theater, and Mie jumped up, shouting, "It's Ida Brown!"

"And Costello!" Smith barked.

Akamatsu was already running for the door, paralyzing pistol in hand. He bolted through onto the sidewalk and raised his gun just as the Ford disappeared around the corner. Akamatsu broke into a sprint in front of the movie theater, but the street was deserted.

"Too late," Smith said, catching up.

"And we're on foot!" Mie complained coming up behind them. She turned around, hoping to see a taxi, and screamed. Smith and Akamatsu swung around, too, and saw the people in line falling over like bowling pins. As soon as they touched the ground they broke like glass, pouring into the gutter, vanishing from their clothes, which were scattered over the sidewalk. One woman's head was miraculously spared; it rolled off the sidewalk in front of a passing car and was crushed like a nutshell.

With a pale face, Beffort turned to Yosho. "Natural phenomenon, eh?"

Mie was not squeamish, but she could not look at such a hideous, stupefying sight. Akamatsu caught her in time, not really sure whether she would shatter if she hit the pavement...

Chapter II

After the tragedy at the Texas Palo theater, they counted 329 victims by the pairs of shoes lined up along the sidewalk, but as far as the corpses, it was impossible to piece them all together. The bags transported to the morgue had only cubes of flesh, bone fragments, veins and arteries filled with powdered blood... In a few seconds Madame Atomos had just made a dazzling display of her newfound power and reminded all Americans of the good old days of the Atomos Terror!

People abruptly forgot about politics, financial difficulties, the race to the moon, etc. The country's whole attention was focused on Amarillo where reporters were flooding in. Once the pictures were taken and the witnesses of the unbelievable massacre were questioned, the press, radio and television people started milling about the overcrowded city. Disasters always attract the curious. With the approach of Christmas, the city was booming and even John Stephano saw his turnover increase by 18.2%!

But the newcomers were not all tourists in search of kicks or newsmen. There were also the commando teams of the Green Dragon Force, the FBI and a special strike team recently formed by Smith Beffort. This team was made up of veterans of the anti-Atomos fight: Eddy Witter, Charlie Hyde, Max Ritter, Owen Bernitz, Ben Brady, Ralph Stutton, Art Baxter, Hank Seurer and the G-man Dan Stone.

Right now the whole team was in the conference room of the Majestic Hotel where the Befforts and Akamatsu had decided to reside during the operation.

The meeting was called because of a letter received by Smith that very morning. A letter signed by Madame Atomos. Beffort passed around the envelope.

"As you can see, it's dated December 17, that is, yesterday, and was posted at 12:30. Here's what it says:

Dear Mr. Beffort,

I'm sorry I missed the chance to kill you during our last round, but I hope that you aren't thinking of getting away from me again in this final round. So, we are even, going into the ring once more. I killed Miss Lodge just to bring you to Amarillo and tonight I will kill the audience of a theater in the city. And this only to prove to you that I am marching into this battle with an extremely effective weapon!

Unfortunately, I still have only one copy of this marvelous refrigerating rifle, perfected by Professor Amata before the destruction of Atomia Island. It took a long time to fabricate without a laboratory at hand, but I have the pleasure to announce to you that from now on it will be mass-produced!

This good news will fill you with joy, I'm sure. Just think that very soon I will be able to refrigerate, in the blink of an eye, the inhabitants of a city as big as New York or Los Angeles. Isn't it fantastic? Right now we are working on a refrigerating cannon, but its perfection will take a few months. Which saddens me. I had dreamed of wishing the Americans a happy new year by striking airliners in mid-flight... Well! All good things in their time! If I manage to refrigerate you and your charming wife before the new year, it will be satisfaction enough for me.

Here's to wishing you many new deaths! Hiroshima! Nagasaki! Compliments of Madame Atomos!

Smith put down the letter and said, "She kept her word last night. 329 people were killed at the Texas Palo, right in front of us, before we had time to act. Truthfully, we almost caught Ida Brown and Robert Costelllo, but at least their personal appearance proves how small Madame Atomos' team is. Moreover, we think the range of the refrigerating rifle is very short. 10-20 yards, no more. Last night the Ford driven by Ida Brown literally skimmed the sidewalk while Costello sprayed the crowd with his lethal ray."

"Not a certainty but a hypothesis," Hyde intervened.

"Okay, a hypothesis," Beffort admitted. "Still, remember that Miss Lodge was also on the sidewalk when she was frozen. Lots of cars were driving by. In my opinion, Costello refrigerated her at point-blank range from the same Ford with Ida Brown at the wheel. And as a footnote, doesn't this process lead you to believe that the rifle in question is very heavy and unwieldy? With a light, manageable weapon Costello would have been on foot, anonymous in a crowd to protect himself."

Witter frowned. "Even a light rifle isn't easy to hide under an overcoat and almost impossible to use in a crowd without being seen. But I do agree with you about the weight and bulk of the gizmo. To produce such an intense cold, you need some serious equipment... Something like the one that domesticated atoms a little over five years ago..."

Five years! The time astonished everyone. Madame Atomos' first attack against the United States dated back this far. Since then, in spite of the mad hunt, the terrible Japanese woman had always escaped justice.

So, Witter's statement created some waves. Owen Bernitz, the head of the Green Dragon Force, was the first to speak, with his habitually colorful vocabulary, "If Mama Atomos has to haul around her gadgets in an old junker, I can tell you that her days are numbered. My boys will spot her in no time at all."

"Are all your men here?" Beffort asked.

"All of them, with one radio car per head. Stutton set up the dispatch in a house in Pleasant Valley so you can contact him 24/7. By the way, boss, I've brought your Chevelle Malibu."

Beffort nodded his thanks. He did not let it show, but this news pleased him a lot. With the Malibu, radio code *Yellow Mask* to the Green Dragon, FBI and police, he could almost perform miracles. The Malibu could smash through walls 15 inches thick, was fully armored and its top speed was amazing. Beffort remembered, would always remember, the massacre of the Atomos vehicles in Cincinnati[4].

Witter answered Beffort's unspoken invitation to speak, "We're in contact with Washington where Evans is following the new operation with great attention through the teleprinters. His last message said that Louis Radetich is arriving on the next plane and that we should watch over him. Since his wife and kids were killed by Madame Atomos in the Riverside lab, he thinks of nothing but vengeance. Personally, Smith, I think he'll go down in the first round, as Madame Atomos would say."

Beffort understood Louis Radetich. After Bob's death, he and Mie had gone through a period of frenzy and rage that could only be slaked by action.

"Let Radetich go. Right now he has nothing to lose but his life... As for the agenda, first, we have to find a

_____

[4] See *The Seduction of Madame Atomos* in *The Resurrection of Madame Atomos*.

gray Ford whose license plate starts with 339, a '68 or '69 sedan. Second, Ida Brown and Robert Costello are not in Amarillo by chance. Every time Madame Atomos strikes anywhere, it means she has a refuge close by. Like in Riverside, we have to explore the area. It's 10 am, December 18. The issue needs to be resolved before Christmas! You all know what you have to do."

While Beffort was holding his council of war at the Majestic Hotel, Madame Atomos was doing the same in her new laboratory in Dalhart. A building above ground, which was exceptional, with a corporate name as normal as could be: Bells & Lustig Laboratories.

Mr. Bells and Mr. Lustig had been around for 50 years and were very well respected. Their houses were between Dalhart and Hartley and no one could have imagined that these two upstanding men could be working for Madame Atomos. But the ferocious Japanese woman had the means and the skill to force these men to serve her. Bells and Lustig both had children and grandchildren who could fall victim to an accident in case of problems... Madame Atomos did not play around. The fate of the Radetich family a month earlier was still on everyone's minds.

Therefore, the Bells & Lustig laboratory was well established with perfectly honest employees and basements where other employees worked only at night. But this, of course, was unknown to people. Moreover, the Atomos team was scaled down, as was the equipment. In short, contrary to what the letter received by Smith Beffort strongly implied, the sinister woman was still only making things by hand.

The present state of affairs, however, did not discourage her. Since the destruction of Atomia Island, this was the first time that she was capable of bringing out a new arm, beyond traditional weaponry, that could assure her unquestionable superiority over her enemies. But Madame Atomos was no believer in utopia or illusions. She knew that she would get nowhere without more refrigerating rifles. And just as Beffort and Witter had guessed, she did need a vehicle to transport the heavy cold generator. Without a car, the rifle was really good for nothing.

Across the table from Madame Atomos were Ida Brown, more seductive than ever, Robert Costello with his disturbing face, and a young, black, muscular man, Robert Armstrong, for whom Madame Atomos was an idol. And it's true that in her new skin Madame Atomos was worth the trip! On a runway she would easily win first prize, even next to Ida Brown, as long as she kept her glaring eyes hidden behind dark sunglasses. For, in this glare was all the meanness in the world, all the cruelty in the universe, all the hatred in the void. In such a beautiful face it was earth-shattering.

"I have to congratulate you for your clever action last night," Madame Atomos said in a melodious voice. "But are you absolutely certain that Beffort saw your car?"

"No doubt about it, Madame, Ida Brown said respectfully. "In my rear-view mirror I clearly saw Akamatsu running down the street with his gun out and Smith and Mie were right behind him. I had to speed up to stay out of range of their paralyzing guns."

Madame Atomos' lips relaxed in a gorgeous smile. "Perfect. Just as we hoped. What do you have on the Befforts, Robert?"

"They're staying in the Majestic, room 25, second floor, and Akamatsu's on the fourth. Halton says there's all sorts of traffic in and out of the hotel."

Madame Atomos pulled out a cigarette and Armstrong leaned over to light it. Ida Brown and Costello glanced briefly at each other. Something was going on between the young black and their boss... behind closed doors.

"The Ford will lure Smith and Akamatsu far away from the hotel. Ida will give an anonymous call tonight around 3 in the morning, say. To fool Beffort you'll have to tell him a plausible story, in a sincere voice, just just panicky enough to pass for an authentic SOS. Faced with an emergency, it's likely that Beffort won't think it necessary to wake Mie. He'll tell Akamatsu and no doubt bring along a couple of partners when he hits the road in his Malibu."

Madame Atomos paused and lowered her eyes. "Once Mie Azusa-Beffort is alone, Armstrong will use this." She opened a drawer and put a heavy, round object on the table. It looked like a grenade. "This device is just a little bomb with sleeping gas. The slightest bump will split its shell and let out the gas with immediate effects. The problem is to make Mie breath it in. With Halton's help it shouldn't be too hard, right?"

Robert Costello nodded. "If she's alone, it'll be a piece of cake. Halton can get hold of a passkey and take Armstrong to room 25. Only a few seconds to open the door, throw the thing in and close it again. But then?"

"Then," Madame Atomos said, "we have to get Mie out of the Majestic. Here's how we'll do it..."

Louis Radetich stepped out of the plane at 11 o'clock and took a taxi to the Majestic Hotel. He had lost a lot of weight and his hair had turned white, but he carried himself with iron determination. Radetich had only one goal in life now: to kill Madame Atomos.

He had sworn to it on the graves of his wife and six children in the Oakland cemetery and nothing would stop him as long as he was alive. He had sold his house, quit his job and packed his suitcase with the bare necessities of a homeless man. Now he was living in hotels, on trains, planes and in cars. A first class sharpshooter, state champion, he knew that he would kill Madame Atomos with a single shot when she got in his line of fire. It was only a matter of time.

At the Majestic Radetich asked for Beffort, climbed up to the second floor and knocked on the door. Mie opened it and brought him into the small sitting room where Smith and Yosho were still talking.

"Hello," Radetich said. "Surprised to see me?"

"No. Washington told us you'd be coming," Beffort responded. "Besides, aren't you a member of the Green Dragon Force?"

Radetich nodded and added right away, "By the way, Smith, I'd like you to leave me a pretty free hand in the future actions of the anti-Atomos fight."

"Freelance?"

"In a way… but it's not to make a name for myself. I feel like I'd be more effective if I worked alone."

Akamatsu stared at him. "You can't win like that, Mr. Radetich. Against Madame Atomos, her organization and the A.O.F.M.A. you need to fight them with another organization. That's why Smith created the Green Dragon Force, which has an entire system of weapons and information. If you work on the fringe, you'll miss out on a bunch of vital information."

"Yosho's right," Beffort agreed. "Besides the fact that you can't go playing secret agent since Madame Atomos and her cronies know you. At best you'll just get yourself killed for no reason."

Radetich sat down with a troubled heart. His bitter hatred was making him lose sight of the practical side of the battle he was preparing to fight. "So, what do I do?"

Beffort reassured him immediately. "I'm going to give you a Green Dragon car equipped with a radio so you can stay in touch with our dispatch. Right now Owen Bernitz and his men are looking for a gray Ford whose plates start with 339, a '68 or '69 sedan. Likewise the FBI and the police are on the lookout for Ida Brown, Robert Costello and a young black guy whose name we don't know. Get in on the work and you'll be on the right track. By following the Ford or one of the suspects you'll inevitably run into Madame Atomos. Do you need money?"

"No, I've got enough. Where's the car?"

Akamatsu pulled out a key ring and took Radetich to the window. "It's that black Chevy in the lot. Here's the key."

Radetich took the key ring and walked toward the door. "See you later" is all he said.

"Are you armed?" Beffort asked.

"Of course I'm armed," Radetich smiled. And he left, looking like a gunner with his finger on the trigger.

Chapter Three

All day long on December 18 the Green Dragon Force and the FBI, as well as the Amarillo police, conducted a fruitless investigation inside a perimeter that was approximately double the size of the city. Garages, parking lots and private roads were examined in vain. The gray Ford with the license plate starting 339 was nowhere to be found. Moreover, countless factories, workshops and commercial buildings were visited by policemen, but again the anti-Atomos groups failed to find anything.

In the evening of this disappointing day, Smith Beffort, his wife and Akamatsu ate at the restaurant in the Majestic Hotel.

"All that for nothing," Smith said. "We'll try again tomorrow." His voice was calm, not at all discouraged. Against Madame Atomos you could never hope to win by K.O.

Akamatsu swallowed an oyster and said, "Madame Atomos wrote in her letter, *I killed Miss Lodge just to bring you to Amarillo.* I'm asking myself Why?"

Beffort shrugged. "It's obvious. She's going to try to kill us once and for all, in some spectacular way, to demonstrate her power and panic the citizens. With us alive she can't concentrate on wreaking vengeance on the United States. You know that, Yosho."

"Yes, but I have to say that the threat looming over you and Mie doesn't seem to be bothering you very much. Don't you think it would be wise to take some precautions?"

Smith and Mie had the same smile. They were hunting Madame Atomos and Madame Atomos was hunting them. That was how things worked.

"You know, Yosho," Mie responded, "she can't just kill us in any old way, as Smith just reminded you. So, we're safe from any ordinary traps and in a way that puts us in a favorable position. The day Madame Atomos decides to go into action, you can bet that the USA and the rest of the world will know all about it." She took a sip of white wine and added, "Personally, considering the present state of affairs in this new battle, I would tend to watch out for the number three."

Smith and Yosho stared at her in amazement.

Mie explained, "300 degrees centigrade, 329 victims at the Texas Palo, 339 on the Ford's license plate. You think it's crazy? Not to mention that there's three of us on her black list."

They did not know if she was joking or not, but they had a good laugh. They should have been more mindful. Under certain circumstances Mie had a kind of sixth sense.

Smith heard a ring and reached for the alarm clock, but quickly realized that it was the phone. He turned on the bedside lamp and picked up.

"Sorry to bother you, Sir," the night operator apologized, "but they insisted on speaking with you. The call is coming from Tulia. Will you take it?"

"I'll take it," Beffort said.

Tulia was around 40 miles from Amarillo on Highway 87 and Beffort wondered who could be calling him without going through Ralph Stutton's dispatch.

"Mr. Beffort?" It was a woman's voice, very tense, almost in distress.

"That's me. What do you want?"

The woman sighed deeply, paused, and then started talking very fast. It sounded like time was running out for her. Smith instantly thought that danger was afoot.

"My name's Ericka Kirsten, Mr. Beffort, and I live in Tulia, not far from Vigo Park, on Highway 146. Are you listening?"

"Go on."

"Like everyone I know that Madame Atomos is in our area and that her new weapon freezes people to death. Well, now, maybe ten minutes ago I was woken up by my chickens. They were clucking and cackling…"

"Your chickens?" Beffort interrupted. "Listen, if this is a joke…"

"You listen!" the woman shouted. "I wouldn't disturb you at such an hour if it wasn't very important! In fact, I'm scared stiff! I went to see what was going on, but my chickens had quieted down. Well, I was worried…"

Beffort almost hung up. He was obviously dealing with a crazy woman. Mie opened her eyes and propped herself up on an elbow.

"In the chicken coop," Ericka Kirsten continued, "they were asleep with their eyes open! I touched one and it broke, Mr. Beffort. It broke!"

Smith was already out of bed. The woman at the other end of the line was sniffling. She was terrified, for sure.

"Did you see anyone, Mrs. Kirsten?"

"No, but a car was parked next door. Its lights were off, but I could see that it was a gray Ford, like the one everyone's talking about."

Smith put on his pants, still holding the phone. "Stay where you are," he said. "What's your telephone number?"

"I don't have a telephone. I'm in a public phone booth near my house and I'm not going to stay here. There are people in that car, Mr. Beffort! First my chickens, why not me?"

"Don't leave!" Smith ordered. "Without you we won't be able to find the Ford fast enough. Can you wait at the intersection of 87 and 146?"

"Okay, but hurry up!"

She hung up and Smith got dressed in a jiffy.

"Where are you going?" Mie asked.

"Tulia. There's a woman going crazy there because her chickens were refrigerated and she claims there's a gray Ford parked next door to her."

Mie smiled. "It's a hoax. Besides, the local police can be there before you."

"I can't leave anything unchecked, Mie. And with the Malibu I'll be there in 25 minutes. While I'm tying my shoes can you inform Stutton?"

Mie picked up the phone and quickly got through the operator and was talking to the 555-6289 dispatch. "Hello, Ralph? Mie here. My husband is leaving for Tulia where a gray Ford's just been sighted."

Smith leaned toward the handset and said, "Close off the sector, Stutton! Discreet roadblocks on 87 and 146. I'll contact you from Yellow Mask."

"Okay," Stutton said.

Mie hung up and glanced at the alarm clock. "Be careful, Smith, it's 3 am." Beffort headed for the door. "And Yosho?" Mie asked.

"Stutton should be waking him up right now, but I can't wait. Turn off the lights and go back to sleep. See you later." The door slammed behind him.

Mie got up to lock the door before going back to bed and turning off the lights. The sound of a roaring engine could be heard in the street. The Malibu was off to Tulia...

Five minutes later there was a knock at the door. Without moving, Mie asked, "Is that you, Yosho?"

"Yes. Has Smith already left?"

"Like a rocket!"

"Thanks."

Mie listened to his footsteps fade away and then silence once again fell over the Majestic, which was not the quiet hotel its advertising claimed. Mie dozed a little, but could not fall to sleep. Something was nagging her: how did this woman in Tulia know that Beffort was staying at the Majestic? The question drifted in her mind for a minute before settling down for good. She sat up. Now was completely awake.

The story was screwy. Chickens, the gray Ford... all this at 3 am.

Now the luminous dial read 3:35. Smith must have made it there by now. Mie picked up the phone without bothering to turn on the lights. She was planning to call Stutton at dispatch to get the latest news from Tulia, but she froze when she realized there was no dial tone.

Quietly she put the phone back down, got out of bed and tiptoed across the room. She had been fighting against Madame Atomos and her organization for a long time and knew to be wary of anomalies. Now, the call from Tulia and the sudden breakdown of the telephone made two first-class anomalies. She noiselessly opened a drawer and took out the weapon she found there. By its weight and shape she figured it was a 38 special. She would have preferred a paralyzing pistol, but knew that she did not time to search for one.

In the darkness, feeling around a little because she was not yet familiar with the room, she headed for the bathroom. She did so without thinking, purely on instinct, like an animal fleeing before a distant threat, not yet seen but felt.

She was stepping into the bathroom when it happened. It was very fast: the door of the apartment swung open, an object exploded on the carpet and the door shut immediately.

Without thinking, Mie slammed the bathroom door and leaned against it. She was expecting a violent blast, but nothing happened. The first explosion had been very weak, like a light bulb popping, and Mie figured that the second, though late in coming, would shake the building to its foundation. Some dead time passed before she heard the unmistakable creaking of door hinges. This time they were sneaking into her room.

Mie cracked open the bathroom door very carefully, saw the pale beam of a flashlight and then two silhouettes behind it. Two men. One white and one black. The second was carrying a big bag, the first a machine gun.

Mie opened fire on the spot, shooting from the hip and turning on the light at the same time. The roar of her gun echoed through the Majestic from the basement to the penthouse as the man with the machine gun was jolted by the bullets. He dropped his weapon and collapsed to the ground. The black started forward.

"Don't move," Mie warned calmly.

Armstrong dropped his bag and raised his arms. Mie Azusa-Beffort, the ex-Miss Atomos, scared him almost as much as Madame Atomos…

At 5 am Armstrong was sitting in the office of John Martens, the head of the local FBI, with the blinding light of a halogen lamp shining in his eyes. Facing him were Smith Beffort, Akamatsu, Mie, Witter and Hyde. Armstrong had not been in the hot seat for long, but sweat was already covering his forehead. He knew he was stuck, far from Madame Atomos and her tricks, left to himself from now on. This did not lift his spirits. Plus he had heard that the G-men were not choir boys when it came to making tough guys talk.

"Who's Erika Kirsten?" Beffort asked.

"Ida Brown," Armstrong answered straight off. He caved in on the first question because of the long practiced experience of a master.

Beffort relaxed a little. He was expecting a much more stubborn resistance. In a casual tone he said, "I suspected as much and I know the rest. With Halton's help, who was recently hired at the Majestic as a waiter and lived there, you cut off my room's telephone after I left as well as Akamatsu's. Thanks to his passkey, Halton could open the door, then you threw that sleeping gas grenade inside. Where were you supposed to take my wife?"

Now they were entering taboo territory and Armstrong stiffened up. If he talked, his hide was worthless. Sooner or later Madame Atomos would take him out, even in jail, even in prison! Armstrong was sure of this.

"I don't know," he said.

Beffort tossed away his cigarette butt. Through experience he knew exactly what Armstrong was feeling. He was not the first member of the Atomos Organization to react like this. The infernal Madame Atomos controlled her world through terror.

"That's a stupid answer, Armstrong. You were supposed to kidnap my wife, which is no walk in the park, and now you're saying you didn't know where you were supposed to take her..." He stood right in front of the black man. "Really you're scared that your boss will mark you for death and that's exactly what will happen if you live, which is an unlikely prospect. Next door there's an electric chair that we intend to use if you keep protecting Madame Atomos! She's the greatest criminal of all time! Did you ever think about that?"

Armstrong said nothing. Madame Atomos' brutality was unquestionable. The G-men's remained to be seen.

"Okay," Beffort said, take him next door.

Witter and Hyde leaned forward. Armstrong jumped up, shoved the two men and ran for the door, pushing Mie hard on his way. Beffort and Akamatsu dove at him in time, but he was unusually strong. He almost knocked Akamatsu unconscious before dealing with Smith, who was desperately hanging onto one of his legs. Everything happened in a flash. Witter, Hyde, Mie and Akamatsu were still on the ground. If Armstrong got out of the office, he would be shot dead by the guards. But Smith wanted him alive. He blocked a lethal punch with his elbow and stood up, still holding the black's leg. Thrown off balance the man made an incredible spin, got free and grabbed the door handle just as Witter and Hyde came to the rescue, making short work of it, and Armstrong was contained in spite of his strength.

Two minutes later his eyes were rolling in his head as the straps of the electric chair were tightened around his body. If he were more intelligent, he would have known it was all a fake. They did not shave his head; he had no helmet; only two electrodes were hooked up to carry the current into his body. But Armstrong was too terrified to notice these details. Especially since the people around him all looked very serious, formal even, and Mie was not allowed into the room.

"So," Beffort asked, "still mute?"

"You don't have the right!" Armstrong shouted. "I haven't seen a judge!"

Smith pointed his finger. "We're taking the right. One of my men has his hand on the knob over there. If he clicks it over, you'll receive a painful electric shock. If he keeps going, the shock will be unbearable and you'll writhe and scream. The third notch is lethal. Now, before torturing you, I'll repeat my question: Where were you supposed to take my wife?"

Armstrong looked over his shoulder at Charles Hyde who was standing in front of a frighteningly complicated control board.

"Talk, buddy," Witter advised, "or else this room's gonna stink of burned meat in a few minutes."

Armstrong was sweating fear. His head bobbed like stunned boxer, then stopped moving when he said, "I was supposed to take Mie Azusa to the Bells & Lustig Laboratory."

"Where's this lab?"

"Near Dalhart. That's where Madame Atomos makes the refrigerating rifles and the cold generators."

The dam had broken and he told everything. But paradoxically he could not give the exact location of the laboratory, so Beffort had to waste precious time looking through the yellow pages. Nevertheless, it was only 5:40 when the Malibu and six cars stuffed with G-men set off for Dalhart.

Smith drove fast without thinking of the other cars. When he took a turn at full speed, Mie prophesized, "No need to tempt death, Smith. When we get there the birds will have flown the coop. If we can pick up all the equipment, we'll have done well."

Beffort gave her a grim look. Even when she was right, he hated when she played the sibyl!

Chapter Four

Just as Mie had predicted, the Bells & Lustig Laboratory had been evacuated by Madame Atomos and her team. It had been done in a rush because the mysterious machines piled in the basement were systematically put out of order. But even though it was late, the raid was still an undeniable victory for the forces of order. From now on, unless there was another laboratory, which was doubtful, Madame Atomos could not continue producing her new weapon. Therefore, with this in mind, the capture of Armstrong was pretty valuable.

However, Smith had a long face. The trail of the sinister woman was lost again. She had plenty of time to get away and God only knew where she had gone. God, not Armstrong!

Beffort imagined her hundreds of miles away and he would have been very surprised to see Madame Atomos pacing back and forth in a beautiful apartment in Amarillo. Madame Atomos was steaming. They had taken away her pet, her thing, her toy! But they were going to pay for it… with interest! Stupid Armstrong!

"Where is he, Robert?"

"At FBI headquarters, Madame."

"Halton?"

"At the morgue."

Robert Costello and Ida Brown were not very confident. The Atomos team had gotten smaller over the months and their boss did not speak about increasing the personnel. Thanks to the A.O.F.M.A. she had plenty of money and researchers, which had allowed her to perfect the refrigerating rifle, but human material was something else altogether. Then she had to leave the Bells & Lustig laboratory after destroying the machines and the specialists had scattered. How long would it be before they met again?

On the verge of rage, Madame Atomos sat down. "We're going to attack," she said.

Costello turned pale. "Attack what, Madame?"

"FBI headquarters, Robert."

This shut them up. Costello and Ida Brown exchanged a knowing glance. Apparently the boss could not leave behind her *boy toy*! Arguing with Madame Atomos was highly unrecommended, but Costello was starting to get fed up.

"That's madness. FBI headquarters is full of G-men and the streets are full of police and the Green Dragon Force. They all have our pictures. If we take one foot outside, it'll be suicide."

Madame Atomos crossed her legs and lit a cigarette. "You're driving the van. Ida and I will sit in the back and we'll cruise right up to their headquarters. The cold generator weighs 75 pounds, so don't tell me you want to carry it on foot. When we get there…"

Never in the memory of man has anyone ever dared to attack an FBI office because in the first place, there is no point and secondly, the retaliation could be brutal. Therefore, there was no special surveillance of the FBI headquarters. It looked like any other commercial building. A visitor gave his name and an ID at the reception, stated his business and went to the appropriate department.

However, inside the bureau it was another matter. There were zones *only for FBI personnel* and *forbidden to enter* and *no loitering in the hallway*, etc., so that it was almost impossible to wander off the acceptable path without meeting the black eye of a 38 special.

Like in any administrative office in the United States, the real workday does not start before 9 am. But because of its particular vocation, an FBI bureau is on duty 24/7. So, the three receptionists were not at all surprised to see a man and two women enter the lobby at 7:10 before the day had started.

The man was carrying a heavy, cumbersome case from which two wires stuck out, attached to a chrome tube that looked like the end of a big electric hairdryer. One of the women was holding this tube. The other woman carried nothing but a handbag. But the receptionists had no fear because all three of them were wearing dark sunglasses and using white guide canes...

One of the receptionists stood up to help the poor folks, but a vibrating sound stopped her. The end of the *electric hairdryer* sparked and the receptionists, two sitting and one standing, were frozen forever.

Now the fake blind people were alone in the lobby. Madame Atomos went back to lock the main entrance. When she came back to Costello and Ida Brown she asked, "The cells?"

"Underground," Costello answered. "The staircase is over there on the left."

Madame Atomos took the paralyzing pistol she had swiped off the corpse of Lucky Simms a few months earlier[5] out of her handbag and said, "Don't move from here. You're blind. Go and talk with the receptionists. If any G-men enter the lobby, refrigerate them. In three or four minutes I'll be back."

---

[5] See *The Evil of Madame Atomos* in *The Revenge of Madame Atomos*.

She crossed the lobby, went down the stairs and came into a small room where two G-men were standing guard. "What do you want?"

Madame Atomos paralyzed them with a press of the trigger, grabbed a ring of keys and pushed open the door. Doors lined the wide hallway.

"Bob?" By herself, Madame Atomos could be casual.

There was a groan, a noise, and Armstrong stuck his face against the bars. "Boss?" His mouth dropped.

Madame Atomos smiled. Bob was stunned, but Smith Beffort would no doubt have a heart attack. She held out the keys. "Get out of there, would you?"

Armstrong tried the keys while Madame Atomos watched the hallway. He found the right key and in no time at all was out, hesitating, not really sure whether his boss had come there to kill him.

Madame Atomos looked at him and smiled. Her plaything was unharmed, still a beautiful animal, complete with his stupidity and fidelity. "Follow me, Bob."

They went upstairs without incident, but when they entered the lobby it was full of frozen men. They were lined up along the staircase going up to the first floor and all around the doorway leading to the guardroom. Ida Brown and Costello had done their duty but were peaked. Even frozen all these G-men were impressive.

"Let's get out of here," Madame Atomos ordered. "Armstrong, open the door." In front of the others, she no longer called him Bob. Modesty....

Costello stepped forward, picked up the cold generator and followed Ida Brown who struck the rifle through the double doors. Armstrong opened them the all the way. No one on the sidewalk. Madame Atomos made a sign to them, put her paralyzing pistol back in her handbag and headed for the van parked there in front. It was 7:20 am when the vehicle took off.

Madame Atomos left 20 dead behind her, a jail cell wide open and two G-men paralyzed for 60 minutes. Later they would tell Smith Beffort what had happened. Publicity...

Hiroshima! Nagasaki!

Madame Atomos burst out laughing.

While Madame Atomos was taking risks to save her lover from a life sentence in prison, maybe even the electric chair, Smith Beffort and his men were very carefully going through the basement of the Bells & Lustig Laboratory. When escaping in a hurry, it is very rare that you think of everything. Why could Madame Atomos not have left behind some compromising clues? Forced to destroy her precious machines, pressed by time, she might have forgotten to take certain basic precautions.

The basement of the laboratory was huge. They had divided it into five separate parts: the workshop, the living quarters, the research room, the testing chamber and the office. It was far from the ultra-modern refuges of the grand Atomos period, but given the circumstances, Beffort judged it a remarkable realization. Only Madame Atomos could do this right under the noses of Americans...

According to all evidence the office had been the private property of the terrible Japanese woman and it was here that Smith and Mie were searching while the rest of the team took care of the other rooms. But the task was tricky because contrary to her usual practice, Madame Atomos had left piles of paper behind. There were plans and blueprints covered with numbers, files as thick as logs, but the trouble was that everything had been written in Japanese!

Akamatsu and Mie were the only ones who could read them, but they could obviously not translate the mountain of documents in sufficient time. Yosho said so. Beffort nodded and responded, "It's more likely that these files and plans are useless, otherwise Madame Atomos would have destroyed them. Still, we have to go through them all. We just might find the formula for the refrigerating ray."

Akamatsu was not so sure, but would not swear to it. As usual, Madame Atomos had managed to sow doubt in the minds of her enemies, slow down their action and force them to run around in circles while she had time to get away.

While they were pondering things, Owen Bernitz burst into the basement at 7:30 and shouted, "Madame Atomos just attacked the headquarters in Amarillo. She freed Armstrong and refrigerated 20 G-men. A newspaper seller mentioned a van…"

Smith interrupted him. "Any survivors at headquarters?"

"Two guys were paralyzing in the holding cells, but we won't be hearing from them for an hour."

"The newsdealer?"

"He said Madame Atomos and Armstrong were with a man and a woman who could be Costello and Ida Brown."

Beffort slammed his fist down on the table. "This woman is diabolical! She knew the lab would lure us like flies to jam and that most of our team would leave the city, giving her free rein. We've got to get back to Amarillo! Everyone to the cars!"

He ran up the stairs. Everyone followed him except for Mie, who went back to the office. She heard the engines roar, she smiled and took off her coat. Then she emptied a folder onto the floor. Without any rhyme reason she felt that this room held the key that would put them back on the trail of Madame Atomos or one of the members of the A.O.F.M.A. Besides, they did not need her in Amarillo.

In total silence she started working and found rather quickly that the plans had nothing to do with the refrigerating ray. They were all about a mysterious installation of electric motors and telephone lines with reference to files that were titled *New Africa*.

Mie pushed all this stuff aside and leaned over the now empty desk. A map of Mississippi, Alabama, Georgia, Louisiana and South Carolina. Five states clearly separated from the United States, even from Florida, along with property titles from the acquisition of 8,000 hectares of land in Mississippi.

New Africa?

Mie continued her search without getting distracted by the new problem. Her watch read 9:30 when she found a piece of paper stuck under the bottom drawer of the desk. He was a rental contract for three apartments in Amarillo belonging to Arthur Benjamin. The contract was signed back in June 1967 for a duration of three years to Miss Ida Brown and the right to sublet.

Mie suddenly became flushed. There was no way she could believe that Ida Brown and Costello still lived in one of the three apartments, but she was hoping that a visit might bring the next link in the chain that was starting to form.

She slipped the paper into her bag next to her paralyzing pistol, left the basement and got one of the policemen guarding the lab to take her to Amarillo. In the suburbs she hailed a cab, and when she gave the address on the rental contract she realized that two of the apartments were located on 15th Avenue, near Elwood Park, whereas the third was on 16th Avenue. This detail had not struck her at first and she was too involved in her research now to think it very important.

She climbed out of the cab in front of 214 15th Avenue and entered the building without the slightest hesitation, thinking of Smith's surprise when she would tell him how she had chanced upon an Atomos refuge in the middle of Amarillo.

She quickly located Arthur Bergmann's mailbox, which indicated the 12th and top floor. She took the elevator up and rang the bell. A minute passed before she heard the sound of muffled footsteps on the other side of the door. Mie stood there calmly while Bergmann looked her over through the peephole. Finally a lock clicked and the door opened, revealing an older man with a tired face, clearly sick.

"What do you want?" he asked brusquely.

Mie showed her FBI ID. "I want to ask you about one of your tenants. Can I come in?"

Bergmann stepped aside grudgingly, closed the door and led Mie into a big living room with huge windows that looked out on Elwood Park.

"Have a seat," Bergmann said, looking more intrigued than angry at being disturbed by Mie. "What tenant are you talking about?"

When Mie showed him the contract, Bergmann's eyes widened a little. Mie noted the reaction. "As you can see, it's about Miss Ida Brown, Mr. Bergmann. I…"

"She doesn't really live here," the man jumped in, suddenly talkative, "and, in fact, I'm still wondering why she rented three apartments for nothing. Especially at such a price! If you're expecting me to give you any information, I can't. I've only seen the woman once. But as long as she's paying the rent, I can at least tell you that she's not dead." He paused abruptly, smiled and asked, "What's she done?"

"Nothing. I just want to visit the three apartments rented by Miss Brown. Tell me, Mr. Bergmann, have you been reading the papers lately?"

"Hmm, well, no."

"I thought so. Otherwise you would've known a long time ago that Ida Brown is a sidekick of Madame Atomos."

The man's face paled and he dropped into the closest chair. "You should've said so, Miss! I've got a heart condition and that kind of news…"

He sucked in air through his gaping mouth. Mie thought he might faint. But he caught his breath, apologized with a smile and said that he should take his medicine right away. Then he went into the kitchen and straight to the fan, which he turned on and then pressed a button. A barely audible voice asked, "I'm here. What do you want, Arthur?"

"Madame," the man whispered. "Mie Azusa-Beffort is here."

"Alone?" Madame Atomos grumbled.

"Alone," Bergmann confirmed.

"Keep her busy a minute," Madame Atomos ordered. "We'll get her in the elevator."

Chapter Five

The elevator shot up to the highest floor calling, which meant that if two people called it at the same time, it first went to the higher floor, but stopped on every floor if need be. There was nothing unusual in this, just like thousands of modern elevators, and Mie was not surprised, even less so alarmed, to see the elevator stopped on the sixth floor. Besides, she was deep in thought about Arthur Bergmann. A strange man who certainly knew more than he let on about Ida Brown. He was obviously very sick, but more scared to death for some reason that Mie did not know.

Then the door opened and Costello and Armstrong were standing there. Mie understood in a flash.

"Would you like to follow us, Mrs. Beffort?" Costello asked nicely.

Mie's hand dove into her bag and grabbed the butt of the paralyzing pistol, but Armstrong seized her instantly. He was unusually strong and Mie did not struggle. Costello snatched her bag and found the pistol. Mie screamed to alert the other residents, but Costello shot her with her own gun and Armstrong just had to lift her up and carry her to the next apartment.

Paralyzed for 60 minutes, but conscious, Mie had all the time in the world to scold herself. Since Madame Atomos first pounced on the United States, none of her enemies had fallen into her trap so willingly.

At the Amarillo headquarters, once Beffort and his men had assessed the damage done by Madame Atomos, they started worrying about Mie. So far they had each thought that the young lady had left in someone else's car. Now they saw that she must have stayed at the Bells & Lustig Laboratory. But when Smith called, they told him that Mie had gone back to the city in a police car.

"Where'd she get out?" Beffort asked.

"In a suburb to the north. Then she took a taxi."

Smith thanked them, hung up and looked at his watch. Mie had been gone for an hour. Troubling…

"If Mie decided to take a taxi instead of staying in the squad car," Akamatsu assumed, "it was as a precaution. In other words, she found a clue in the laboratory basement."

"That's exactly what scares me," Beffort said gloomily. "It's not her way. I think maybe she wanted to verify something before revealing her discovery. I don't like this, Yosho."

"There's nothing to be alarmed about yet," Akamatsu said, who was also starting to feel a little worried. "Your wife has proven that she's capable of taking care of herself. I'm sure we'll hear from her in no time."

Beffort did not comment as he leafed through the report written by Witter. It had the statements of the two G-men paralyzed by Madame Atomos before she freed Armstrong, as well as the newspaper vendor. The latter was far more interesting. The man had a good memory and a gift for observation; his description of the van and its passengers was perfect. Unfortunately, he did not have the time or thought to get the license plate number.

"Gray delivery vans are all over Amarillo," Beffort complained. "How can we start looking for it without more information?"

Akamatsu shrugged. "With or without doesn't much matter. Madame Atomos won't risk using the same vehicle again after…"

The telephone rang, interrupting him. He picked it up, asked them to hold the line and passed it to Beffort, saying, "An outside call."

Beffort took the phone. A man's voice on the other end of the line said, "Do you know where your wife is, Mr. Beffort?"

Smith covered the mouthpiece with his hand and looked at Akamatsu. "Trace this call, Yosho, I'll try to keep him talking." Akamatsu dashed out of the room. Smith said, "Hello, can you speak up? I can't hear you."

"Do you hear me now?" the voice said more loudly.

"Yes. Who is this?"

"Doesn't matter, Mr. Beffort. I'm just supposed to tell you that your wife is being held prisoner by Madame Atomos."

Smith clenched his jaws. From the very first word the stranger spoke he knew what it was about, but the brutal revelation still hit home. Now he had to keep the man talking so they could trace the number.

"Ridiculous!" he said. "My wife is shopping in the city. If you think…"

"Listen," the other cut in, "I don't need to convince you. Madame Atomos wants you to know that Mie will be executed tomorrow night if ten million dollars isn't sitting behind the north gate of San Jacinto Park!"

"Ten million dollars! You're crazy, pal. That's a huge sum and even if I had it, it would be physically impossible to get that much in cash in such a short time."

"With the help of the US government, you can manage it very fast, I'm sure."

"My wife is worth it to me, but for the government of the USA…"

"Madame Atomos thought so. The promise of a thousand deaths on Christmas Eve will certainly help

205

your directors to open their safes, don't you think? We've proven our effectiveness these last few days and we can do it again at any time."

Smith had a tough time keeping calm. "Madame Atomos never keeps her promises except when it's to kill or destroy," he said coldly. "When she has the money, she'll murder my wife and 'refrigerate' a thousand innocent people on Christmas anyway. So, you can tell her right now that there will be no one at the gate in San Jacinto Park!"

There was silence before the other said. "Madame Atomos predicted your reaction, Mr. Beffort. But you'll change your mind when you get Mie Azusa's right hand in the mail tomorrow at midnight. Ten million dollars in clean bills or your wife's hand? Think about it."

He hung up just like that and a little bell rang painfully in Smith's ear. Beffort hung up, too, left the office and almost bumped into Akamatsu coming up from the first floor. "Well, Yosho?"

"Nothing," he moaned. "The call came from a public phone booth, so it takes twice as long to locate. Anyway, the guy would be long gone before our men got there. It was a shot in the dark."

Smith nodded gravely. "It was worth the shot, but I knew we wouldn't get him. Now we only have one way to save Mie: Find that cabbie who picked her up in the suburbs and hope that he'll remember where he dropped her off."

While a team went in search of the taxi driver, which was not an easy job considering the little information they had to go on, Smith and Akamatsu resumed their search of the Laboratory basement. It was a logical reaction. Mie had been kidnapped after finding a clue in the former Atomos lair, so it was not unreasonable to hope to find another. Around noon Akamatsu came upon the *New Africa* file and the map of the five states. He also found the property titles for the purchase of 8,000 hectares in Mississippi.

It was all Greek to Smith, but When Yosho translated for him, he perked up. "I recently read an article by Robert Sherill in *Esquire* that detailed the creation and shenanigans of a movement for the establishment of this *New Africa*."

Akamatsu raised his eyebrows. "It's a joke?"

"I thought so, too, but the fact that Madame Atomos is interested in *New Africa* changes things."

"What's it all about, Smith?"

"A new nation formed by Black Americans that would be established over these five states here. According to *Esquire* the leaders of the movement have already presented a request to the federal government demanding reparation of 400 billion dollars and the transfer of power giving them authority to the govern the states in question. They would name the president of the republic of New Africa as Robert F. Williams, who is presently living in Peking, and the first vice-president as Milton Henry, as well as a cabinet of ministers. Milton Henry and the author of the article say the strategy of this *government in exile* is planning two phases of action. First: Arm the blacks in the cities of the north and west to protect them against the reaction of the whites faced with the demand for secession. Second: Send a million well armed blacks to Mississippi where their job will be to force people to vote for them as sheriffs. Once the police are in their hands, the black armies will enter Mississippi and take over strategic points. After that they'll hit the other four states, Alabama, Georgia, Louisiana and South Carolina and do the same.[6]"

Akamatsu was stunned. "There's something you don't see in Japan," he said.

Smith looked over the property titles and continued, "I also remember that Milton Henry told Robert Sherill, 'We have already started moving forward by purchasing 50 hectares in Mississippi.' It was a little ridiculous, but here we see a real purchase of 8,000 hectares, which is not ridiculous at all."

Akamatsu scratched his head. He had lived in the United States for a good while, but the behavior of the Americans still astonished him. "Don't tell me you're taking this seriously!"

Beffort gave him a feeble smile. "When Madame Atomos is pulling the strings, I take everything seriously, Yosho. There was a time when she was demanding two or three southern states and telling our country to stop the war in Asia. This proves that Madame Atomos is dedicated and her convictions can sometimes take precedence over her vengeance against the USA. Really, what do you think she's going to do with the ten million dollars she's demanding for Mie?"

"Buy more land?"

"Appears to be," Beffort agreed. "She's so desperate for money that she's ready to spare my wife for as long as there's any hope she can get it from us. That's why the caller first said that my wife would be killed tomorrow night if the money wasn't at the north gate of

---

[6] True. After violent run-ins with local and federal authorities the RNA was suppressed and its leaders arrested, but it still exists today as a political organization. [*Note from the translator*]

San Jacinto Park. But faced with my resistance to his blackmail, he only talked about cutting off a hand…"

"Like the wife of Louis Radetich," Akamatsu reminded him. He looked at Beffort and asked, "You said he only talked about cutting off her hand! Do you think that's a lesser evil?"

Beffort threw up his hands in annoyance. "It's just a way of speaking, Yosho! A way of highlighting the fact that Madame Atomos might be ready to make concessions in exchange for a promise of money. She has to defend her prestige with the Black Americans, who have contributed to the A.O.F.M.A. for a long time. On this earth, you don't do something for nothing. They help Madame Atomos who in turn is supposed to help in the creation of New Africa. If she doesn't do it, she'll be alone, without resources, shelters and workers. Damn, when I think about it, I wonder if Mie's kidnapping might not turn out to be Madame Atomos' greatest defeat! By killing the Lodge girl and the moviegoers at the Texas Palo, she had only one idea in mind: to grab Mie so she could blackmail us for millions of dollars! Needless to say that this proves how needy for money Madame Atomos is, right?"

"Apparently so," Akamatsu agreed.

"Therefore," Smith continued, "if she kills Mie…"

"No dough," Yosho finished.

Beffort's face brightened. "So, Mie's life is not in danger?"

Akamatsu warned him instantly, "No, but her right hand is! Then you'll receive her left hand, then a foot or an ear… Sorry, Smith, but I firmly believe that we have a very limited time and we shouldn't be too optimistic. If Madame Atomos wants ten million dollars, she'll have it! Unless we free Mie in the meantime." He put a friendly hand on Smith's shoulder and added, "I understand that you're clinging to the slightest hope because the life of your wife is the most important thing, but you have to look at the situation realistically."

Beffort nodded. "You're right, Yosho. In short, there's nothing we can do except find that taxi driver."

Akamatsu spread his hands. "We've gone through everything here, which means that Mie took the clue with her and we can't follow up on her lead. Let's go back to Amarillo, Smith. Only the taxi driver is important now."

The Malibu sped back to the city in record time, but the search teams had not yet found the driver. However, they did know that he did not belong to a company working by phone, which reduced considerably the number of cabbies to interrogate.

"But," Witter remarked, "it's not in the bag. Our man could have knocked off for the day or found a long fare out of the city. I have a list of all the drivers working in Amarillo, but it'll take us all afternoon to work through it. A radio call would make our job a lot easier."

"Impossible," Beffort ordered. "If Madame Atomos is listening in, she'll know where we're going and do whatever's necessary to foil us. We have to act in secret and keep our cards hidden at any price."

Akamatsu furrowed his brow and objected, "Meanwhile, time is passing and the taxi driver's information will be worthless if Madame Atomos changes locations."

Smith's laugh was hollow. "Not long ago you were advising me not to be overly optimistic and now you're sinking into the opposite. Who could say that Mie gave an exact address to the driver? She could have got out of the cab at an intersection or on a busy street in down-town Amarillo…"

He did not finish his list because there was no use. In truth, everyone had to admit that Mie's position was almost desperate. Without some extraordinary stroke of luck, Madame Atomos was having her vengeance and would be as tenacious as a dog with his bone. Killing Mie would bleed Smith dry…

Chapter Six

Mie was sitting comfortably in a big armchair, but her left ankle was shackled by a short chain to one of the legs of the huge chair. Thus, Mie could stand up or shift positions when she felt a cramp. She even managed to drag her ball over the thick carpet and explore the whole room where she was imprisoned. An armored door with a lock on the outside; a window with six panes of unbreakable glass and fitted with metal shutters and no way to open it; that was all. No furniture, no decorations, but perfectly soundproofed with air conditioning in the ceiling, thereby inaccessible…

Moreover, obviously to frustrate any hope of escape, they had taken her bag, shoes and clothes. She sat in her armchair dressed only in her panties and bra. This was not surprising. On the other hand, she did not understand why they had not killed her yet. By keeping her alive, Madame Atomos was taking a chance because Mie was dead set on fighting to the end to regain her liberty.

After a while, the lock clicked, the door opened and Ida Brown walked in. She was pushing a rolling table with a plate full of food and Costello was right behind her. When Mie sat up, Ida Brown smiled and said, "Lunchtime, Mrs. Beffort. I hope you're hungry."

"I'm hungry, thank you," Mie returned the smile. "I guess it's noon?" Since they had also taken her watch, she had no idea what time it was.

Ida Brown pushed the table up to the armchair saying, "It's 1 pm. We'll give you an hour to eat, they we'll come back. Please note that you don't have a knife or fork and we're giving you paper cups and plates. You'll have to eat with your hands. Bon appétit."

She turned around and left, followed by Costello. The door closed, the lock clicked and Mie was alone in total silence again, sitting in front of a cup of water and a plateful of mush made of mashed potatoes and ground beef. But she had to keep up her strength to be able to take advantage of any eventual slip by her enemies.

She polished off the meal in ten minutes, then examined the rolling table, which had two wooden trays and four chrome legs. There did not seem to be anything worth taking and Mie gave up the idea of breaking it to use a leg as a club. It would serve no purpose as long as she was shackled.

Mie leaned back in the armchair and tried to evaluate the chances that Smith and his men would find her trail, naturally thinking that everything hinged on the taxi driver. She had given number 214 on 15th Avenue when she got in the cab, so if the man remembered this, Smith could find the building. After that, everything would depend on luck because if Madame Atomos and her cronies saw the anti-Atomos forces pouring out, an immediate evacuation would be ordered using the apartment on 16th Avenue.

Mie was still thinking of this when Ida Brown and Costello came to get the rolling table. They looked a little stiff, anxious even, and Ida Brown shuddered when she saw that Mie had not touched her glass of water. She stared at her straight in the eyes and said, "You should drink, Mrs. Beffort, because you won't have any more water before tonight."

Her eyes spoke more than her words. Mie grabbed the paper cup, drank, and felt something solid slip into her mouth. She almost spit it out, but the goggling eyes of Ida Brown stopped her. It was a silent warning, a caution, a cry for help. Mie put the cup down, wedged the mysterious object against the inside of her cheek and asked, "How long are you going to keep me here?"

Suddenly more relaxed, Ida Brown answered, "I don't know. Madame Atomos will make that decision. See you tonight, Mrs. Beffort." She backed up, taking the table and revealing Costello who was holding a small card that said: *Watch out! Mic and cameras above the door!*

Mie blinked her eyes to show that she understood and Costello slipped the card into his coat pocket. The two of them left after one last conspiratorial wink. The door locked again and Mie was back in stillness. She was deeply surprised by the attitude of her guards and was eager to get a closer look at the object they had slipped to her in such a strange way. First, however, she had to get away from the camera and microphone that was probably ultra-sensitive. She waited a minute, then stood up and dragged her armchair in front of the window. Like this she was as far away from the mic as possible and the back of the chair would hide part of her from the spying camera.

Without moving her head she quietly spit the object into her hands and saw that it was a tiny glass tube with a rubber stopper. This kind of tube usually held lighter flints, but now it contained a carefully rolled up message. Mie easily unplugged the tube, took out the paper and unrolled it: *Robert and I have decided to help you because Madame Atomos is crazy. If we stay with her, we'll die. Tonight we're leaving with you. Be ready.*

It was brief but clear. Mie did not know that the morning attack against FBI headquarters was the origin of their decision, but truth to tell it did not matter. She was dealing with two criminals who were in a panic and using this windfall as a possible bargaining chip with justice in the future. Give and take: Mie's life for total amnesty.

Preoccupied with this turn of events, Mie did not hear the quiet whoosh coming from the air conditioner. She simply felt her eyelids getting heavy and thought that she was tired. Then she dropped off to sleep.

It was 6 pm and night had already fallen over Amarillo when the cabbies were brought into Beffort's office at the central police station. He had decided to set up there because of the morning tragedy at FBI headquarters where the preliminary investigation, useless but mandatory, was still being conducted to determine the exact circumstances of the Atomos attack.

There were four of them who, by a strange twist of fate, had picked up Asian women in the northern suburb that morning. Witter asked them to sit down and Smith simply held a picture of Mie over his desk. In a calm voice, far from how he felt, he said, "Here's the woman we're interested in. Who remembers picking her up?"

A silence followed his question. It was the end of the day and the men had all driven long and hard with maybe 20 different fares. They were tired, uncooperative and really having a hard time dredging their memories.

Then one of them said, "I think I recognize that face. At least the woman I had this morning looked a hell of a lot like her."

"Where did you drop her off?" Beffort asked patiently.

"Let's see… I was coming back from the garage where I'd taken a guy with suitcases… I was cruising around the edge of Pleasant Valley when this woman stopped me… I drove across the city to 15th Avenue, then I picked up a guy with two kids…"

"So," Beffort jumped in, "your client got off on 15th Avenue?"

The taxi driver smiled. "Exactly! Now it's coming back. She was going to number 214."

"Are you positive?"

For a minute the cabbie hesitated. It came to him naturally but now he was wondering if he might not be mistaken. He was not sure of anything. "Positive is saying a lot," he hedged.

"Could you recognize the building?"

"I don't know… maybe, yeah, sure."

Beffort stood up and said, "We're going to 15th Avenue. Don't worry about losing time. I'll compensate you no matter what happens there. What's your name?"

"Emerson. If you don't mind, I'd like to call my wife before leaving. Since this Mama Atomos is in the area, she's scared I might be cut into little pieces if I'm ten minutes late for dinner."

Mie had difficulty waking up. Her mouth was pasty and she knew that she had slept for a long time because it was night. A dim light seeped out of the ceiling, but no bulb was visible. It made for a weird ambience. Mie sat up and looked in vain for the small glass tube with the message, understanding very quickly that someone had entered the room during her sleep.

Something crackled behind her. When she turned around a voice she knew all too well said, "Good evening, Mie Azusa. I have some bad news to tell you: Ida Brown and Robert Costello cannot help you escape because they're dead."

Madame Atomos cackled before continuing, "I presided over their execution myself, but you are responsible for their disappearance. If you didn't hide Ida Brown's message, I wouldn't have suspected a thing. Nowadays we can't trust anyone, can we?"

Her nasty laugh shook the speaker again and Mie really thought she was going mad.

"No," Madame Atomos said, as if reading her thoughts, "I'm not crazy! No more than the Americans who atomized the inhabitants of Hiroshima and Nagasaki in cold blood! Since that day human life is no longer important to me, but that doesn't mean I've lost my mind. My goal is still the same and sooner or later I will reduce the United States to ashes... except for five states. There I will create the Atomos Land where only colored people will live. But I'm doing all the talking and you the listening. Don't you have anything to say, Mie Azusa?"

Mie automatically looked up at the wall above the door. "I have nothing to say to you. I just want to know why you haven't killed me yet."

"That time will come, my dear. Beforehand, I'm hoping you will earn me a few million dollars that I need for my future nation."

"New Africa?"

"Glad to hear that you know about it! The more it's known, the more people I'll have on my side."

"In fact, it seems that you're losing your popularity with the A.O.F.M.A.," Mie said, no irony intended. "I was at your refuge in the basement of the Bells & Lustig Laboratories and it was far from perfect. You're lowering your standards every month, aren't you? And your partners are abandoning you one by one. Soon you'll be reduced to joining up with the black racist extremists who are just a bunch of hustlers. They used to give you money. Now, they're asking you for it. You're headed for a fall, my dear."

Mie waited for a response that was a long time coming. Madame Atomos obviously took this kind of criticism very badly. Finally, after swallowing her anger, her voice was full of sweetness. "I will prove to you very soon that my power is intact. I am the strongest. *Kateba kangun, makereba zokugun*, as they say in our country.[7]"

Mie made no reply. She was thinking that the Atomos team watching over her would be very small after the deaths of Ida Brown and Costello. In fact, except for Madame Atomos, there was only the young man, Armstrong, and old Bergmann. The first had colossal strength, but the second could not put up much resistance. If the taxi driver could take Smith to 214 15th Avenue and he could surround the building without being noticed, Madame Atomos' criminal career could be cut short without much difficulty.

Except that between Madame Atomos and the forces of order there was the terrible refrigerating rifle…

Beffort's Malibu pulled up to the sidewalk. Emerson looked around, blinked, and sat thoughtful for a minute. Finally he spoke up, "This is it. I stopped my taxi across the street and the little lady crossed at the light. See, 214 is nearby."

Smith examined the 12-story building. Mie entered this morning, but nothing proved that she was still not inside.

---

[7] Literally, the government's army if you win, the rebel army if you lose. As we say, Might makes right.

"We have to search all the apartments," Akamatsu mumbled, "and interrogate all the tenants. But how will we know if one of them works for Madame Atomos?"

Witter fidgeted in his seat. "In my opinion, we should do it different. Take my advice and surround the block before neutralizing every single person."

Smith turned to the taxi driver, who had turned pale at Akamatsu's mention of Madame Atomos, and handed him a large bill. "We don't need you anymore, Mr. Emerson. Thanks."

"I can go?"

"You can."

The cabbie opened the door, tipped his hat farewell and hurried down the sidewalk.

Witter tossed his cigarette butt on the pavement and said, "There's only three of us and we don't know who we might run into. If they point a cold ray at us…"

Smith turned off the engine and cut the lights. "Nobody's found a better way to use against Madame Atomos, but we usually send in the big guns and troops every time she shows her pinky. Today, we're changing tactics."

He got out of the car, followed by Akamatsu. Witter was supposed to wait in the car and maybe it was this seemingly passive role that was making him bitter.

"Take the wheel, Eddy, and keep an eye out," Beffort advised.

Witter grumbled that he would keep both eyes out as he watched Beffort and Akamatsu enter the building. Then in his rear-view mirror he saw a black Chevrolet stop behind the Malibu. Louis Radetich got out and walked up to him. "On guard duty, Witter?"

"As you see, Louis. What brings you here?"

"I heard your radio calls to Stutton and I was available, so I thought I you might need me. For example I could sit over on 16th Avenue."

"Why 16th?"

"Looking at a map," Radetich explained, "I saw that this building might have a second exit on the other side of the block. It's not impossible…"

Witter shot him a grim look. "With Madame Atomos, the word impossible doesn't exist. Personally I'm glad to see you. Take your place on 16th Avenue, Louis. If it doesn't pan out, at least it can't hurt."

Radetich nodded, got back in his Chevy and left. By a strange twist of fate, Madame Atomos' escape route was now cut off.

Chapter Seven

Safe behind the curtain, Armstrong was watching 15th Avenue when the Malibu pulled up. There was only one car like that and Armstrong did not budge. Then Beffort appeared and the black man felt like someone had socked him in the stomach. He shot up and rushed into the living room where Madame Atomos was fiddling with the buttons of a small two-way radio. He stood in front of her and pointed outside.

"Boss! Smith Beffort!"

Madame Atomos jumped up, ran into the other room and parted the curtains. She recognized the Malibu instantly, as well as Beffort and Akamatsu who were heading for the entrance of the building. Then she also saw Witter. She stood there petrified for a few seconds. She did not understand how Beffort could have come there and she could not take her eyes off the car...

"Boss, we gotta leave!"

Stunned and motionless, Madame Atomos was trying to catch her breath when Louis Radetich walked into her vision. He spoke with Witter, got back in his car and drove around the building.

"Boss, the other exit!"

Suddenly calmer, Madame Atomos turned around. Radetich's move meant the building was surround by the anti-Atomos forces. Therefore, she could not use the 16th Avenue exit anymore.

"Take the cold generator and go up to Bergmann's," she ordered. "I'll join you in five minutes with Mie Azusa."

Armstrong bolted like a rabbit and Madame Atomos breathed more deeply to calm herself. As she pictured Beffort and Akamatsu in the lobby, she had to fight hard against the nagging desire to flee. She adjusted the radio and grabbed the microphone.

"Africa One here! Answer, Dragonfly!"

She was ten minutes early for the appointed session and heard nothing but a quiet hum in her headphones. She repeated the call three times, beads of sweat on her forehead, then suddenly realized that she was panicking for nothing. If Beffort had precise information, he would already have broken down the door and the building would be swarming with G-men from the top to bottom floors. Glued to her seat, she called once more before a loud voice came back, "Dragonfly here. Loud and clear. Go ahead, Africa One."

"I need you immediately!" Madame Atomos barked. "Track 2, sector 18. Immediately!"

"In 15 minutes, Africa One!"

"Immediately!" Madame Atomos yelled.

"Got it, but it'll take time for me to get there. Mark out number 2! Over and out."

Madame Atomos signed out and picked up the two paralyzing pistols, a box containing the clothes of Mie Azusa-Beffort and turned the locks on the room that served as a cell for the young lady. Storming into the room, she startled Mie. Holding a weapon, with a wild look in her eyes, Madame Atomos marched up to the armchair, bent down and unlocked the iron shackle. Then she stepped back and said, "Get dressed. Your clothes are in that box. I'll give you four minutes."

Mie smiled and remained seated. Madame Atomos was acting like a hunted beast and the young lady figured that Smith and the Green Dragon Force were behind her panic.

"Get up!" Madame Atomos squealed. "Or else I'll paralyze you!"

"Go ahead, paralyze me. Then you'll have to leave me here or carry me around in your arms for an hour."

Madame Atomos knew that she would not get the better of Mie. She went out and shut the door. Through the interphone she asked Armstrong to come down and wait on the landing. No sound could be heard from the lower floors and the elevator was empty. This meant that Beffort and Akamatsu were going through the building apartment by apartment, systematically, interrogating every tenant in depth.

At this rate, they would not reach the 6th floor any time soon. Madame Atomos breathed more freely and motioned to Armstrong to come along. She took him back to the cell room, opened the heavy, armored door again and pointed her gun at Mie.

"Now, make up your mind. Either you get dressed and follow me or I'll paralyze you and Armstrong will carry you half-naked in his arms! You'll be at his mercy for one hour and I can't guarantee that he won't rape you."

Armstrong understood his role and reached out his big hands for Mie's chest. She stepped back, saying, "Call off your gorilla. I'll follow you."

She opened the box, but took her time getting dressed. Madame Atomos' apparent calm bothered her. If Smith really were close by, the sinister woman would have pressed her. But catching her enemy looking frequently at her watch, she tried very hard to have trouble buttoning her blouse.

Finally Madame Atomos raised the barrel of her gun and said, "You can finish getting dressed in the stairway. Bob, get her. Make sure she doesn't scream."

Armstrong grabbed Mie's arm, threw around her a coat that she had not yet put on, and pushed her in front of him while slapping his right hand around her mouth. Madame Atomos left the apartment door wide open and followed Armstrong who walked fast in spite of Mie's weight slumped against him.

On the 12th floor landing Arthur Bergmann was waiting, more pale than ever, trembling throughout his body and with his face full of tics. He was scared to death and his teeth were chattering. Armstrong carried Mie into the apartment.

When Madame Atomos entered, she turned around to Bergmann, who was locking the door, and asked curtly, "The ladder?"

"It's ready, Madame, and here are the lights." There were four, big flashlights. As for the ladder, it led to a trap door in the ceiling and opened directly onto the roof.

"Climb up, Bob! I'll take care of the flashlights with Bergmann."

Lifting Mie like a feather, Armstrong shimmied up the ladder, lifted the trapdoor with his head and disappeared onto the roof with his living cargo. Madame Atomos paralyzed Bergmann, who had turned around, and dragged him into the kitchen. She put his head in the oven and turned on the gas. Then she closed the kitchen door before climbing up to the roof where she put down the flashlights, pulled up the ladder and let the trapdoor fall back down.

"And Bergmann?" Armstrong asked without letting go of Mie.

"He's old and deadweight." Madame Atomos answered. She turned on the flashlights, set them up in a square with the beams pointing upward and looked at her watch. If all went well, Dragonfly would appear in three minutes.

Half-strangled by Armstrong's hold, Mie was thinking fast. It looked like Madame Atomos was preparing to escape because danger was near and threatening. With the layout of the flashlights and the flat landing of the roof, she had no doubt about the means of transport that Madame Atomos was planning to use.

Mie tried to move, but Armstrong held her even more tightly, so that she had trouble breathing. Madame Atomos glanced at her, smiled savagely, and looked up at the dark sky. From below came the sounds of the city. Even if Mie could scream, her cry would be lost in the constant rumble. She lost heart and gave up. As things stood, she could do absolutely nothing to oppose Madame Atomos' projects.

Beffort and Akamatsu reached the 6th floor landing. They had worked relatively quickly because the tenants so far were beyond suspicion. Elderly folk, businessmen, a doctor, a tax inspector…

"You see that door, Yosho?"

Armed and ready they snuck into the apartment that was silent but brightly lit. In an instant they saw the radio set up in a corner of the living room.

"This time," Akamatsu whispered, "it looks like we're on the right track." He touched the radio and looked at Beffort. "Still warm. It's been used recently."

Smith went through the apartment and found the room with the armored door furnished with the armchair and shackle. It looked like a prison cell. He turned around, heard Akamatsu shout something and sprinted into the hallway.

"Look, Smith!"

Beffort peeked into the closet and saw the stiff corpses of Ida Brown and Robert Costello.

"Refrigerated!" Akamatsu said. "There's trouble brewing for Madame Atomos."

Without a word Beffort went back to the living room and approached the window. From there he saw the Malibu very clearly with Witter at the wheel. He turned to Akamatsu. "Damn, I'd bet my life that Mie's still in this building! No one's left, seeing that Witter's still there... Come on, Yosho, I've got the feeling that the Atomos team is hiding higher up!"

They left the apartment and started climbing the stairs. When they reached the 10th floor, a weird humming came from above. Beffort froze. "Sounds like a helicopter!"

Akamatsu winced. "It is a helicopter, Smith, and it's going to land on the roof any second now."

Both of them ran at the same time, reached the top floor and were deafened by the roar of the engines set down right above them. Smith went up to a door that obviously opened onto a stairway leading to the roof. He tried the handle and swore loudly when he found it locked. Akamatsu pushed him aside, pulled out his Colt Cobra and opened fire on the lock, which shattered to bits. Smith pulled the door, ran up the straight staircase, pushed open another door and jumped onto the roof just in time to see the helicopter soaring off. Smith raised his weapon, but Akamatsu shouted to him to stop, pointing to a pair of shoes left in the middle of the square of shining flashlights. It was the only way Mie had found to leave a clue for her husband.

Smith picked up the shoes, waved to Yosho to follow him and bounded down the stairs at full speed to the
first floor where the two of them rushed out of the building and up to the Malibu.

"Witter," Akamatsu shouted, "we have to…" He
stopped when he saw the G-man on the radio. As he got
closer he could hear Witter's call over the airwaves:
"Atomos helicopter leaving downtown and heading
west. Mie Azusa is on board! Forget the land race,
Ralph! Track them by radar at all cost! They can't get
away! I repeat…"

Beffort motioned to him to move over and gave
Akamatsu time to climb into the backseat before he
peeled out, heading west, while Witter kept alerting the
dispatch and the local police stations.

On the other side of the block, on 16th Avenue,
Radetich knew as quickly as Witter what was happening
when he saw the lights of the helicopter, but he reacted
quite differently. He sped off through the intersection,
ran three red lights and shot off toward the west, keeping
an eye on the skies. It was a hopeless chase, a rash
move, but Radetich was not surprised to see the helicopter lights again as he left the city. He lost sight of them
presently, but kept going while listening to the updates
coming over the radio. The copter was spotted flying
west toward Wildorado.

Radetich put the pedal to the metal. If anyone was
going to find where Madame Atomos was going, it
would be him.

After a 15-minute flight the helicopter set down
near a dark building in what looked like a farmyard. Mie
made out a tractor, a truck with a covered bed and then

six men came running up. They were carrying flashlights and opened the double doors of the hangar to move in the helicopter.

"Get out," Madame Atomos said. "Bob, you take Mrs. Beffort to the *Chapel*."

Madame Atomos jumped out and walked away. Armstrong pushed Mie out and led her toward the building, keeping an iron grip on her arm. Without shoes, Mie felt the painful bumps in the ground with every step and she was relieved on feeling the smooth touch of concrete under her feet. Armstrong pushed her brusquely forward. They crossed a deserted room into a bigger room with a dreadful stench.

In the dim glow of the scarce lights Mie saw several rows of beds where black men were sleeping. The heat was suffocating and most of the men were naked. Along one wall there was a rack of assault rifles and machine guns. On the ground, straw, dried mud, food scraps…

The first section of the future Atomos army!

Armstrong opened a door onto another room and shoved Mie in. "This is the *Chapel*, Mrs. Beffort. The window's barred and on the other side of the wall is a big manure pit. This disgusting dormitory always has 50 men inside while the others are working. There's no other women here, so if I were you, I wouldn't attract attention." He left, locked the door and slipped away.

Mie walked around her new, darkened prison. She bumped into a table, a chair, finally found a bed and lay down. The window was closed and the young lady was quickly swimming in sweat. She took off her coat and skirt and lay down again. Just as she was nodding off, she heard scuffling and murmurs coming from the other side of the cracked and battered door. Rays of light filtered through. Mie sat up on an elbow and watched the shadows crossing the light, listened to the low laughter and then something banged into the door.

Mie huddled against the wall and hoped that the door would hold. On the other side of it was a gang of brutes hungry for fresh meat…

Louis Radetich was cruising around by guesswork. The radio was no longer reporting useless information because the radars had lost track of the helicopter a while ago. Radetich could not have said why, but he was sure that the helicopter had landed there. The zone where Radetich was driving was deserted, scratched out by little used or unused side roads. In fact, it was the perfect setting for an Atomos base. To concentrate better Radetich turned off the radio. He stopped often, cut the engine, got out and listened.

The night was silent and dark. He clearly heard the sound of an engine rumbling. The roar got louder and headlights popped into sight, turned and headed down the bad road. Radetich jumped into his car, drove it into a clump of trees, and ran back to the road. The truck appeared, rumbled by and kept going. Its bed was covered, but Radetich had time to see two or three black faces sticking out of the canvas.

In itself this meant nothing and anyone but Radetich would have let it alone. He decided to leave his car and head out on foot down the dirt road toward where the truck had come from. He had two competition pistols and twelve packs of ammunition in his pockets.

Chapter Eight

The truck's departure was the result of an unthinkable mistake committed by Bob Armstrong. After locking up Mie in the *Chapel*, he went to join Madame Atomos in her small underground HQ, air-conditioned and soundproof, with three exits. She had a telephone, a two-way radio powerful enough to reach the New Africa HQ in Louisiana, and at the end of an escape tunnel, she had parked a fast sports car, which, in case of a serious emergency, could take her to New Mexico in less than 20 minutes.

Armstrong rang the buzzer and waited for the green light that gave him permission to enter. He pushed the door open and stood face to face with his boss.

"Well, Bob?" Madame Atomos was wearing a see-through nightie and her shining eyes were inviting Armstrong to a few hours of fun. When Madame Atomos was in this kind of mood, Armstrong could relax a little. He sat down, lit a cigarette and casually crossed his legs. "Mie's in the *Chapel*, but the men are already knocking on her door. If you leave her there, she's gonna have a rough time."

"Not so bad as all that," Madame Atomos murmured as she stretched and showed off her hefty chest. "How many are in the dorm?"

"Maybe 50."

Madame Atomos' eyes lit up and she licked her lips with an agile tongue. Erotic thoughts were drowning her brain, making her hands tremble slightly. When she was not killing people, Madame Atomos could be incredibly sensual. "Bob, come over here…"

Armstrong stood up, crushed his cigarette in the nearest ashtray and took his mistress in his arms. Madame Atomos kissed him, bit him and whispered in her last, clear-headed moment, "Did you put the cold generator somewhere safe, Bob?"

Armstrong's body turned into a steel bar. He wriggled free and just stood there, his eyes popping out of his head, saying nothing, scared stiff. Instantly Madame Atomos forgot the burning desires that were inflaming her heart. "What have you done, Bob?"

Armstrong took a deep breath and said, "The cold generator is still at Arthur Bergmann's!"

"What?" Madame Atomos pounced and slapped him hard. "Idiot! Stupid slave boy! Stinking swine!"

Armstrong was devastated. He shook his head and tried to find excuses. "I was making sure Mie didn't scream and…"

Madame Atomos slapped him again, in rage, her mouth twisted by anger. Just like that, despite her sexy negligee, she became repulsive. Armstrong thought his final moment had come when Madame Atomos grabbed her big Luger, but she calmed down suddenly, lowered the weapon, forced a smile and said in a sweet voice, "Why don't you go back there, Bob. Take a dozen armed men and a vehicle. If you come back without the generator, I'll order them to hang you. Go!"

Armstrong lowered his head and left without saying a word. A few minutes later, on board the truck, he passed by Louis Radetich and thus gave him precise directions to the training camp where Mie and Madame Atomos were holed up.

In the Malibu Beffort, Akamatsu and Witter had just entered Wildorado. There was still some activity going on in the town, but at this time of the day the streets were slowly vacating. The people were watching television and the lights in the shops were starting to blink off.

Beffort stopped the car on a hill and flipped a switch on the radiotelephone. "Yellow Mask here. Any news, 6289?"

"Nothing," Ralph Stutton answered right away. "The radars have completely lost track of the helicopter. It could have set down or kept flying very low. But it won't go far."

"It doesn't need to go far," Beffort grumbled. "It just needs to let Madame Atomos off near a car or train or airport and that's all she wrote. Give it to Green Dragon. Tell Owen Bernitz to leave Amarillo. From now on we're working a 60-mile radius around the city."

"Got it and I'll pass it on. Position?"

"Wildorado. I'm sticking between here and the western exit of Amarillo. Over and out, 6289."

Beffort left the radio on, but hung the mic up. He turned to Akamatsu who was examining a detailed map of the Wildorado area in Oldham county. When he saw Beffort's questioning look, Yosho grimaced and said, "What's for sure is that we're inching toward New Mexico. Moreover, this point in Texas has a huge strategic value. In no time at all you can reach Oklahoma, Kansas or Colorado."

Witter groaned and spoke bitterly, "If Mama What's-Her-Face is a hop, skip and jump away from four states, then we're up the creek! I'd be surprised if she had another refuge around here."

Beffort got the Malibu running again and turned around.

"Where you going, Smith?" Akamatsu asked.

"Just driving around. This county is full of farms and a bunch of little side roads. Madame Atomos loves this kind of place."

Akamatsu stayed silent. Witter sat back comfortably. Both were thinking that to search for Madame Atomos at random was like searching for that famous needle in a haystack.

Radetich progressed cautiously. He could see the dark shape of a big building that was nothing extraordinary in itself but that the motionless forms (obviously sentinels) gave the impression of a fortified camp. Radetich moved silently to find another view of the place. Now he saw that the property was divided into three separate parts, in the form of a three-pointed star with a paved central court in the middle. Between each branch, two armed men paced up and down. In spite of the thick, heavy curtains thin rays of light filtered out through the windows, which Radetich counted and easily deduced that a large number of people were living under the flat roof of the south building.

Thanks to the cloudy sky he got closer without being spotted. He managed to crawl between two sentinels and flatten himself against the gray wall of the east building. Now Radetich was holding a gun and his second was in his belt. He knew perfectly well that they would show no mercy, so he had to shoot first. Of course, he was not absolutely sure that the camp belonged to Madame Atomos, but somehow, strangely he could sense it.

Like a shadow he inched along the gray wall until he felt the rough wood of a double door. With all senses alert, Radetich pulled one of the doors, which creaked softly but too loudly in the surrounding silence. He swung around, caught sight of the two sentinels and was relieved to see them continuing their tireless march. He opened the door a little more and smelled the sticky odor of warm oil. He entered without further ado, sweeping open his overcoat.

His lighter glowed dimly but enough to reveal the big helicopter. Radetich put away his lighter and waited for a few seconds. Now he had two choices: he could go back to his car and alert the dispatch of his find, which would surely bring them here in force, with the usual commotion, and the probable flight of Madame Atomos who was still on guard. Or he could stay there, find her lair, kill her and inform 6289 afterward.

By instinct and by hatred Radetich choose the second. He had sworn on the fresh graves of his wife and six children that he would kill Madame Atomos...

Radetich left the hangar and was back in the cold night air. After closing the door he went farther along the wall, almost to the end of the building, where he found some uneven land that he used to get to the south building. Lizard-like he leapt, dove, flattened himself on the ground and stayed still. He heard a conversation behind him, the snap of a rifle bolt and then a long, unbearable silence. The two sentinels finally separated and went back to their rounds. Radetich let the air out of his lungs and crawled until he could stand up in the darker shadow of the south building.

Immediately he heard faint voices. Inside the building some men were chatting as softly as possible. Radetich leaned over and glanced through the slit in the curtains. He saw twenty or so blacks huddled around a gas lamp. They were all staring at a door that two other blacks were trying to force open. By their attitude and obscene expressions Radetich suddenly thought of Mie

Azusa-Beffort and had to admit that he had completely forgotten her. However, the young lady must have been in one of these three buildings.

Radetich moved along to the corner of the building and almost fell into a manure pit. As he walked around it, he saw the barred window. The inside of the room was dark, but through the cracks in a door in the background he could plainly see the unmistakable white glow of the gas lamp. Still using extreme caution Radetich went up to the wall where he used a narrow ridge of ground to reach up and grab the bars. He pulled himself up and tapped on the window with the butt of his pistol. He was only slightly surprised, but very happy, to see Mie's face appear a foot away from his.

He could see in her face that the young lady was having a hard time, but she still found the energy to smile. Radetich asked her to open the window. Mie waved to him that it was impossible, that the window was jammed and the bars too strong. In a situation like this, a fruitful conversation was naturally unthinkable. Since Radetich could not attack all the men on the other side of the door, there was only one way for Mie to defend her life—if not her honor—while waiting for help to arrive.

Radetich wrapped the pistol butt in his handkerchief and asked Mie to cushion the impact. She nodded, disappeared and reappeared right away with her coat, which she put up against the window when Radetich smashed it with his gun. It made little noise and caused a star-shaped crack around a hole in the center about two or three inches wide. Mie caught the shards in her coat, which she put on the ground, as Radetich widened the hole by breaking off the slivers and dropping them in the manure pit. The operation was practically silent and the dialogue that took place was no less so.

"Here's a gun," Radetich whispered, "and two boxes of ammunition. But don't wait for the last minute to shoot this gang of savages."

"Thanks, Louis. How'd you end up here?"

"No time to explain. Is Madame Atomos in the camp?"

"She was not long ago, but since I've been locked up in here, I don't know what's become of her." Over Radetich's shoulder she saw the two sentinels' outlines cut out on the horizon. She shivered. "You're risking your life by staying here. Where are the others?"

Radetich's teeth shined in the dark. "I'm alone. I came to kill Madame Atomos, but I have to make sure you're safe first. My car isn't far from here... Defend yourself while I call for help."

Mie squeezed his hand and her voice was full of emotion when she said, "Be careful, Louis."

Radetich laughed hollowly before disappearing from the window and dropping down to the ground. He snuck along the building heading west. He had no intention of taking the same route back and was not so stupid as to run the gauntlet of the two sentinels again. Even though he had to cover twice as much ground, he preferred to skirt around the camp.

Inside the area guarded by the sentinels, he made a wide detour that brought him safely to the corner of the north building. Having roughly staked out the area and the placement of sentinels, he could now move more quickly, with more confidence, but unfortunately without the extreme wariness with which he had accomplished his previous feat. Moreover, the urgency of his mission was pushing him on. Mie's life was in his hands, as well as the capture of Madame Atomos. It was a lot of responsibility for one man. Radetich skimmed along the wall of the north building until he came to a door that flew open, flooding him with light. He was the victim of the stupidest accident, but his lack of training with the Green Dragon commandoes was bound to prove fatal. He heard a cry of alarm, he shot, he killed a man, but pounding footsteps and shouts bore down from every side. Radetich took off, his weapon at his hip, and ran straight for the hangar.

All of a sudden the camp was awake and a small searchlight lit up and scoured the land. It found Radetich, who dove. Explosions all around and bullets whistling by. He rolled onto his stomach and turned off the light with a single shot.

Only 30 feet from the hangar he was at the door in a jiffy. He pulled the door, slipped through the opening and took up position. From here he could cover practically the whole courtyard. He brought down two reckless blacks who ran at him like idiots, kamikaze style. Their fall temporarily put a halt to the havoc and the camp fell silent. Radetich thought it made no sense, but then he laughed: the helicopter was behind him with a tank full of fuel ready to explode! This explained everything, but the calm would not last. Madame Atomos would take matters into her own hands if the Radetich situation became too risky. Nevertheless, as long as he was alive, he would force the others to shoot, which might be good if someone heard the gunfire. The camp was isolated, but not as much as it could have been. The Green Dragon Force, the G-men and the police should have been roaming around the region since the helicopter had disappeared over Wildorado.

Radetich emptied his clip to goad the others into shooting, but when no shot answered, he started getting worried. They knew he was alone, caught in the hangar with limited firepower and obviously not enough ammunition. As things stood, he was harmless and the easiest thing to do was to let him rot in his corner. Without water or food he would not last long without outside help coming to save him.

Plus, he could not stay awake all day and night. They would put feelers out now and again and if he was sleeping, it would be a sleep turned into eternal night.

Radetich reloaded his pistol and glanced thoughtfully at the helicopter, wondering how he could use it to his advantage. Then he caught sight of movement and made out a group of men setting up on either side of the north building. A moment of silence passed before the sound of footsteps could be heard behind the hangar.

Now he was trapped and even though he was not hurt, he could consider himself already dead.

Chapter Nine

In the *Chapel* Mie heard the shouting and explosions, then the blacks who were trying to break through her door scampered off like rabbits. By the metal clacking she knew that the gun racks were being emptied and then she heard the sound of bare feet slapping against the pavement outside. Because of the broken window the noises came with the air into the small room. Listening and wathcing at the window, gripping Radetich's pistol, Mie waited with her heart racing.

There was silence, another round of gunfire and then everything was calm in the camp. Mie guessed that Radetich had not been caught and that he was holed up in the hangar when she saw groups of men surrounding the building, which had become the center of their attention. Moreover, considering the precautions that the Atomos men usually take, it was obvious that Radetich was a danger to them. Therefore, although he was helpless, he must not have been hurt and if need be he could still make an impact.

A while passed without anything new happening and then something metallic slipped into the lock of the *Chapel* door. Mie left the window and tiptoed over to the door where she peeked through one of the cracks. There were no more than four of them around the gas lamp, but their determination to get hold of Mie was written all over their faces. They had put their weapons on the ground, only interested in getting the door open. The hook they were using on the lock clicked around, scratching the metal noisily.

"Quiet, Sam, quiet… no need to wake her."

"What's the difference? Everybody's worried about the other guy."

"She can scream. If she screams, Madame Atomos will hear her and there goes our fun. Be quiet and get it open... After we can close the door and nobody's any the wiser."

Mie backed away slowly, put on her skirt and coat and stretched out on the bed. She was thinking that the sound of her pistol might alert the others, so she rolled the end of the sheet around it and put the blanket over the barrel. It was not a perfect silencer, but the young lady knew by experience that this was good enough to muffle the blasts. Except that one of her arms was immobilized. If she missed her targets with the first shots, she would not have time for another round. The men would be on her immediately, disarm her and pin her to the bed while gagging her... Mie tried not to think of this. Her eyes were riveted on the door.

The hook kept digging at the lock, but it held tight, even though it was an old model—the worker must really have been a novice not to open it more easily. Behind him the others were getting angry, unconsciously speaking more loudly. In spite of Mie's precarious position, she smiled. Between the rattling and the voices they would have woken up the dead!

Then the bolt clicked and wiped the smile off Mie's face. The moment of truth had arrived.

The men became silent as they slowly pushed the door open. In the darkness the light from the gas lamp cast a triangle on the ground that got bigger as the wooden board pivoted. Mie did not move. She just raised the barrel of the gun.

A man stuck his head through and peered into the shadows. His teeth shined as he entered, waving to his friends that the coast was clear. The three others poured into the room and the last of them closed the door. Through her half-closed eyes Mie watched them milling about. They were only six feet away, naked as jaybirds, stinking of sweat and oozing desire.

"Go on, Sam!"

Mie opened fire almost at point blank range, squeezing the trigger rapidly, practically without aiming. She heard the fleshy impact of the bullets, then they snatched away her weapon and a big slimy thing fell on top of her. She held back a scream, but could not stop a knee from slipping between her thighs. She fought against the mouth that was searching for her lips and stuck her hand into a gooey liquid. Then she almost passed out when she realized that she was struggling with a corpse.

Feeling sick, she freed herself and saw in the lamp-light that she was covered with blood. Her bullets had hit home. Three of the attackers had been killed on the spot. The fourth was leaping for the bed when he was shot and died between Mie's legs.

Outside, there was no sound, proof that the battle had gone unnoticed. Mie straightened herself up, went into dormitory, picked out a machine gun and stuffed her pockets with clips. But she stopped at the door to take off her coat, which she simply hung around her shoulders, and took a deep breath, waiting for her trembling hands to settle down. When she figured she was calm enough, she opened the door, left and started walking casually, naturally toward the building where Radetich was holed up.

A few lights were burning here and there, but the courtyard remained relatively dark, so she was already halfway there when they spotted her. A shot rang out.

The bullet missed her by a mile, but a voice shouted right away, "Don't shoot! Take her alive!" Unseen, Madame Atomos was giving orders through a megaphone. Mie smiled, glad to have judged correctly her value as a precious hostage. Not stopping, she lowered the machine gun. A dozen men snuck up, cautiously, hunched over, aware that they were putting themselves in Radetich's line of fire, but they saw to it that Mie was also vulnerable.

"Watch out!" Radetich yelled.

Very agilely Mie opened her coat, raised her weapon and shot two quick rounds, clearing the way in front of her in a general stupor. She took advantage of the break to start running and shooting, hacking down everything around her. Men fell, windows shattered, but no one shot back.

Out of breath she bolted into the hangar and tripped into Radetich's arms. He helped her regain her balance and shook her a little. "Let go of your weapon, Mie. You're safe here."

She realized that her teeth were chattering and her finger was welded to the trigger of the machine gun. She had been hard tested, but she had killed a dozen enemies and wore their blood on her; the sharp odor from the gunfire filled her nostrils...

"Okay," Radetich said, "calm down, it's over. Sit down and take this cigarette." She obeyed unthinkingly. He lit the smoke and watched her take a long, deep drag. "You're a tough girl, Mie. Hat's off!"

She finally smiled and visibly relaxed. When she saw that she was sitting on a can covered in oil, she smiled a little more. Her coat was ruined, but she had come through with honors...

"Not too hurt?" Radetich asked, staring into the darkness.

Mie shook her head. "They were dead before they touched me. If it wasn't for you, I don't know what would've happened. Thank you, Louis."

He turned back to inspect the courtyard through the door left ajar. Now they had turned off all the lights and except for the corpses scattered on the pavement, no one could be seen. Radetich listened, but heard no sound. The camp must have been more isolated than he had thought because Mie's gunfire would certainly have woken up any neighbors. So, there were no neighbors...

"What are we going to do, Louis?"

"Wait. Unless you know how to fly this machine?" Radetich said, pointing at the helicopter.

Mie shook her head. Radetich smiled. "It doesn't matter. I'm joking. Anyway, they'd stop us. In fact, our situation hasn't improved. We're together now, that's all."

Mie raised her machine gun and put the six clips on a crate. "With this we can make it last."

"We have no food or water."

Mie raised her eyebrows. "You're getting ahead of yourself, Louis. Smith will find us before long."

Radetich hoped so, but did not believe it.

Chomping on his eternally unlit cigar stub, big Owen Bernitz was cruising toward Route 66. It was right after the call from 555-6289 that retransmitted Beffort's orders, instructing the Green Dragon Force to search within a 60-mile radius around Amarillo. As head of the Green Dragon, Bernitz had to spread his men around the sector before heading west himself. Right now he was barely out of Amarillo on a four-lane highway connecting the city to Route 66 itself.

There were few cars, if any, which was no doubt why Bernitz noticed the truck coming from the opposite direction in the far lane. At first sight it was just a vehicle like any other and Bernitz was about to look away when a bright streetlight lit up the cab. It was only a flash, but Owen Bernitz instantly identified the dark face of Bob Armstrong.

It was surprising, unexpected, against all logic. Knowing she was being hunted, Madame Atomos could not have sent her closest partner into the city when that very morning she had taken outlandish risks to get him out of the FBI cell! This planted a doubt in Bernitz' mind and kept him from flipping the switch on his radio to send out a call over the airwaves. After all, maybe it was just a striking resemblance. His vision from the far right lane was in no way helped by the night. However, Bernitz was not the kind of guy to ask himself too many questions. When he had an itch, he had to scratch it.

He sped up, took the nearest off ramp, crossed through the tunnel and floored it back to Amarillo. The truck had taken off in an unknown direction and finding it again was no piece of cake. Bernitz drove down the streets at random, ending up on the main streets in spite of himself, until he saw a pair of red taillights stopped way down on 8th Avenue. He got closer to it without paying too much attention to the traffic laws and breathed deeply when he recognized the truck. It went south down Buchanan Street, but when it turned sharply onto 15th Avenue, Bernitz got a big smile. Even though he had not been in on the action that ended with the helicopter's flight, he had followed the whole event over the radio and was fully aware that Madame Atomos' former apartment was guarded by the police. So, he was curious to know what Armstrong was hoping for in coming back to a place that he should have avoided like the plague…

The truck pulled up along the sidewalk in front of number 214 in a legal parking space. Armstrong got out and walked straight into the building. Bernitz also stopped, but he was not quite sure what to do. Wouldn't it be smarter to follow the guy back to his refuge than to arrest him here and now?

Owen was considering this when the second black man, probably the driver, stepped onto the sidewalk. He looked inquisitively around, saw nothing suspicious and entered the building. A few minutes later the covered bed opened. Two other blacks jumped out and disappeared inside the building. Owen Bernitz sat there without moving, just thinking.

If these four men were planning to visit Madame Atomos' former apartment, they would run into the policemen guarding it. Sparks would fly, damage would be done and Owen could do nothing but pick up the pieces. He threw out his stub, lit a new cigar—which was a rare act—and waited patiently. Not long, barely 15 minutes, and the four blacks came into sight. Armstrong and the driver had their arms free, but the two other were carrying a kind of case that they put in the truck before climbing in and closing up the cover. Then the truck took off and turned at the end of the street to get back to 8th Avenue. A little stunned, Owen followed a few car lengths behind. There had been no shots fired, no commotion; it was as if the Atomos men had come and gone after loitering in the hallway.

However the mysterious case was there to prove the opposite. In front of Bernitz, the truck was just rolling along, staying under the speed limit, in its own lane, looking like it was making a late delivery in some far suburb.

Then Bernitz remembered. He got on his radio and said, "Calling 6289. Bernitz here."

"I hear you, Owen," Ralph Stutton answered right away. "What's new?"

"A little something, pal. I'm on the tail of a truck hauling around Armstrong and a bunch of scruffy boys. Hey, what's this refrigerating thingy like like?"

"Not sure about that. The newspaper seller who saw Madame Atomos leave this morning just said that Armstrong and Costello put a case in the truck."

"There's a weird case in my truck, too."

While driving he told him about what he had seen and was put directly in touch with Smith Beffort through the dispatch relay in Pleasant Valley.

"Hey, Owen," Beffort barked, "what kept you from telling us about this earlier?"

"Caution, boss. You heard my story?"

"I heard. Damn, you should've alerted us when you spotted the truck! That case is certainly carrying the cold generator. If I'm getting it straight, Armstrong is bringing the device back to Madame Atomos. If he makes it, she'll have a formidable weapon!"

Bernitz did not get flustered. "Exactly. But if he doesn't make it, you might never know where your wife is being held prisoner. Me, I can take Armstrong, his truck and the whole shebang off the road. But what then?"

Once again Beffort was stuck in the awful battle between personal interest and the general good. In other words, he had to make a fast choice between Mie's life and that of thousands of Americans whom Madame Atomos had sworn to refrigerate on Christmas Eve.

Since there was no answer, Bernitz proposed, "We can fix everything. Let me tail this truck to wherever it's going. In the meantime, I'll keep you abreast of my position so that we can arrive at the same time for the party when…"

Bernitz stopped talking because his windshield had just disintegrated. Bits of glass flew in his face as a gust of wind blasted his car. He had to grip the steering wheel hard to avoid running into a ditch.

"Owen?" Beffort shouted.

But Bernitz was too busy to answer. The truck was hitting him hard, gunfire screamed by his ears before fading off into the night. The rest, what he did not hear, was hammering the car, piercing the radiator, ricocheting off the engine. A tire blew out, then another, and the car flipped over before landing on the shoulder of the road. Dazed and amazed that he had survived the barrage, Bernitz just sat down on the frozen ground.

When he finally thought of telling Beffort, he found his radio turned into sieve. He looked at the road and lost heart. As far as the eye could see, there was no truck in sight.

Chapter Ten

The man approached Madame Atomos and told her that Armstrong was asking for her on the telephone. The terrible woman went down to her lair and picked up the phone sitting on the table. "Bob? What's happening?"

"I've got the machine, boss, but we had to get rid of a car that was following us out of Amarillo. I'm calling from a phone booth at a gas station on Route 66. What should I do?"

"Get back here as quickly as possible!"

"I don't know if that's such a good idea," Armstrong sounded nervous. "The guy following us looked like a twin of Owen Bernitz and his car had a radio... If he gave away our position, the rest of the Green Dragon and maybe Smith Beffort himself will be waiting for us farther down the road."

Madame Atomos was grinding her teeth. She had enough to worry about with Mie and Radetich without needing to take this idiot Armstrong by the hand... She had to decide everything, supervise everything! Oh, the time of the Great Brain was long gone!

"You already have orders for what to do in case of trouble, Bob. Look at your little list and act accordingly. Wherever you are, there ought to be an A.O.F.M.A. sympathizer nearby. Most importantly, put the cold generator in a safe place. Then change cars and come back here with your men. See you soon."

She hung up, went back up to the first floor and stationed herself behind the blinds where she could watch the hangar through night-vision binoculars. By joining Radetich, Mie had complicated her life considerably. If

Mie was not in there, Madame Atomos would have been preparing to blow up the hangar, helicopter and all. Now she could not take out Radetich without risking Mie's life. And if things went sour, Mie's life would no doubt prolong Madame Atomos' life.

"Tom, get your best shooters into position. Get them to put their scopes on the cracked open door. Radetich looks out sometimes, so the next time his head appears I want it shot off!"

Tom turned around. Madame Atomos stopped him with a click of her tongue. "Tell your shooters not to miss! If they kill Mrs. Beffort, they'll be burned alive! And I won't even say what will happen to you..."

Tom swallowed hard, nodded and went to gather his eight best shooters to whom he gave rifles with scopes. He also gave them their orders and the threats of their boss, letting them post themselves as they wanted around the camp.

Behind the door Radetich caught some movement around the other building and saw two or three shadows fall to the ground, but the darkness and distance kept him from seeing more. Besides, he was not alarmed by it. As long as nobody tried an all out assault on the hangar, nothing could really bother him.

"What time is it?" Mie asked.

Radetich stepped back from the door and glanced at the luminous face of his watch. "Almost 11 pm and it's still December 19th."

Mie shook her head. "Thanks for being precise, Louis. I feel like it's been months since my visit to Bells & Lustig. What's it like outside?"

"Dead calm," Radetich said curtly.

Mie listened. The silence was extraordinary, only disturbed by the weak but bitter cold gusts of wind coming from the north. If this kept up, the clouds would soon be blown away and in the moonlight the assault Radetich feared would turn into mass suicide.

Mie did not understand Madame Atomos' unusual patience. She told this to Radetich who just shrugged his shoulders. "Why should she be in such a hurry? We're surrounded in this hangar and our friends have absolutely no idea where we are." He smiled wryly. "I'm responsible for this predicament. When I figured out that this place was an Atomos hideout, I should've contacted the dispatch right away. Hate is always a bad counselor."

Mie did not comment. Their situation could be changed and it was totally useless to regret past actions. Besides, she understood how Radetich felt. After his family was murdered, he could not act normally. Mie knew what this felt like because after the death of her son, she went after Madame Atomos alone, forgetting about the rest of the world.

Radetich looked around the hangar and pointed to the only window, a skylight leading to the roof. "I wonder if…"

"Don't wonder about anything," Mie interrupted. "If you try to get out of here, they'll kill you. Did you forget that the building is completely surrounded? And there are probably lookouts posted on the roof."

"I'm not so sure," Radetich said, looking up. And I don't think the building is completely surrounded. There are men behind the hangar, but the part across from the building is probably empty. I can climb up on the roof, drop down in an area not being watched and get out of the camp. You know, Mie, my car's only 100 yards or so away."

The young lady grabbed his arm. "Don't do it, Louis, I beg you. We're not in any immediate danger right here and I'm sure that Smith will find our trail soon."

"How?"

"Someone has to see your car."

Radetich shook his head. "No chance. I hid it in the woods when Armstrong's truck passed by. You can't see it from the road, even in daylight. I'll leave you the machine gun and they won't be able to touch you."

"It's too risky!"

"Nothing ventured, nothing gained, Mie. Look, I can reach the skylight by climbing up and then across that central beam. After that it's as easy as pie."

Now Mie was hesitating, but she still objected. "And if there are lookouts on the roof?"

"I'll forget the whole thing," Radetich promised.

He checked his pistol and took off his overcoat, saying, "Watch the courtyard, okay? If they spot me, you can cover me so I can get back to the skylight. Ready?"

Mie took the machine gun and stood next to the door. When she motioned that she was ready, Radetich climbed up the rough wall and onto the beam, scurrying rapidly over to the skylight. From below the roof looked flat, but up close he saw that it was sloping slightly. The skylight opened opposite the other building and Radetich hoped that the ridge of the roof, though low, would hide him from enemy eyes.

He unhooked the old opener, pushed and slowly lifted the window. When she saw him glancing out on the deserted roof, Mie whispered, "Anyone?"

Radetich gave a thumb's up and then waved goodbye before climbing onto the roof. He did not open the skylight completely because in a vertical position it probably could have been seen above the roof ridge. So, he crawled through, letting the window rest against his body, then his legs until he finally let it down softly with one foot. It did not take much effort, but in spite of the cold, Radetich was sweating. Luckily the sheet metal roof made his job easier. His body slid nice and quiet except for the buttons of his coat, which scratched against the metal. But the sound was nothing, especially with the wind blowing harder now.

The lookouts must have had their teeth chattering in the icy breeze. They were ill-equipped and not used to the cold. The endless nocturnal watch had certainly dulled their senses. Given all the circumstances Radetich calculated his chances at 60%. He continued his slow progress, getting closer, little by little, to the edge of the roof. Only now, even after all the problems he had had getting into the camp, Radetich was sorry that he had not accepted Smith Beffort's offer of a paralyzing pistol a few weeks earlier. With a weapon like that he could have cleared a path a long time ago, silently, invisibly, and especially without killing everyone.

After ten minutes Radetich reached the edge of the roof. He had accomplished the first part of his plan, leaving most of the Atomos forces behind him, hypnotized by the hangar door, and now he saw nothing before him but a land of darkness that he figured must be safe. However, to escape in the night he still had to get off the roof without being noticed. Getting to the ground posed no great problem. Hanging off the roof and letting himself drop to the ground was child's play. The hard part was avoiding any guards who might be roaming around.

Radetich inched up to the gutter and snuck a peek around the ground below and the countryside beyond. It looked deserted, but when he looked toward the hangar he saw the lights from a few cigarettes burning. So, just as he had guessed, Madame Atomos was happy with the lockdown, probably thinking that the roof was inaccessible.

But this made Radetich think. Unless she did not know about the existence of the skylight, it was unthinkable that the terrible woman would have left such an escape route wide open. This certainty put a damper on his plans. In the cold light of reason, that is to say not taking his desires for reality, he had to admit that the roof exit was probably a death trap. In his argument with Mie he had once again underestimated the Atomos Organization.

Radetich missed his chance by staying still. Knowing what he knew, he should have turned around immediately. Instead he kept watching the darkness and when he saw and heard nothing, he ended up convincing himself that his imagination was getting the best of him. Like every coin, his previous thought had a flipside, just as strong: in fact, since Madame Atomos did not used to live here, why would she know about the skylight? Others knew about it, for sure, but when Madame Atomos gave orders, who had the balls to contradict her?

Radetich was starting to feel the effects of the cold. He decided to risk everything. Putting his legs over the edge, he hung on with his hands, then let go and landed softly on the ground...

Mie felt totally alone after Radetich left. She fought against the discouragement that was growing in her and tried to divert her attention by watching the courtyard. But nothing was moving there and time was ticking more and more slowly. Nevertheless, as the minutes passed, Mie became more confident about Radetich. If Madame Atomos' men had caught him, there would have been gunshots and shouting. Therefore, the silence was reassuring.

A half hour passed like that and then a shuffling noise from the roof made her look up. She left the door, stood under the skylight and saw a man's torso behind it. It was only a shadow, but strangely she did not recognize it as Radetich. Her throat was dry when she called out, "Louis?"

Up above, the shadow waved desperately to keep silent and that the window was closed from the inside, which meant he could not get back in. Mie was wondering why Radetich did not answer, then she understood when a cloud, swept off by the wind, let a ray of moonlight through to reveal the black face leaning over the skylight. The man realized the danger right away and tried to step back, but Mie's machine gun blew his head away and shattered the window for good. His body rolled down the roof and flopped to the ground behind the hangar.

Mie jumped and reached the door just in time to mow down a group of attackers, a few of whom scurried away leaving the corpses on the pavement. No more noise on the roof and the courtyard was dead calm. She shot out a few windows and destroyed some plaster before taking her finger off the trigger, knowing she was wasting ammunition for nothing. She sat on the crate. Louis Radetich was dead and from now on she only had herself to count on. But how could she keep from closing her eyes when she became tired?

By capturing and murdering Radetich, Madame Atomos had won an undeniable victory and Mie was, in a way, in the palm of her hand. The young lady closed her eyes, exhausted, but snapped them open when she heard Madame Atomos' voice coming through a megaphone.

"Mie Azusa, as you know, Louis Radetich has fallen into our hands. Contrary to what you are no doubt thinking, we did not execute him. He is right here, next to me, perfectly safe and sound. It's up to you to keep him that way. In fact, if you don't give up in five minutes, your friend will be tortured. We'll start by gouging out his right eye. After another five minutes, if you're still in there, we'll pluck out his left eye..." Madame Atomos paused to give her words time to soak in, then she resumed, "Anyway, your chances of seeing help arrive are nil. There's only one road leading here, but to avoid any undesirable surprises, we closed it off with road signs forbidding access because of construction. Now I'm starting my stopwatch. It's exactly... 11:45. Knowing that you have no watch, I'll give you the time remaining every 60 seconds. Think hard! If Radetich becomes blind, it'll be your fault."

She stopped talking and the unbearable silence fell over the camp again. Mie knew that she would surrender. Even if Madame Atomos was bound to kill her and Radetich both, she could not act otherwise. However, before that, she had to try something. Five minutes! It was far from enough time.

Mie threw the machine gun around her shoulder, climbed the rough wall and just as Radetich had recently done, she shimmied across the beam.

"One minute!" Madame Atomos said.

Mie cleared her mind and approached the skylight. Because the frame had no more glass, she was able to get on the roof quickly. She crawled, protected by the ridge.

"Two minutes!"

Mie was not as cautious as Radetich because she was sure that they would not shoot her, so she reached the edge of the roof in record time.

"Three minutes!"

Mie went another 20 yards and saw the other building from a different angle. An angle that Madame Atomos and her men had no reason to worry about. You position your defense with respect to your enemy's position and rarely on your flanks. Now, Mie had just arrived on her enemy's flank.

"Four minutes!"

Mie located the approximate position where Madame Atomos was counting the seconds. She raised her machine gun and aimed carefully. On the next announcement she would fire like hell in the direction of...

There was a scream and the sound of a scuffle amplified by the megaphone. Then the voice of Louis Radetich yelled, "Don't surrender, Mie! They've already gouged out my eyes! I'd rather die! Don't surrender!" A shot rang out and Radetich fell silent.

Mie turned pale and slipped a little lower. This time Louis Radetich was dead and nothing would stop her from playing her final card.

Chapter Eleven

His eyes gouged out, gagged and held by two men, Radetich had managed to get free and get his hands around Madame Atomos' throat. In spite of the agony he suffered, Radetich had shouted his warning after ripping off his gag, even while strangling Madame Atomos, who could not wriggle free of his desperate grip. Finally one of the men had saved his boss by putting a bullet in Radetich's head.

Now Madame Atomos was recovering, rubbing her throat, trying to chase away the stars dancing before her eyes, and wondering where Radetich had found the strength… She had decided to keep him with her in case Mie doubted he was still alive, but Radetich had ruined her plan so that the situation stood as it was.

Madame Atomos pulled herself together, aware that all eyes were on her, and waved Tom over. "Tear gas," she croaked.

She felt like her larynx was crushed, her vocal chords forever damaged, and something snapped in the most troubling way when she swallowed.

She pointed at the hangar and in a voiceless whisper that Tom had to lean closer to hear, "Get her out of that building no matter what. If she keeps shooting, the sound of her gunfire will end up bringing Smith Beffort and his men here. But don't kill her!" She paused before making the effort to continue, "When you get her, take her to the basement. Whoever captures her can do what they want with her. Go!"

Tom went out and came back with a bag full tear gas grenades. He handed them out to five of his best men but kept two for himself. He wanted to be the first in line for the rape of Mie Beffort.

Mie landed on the ground. She got up, grabbed her machine gun and snuck along the wall. Without shoes she made no noise, but her feet were ice-cold. Staying in the shadow of the building, she anxiously examined the open ground that she would have to cross. Around 50 yards before the start of the road and the edge of the woods. An hour earlier, before the wind had chased away the clouds, it would have been easy. Now the moon was shining brightly on the smallest details of the nocturnal landscape and to go without being seen would take unimaginable luck.

She stood still, unable to decide, and heard a faint commotion coming from the other building. She craned her neck and saw dancing lights heading south. Thanks to the moonlight she also saw that the six-man commando team was keeping out of sight of the hangar. She did not know the reason for this move, but she understood that it was creating a diversion that she could not pass up.

She backed away, farther and farther, using the corner of the wall as a screen between her and the other building. After 15 yards her blind spot to the men behind the hangar was finished. Since it was impossible to avoid being seen by someone, all she could do now was run. She did so boldly, sprinting without looking back, until she reached the safety of the trees without hearing the shouts of alarm that she feared. She stopped to catch her breath. If she got out of this, it was thanks to Radetich who had made the ultimate personal sacrifice, twice. In the end he died and Mie could not let his death be futile by getting herself caught.

She glided between the tree trunks, just off the neglected road. Brambles stuck to her clothes and her feet were bleeding, but she was in a state where she felt no pain.

Four or five loud bursts came from the camp, which she recognized right away: grenades! At the same time she realized that the commando team had probably circled the hangar from the south and climbed onto the roof to drop tear gas in through the broken skylight. Here again, Mie figured that luck was on her side. The commando team could just as easily have chosen to come in from the north...

She knew it would not take long for them to realized she was gone, so she left the woods and walked more easily, more quickly down the road. Within the next 15 minutes, she should find Radetich's car. He had told her that it was only 100 yards away or so and hidden from the road... and that no one could see it even in daylight!

Therefore, to find his car under such circumstances would take a miracle. Mie gave up the idea and walked faster even though the weight of the machine gun was starting to tire her. When she came around a curve she saw the lights of the roadblock Madame Atomos had mentioned. A red and white barrier with four lights blowing in the wind and signs on either side. Mie was about to step around it when the sound of an engine made her dive into the ditch. She almost ran off on foot at the idea of Madame Atomos on the hunt, but she stayed hidden when she saw that the car was coming from the other direction. The headlights shined on the barrier and the car slowed down until it stopped in front of Mie. She saw a black man get out, then Armstrong's nervous voice said, "Step on it!"

In the headlights, as well as the interior light that turned on when the door opened, Mie saw that there were five men in the car. Six counting the one moving the barrier. A walk in the park!

Mie opened fire, fast and furious. At ten feet away it was a massacre, but the hardest part was getting the corpses out of the Cadillac. After that Mie turned around, drove over her victims, and sped off toward a more civilized destination. Louis Radetich was dead, but taking out Armstrong and his men was a most satisfying revenge. Mie had to smile as she bumped down the long, straight road, which suddenly intersected with a wide highway as smooth as a pool table. A road sign informed her that she was on Route 66, not far from Wildorado, and only 20 miles from Amarillo. This, along with the emergency roadside telephone, made her smile bigger. She had been on edge for too long. She pulled up to the phone, got out of the car still holding the machine gun, and picked up the phone while keeping her eyes on the side road where an Atomos team might show up at any second.

On the phone someone coughed before reciting, "Roadside emergency here. What's the number of your post?"

"69," Mie said, "but I'm not broken down. My name is Mie Azusa-Beffort and I just escaped from Madame Atomos. Inform the dispatch at 555-6289 on the double, please!"

The guy did not shout and did not get upset. "Okay, Mrs. Beffort, don't move."

Brief as it was, Mie thought she understood why he asked her to hold the line. So, she stayed there, a little disappointed that she had not shaken him up a little, and she heard the faint murmur of voices through the phone.

It lasted a minute, then the guy came back on the line. "Mrs. Beffort?"

"I'm here."

"A car is coming for you. It's coming from Wildorado and you should see its headlights anytime now. Your husband's behind the wheel. Do you see it?"

"There it is! Oh, thank you!"

Mie dropped the telephone and the machine gun and ran up to the car in a childlike reflex that came straight from her heart. When the Malibu braked, Smith jumped out and lifted his wife in his arms. They did not say a word to each other because their lips were glued together.

In the Malibu Akamatsu and Bernitz were looking at the stars.

The van entered the camp. Madame Atomos rushed out of the building and up to Tom, who was opening the door. "Don't tell me she escaped!" At least her throat was feeling better.

Tom looked down and grumbled, "She escaped in Armstrong's car."

Madame Atomos stiffened up. "Where's Armstrong?"

Tom pointed to the van with his thumb. "In the back with the others. Mie Azusa slaughtered them at point blank range. They were dead when we got there, after the gunfire…"

Madame Atomos said nothing. She went around the truck, asked for a light and looked in without touching the six corpses piled up. Armstrong was on top. The bullets had riddled his neck, right under his chin, so his head was hanging by few strips of flesh.

Clenching her jaws Madame Atomos walked away. She did not really love Armstrong, but she felt his death like a personal offense. What's more, it was Mie, her ex-Miss Atomos, who had dealt the blow. The height of paradox!

"Madame," Tom said shyly, "I think we should evacuate the camp."

Madame Atomos nodded. It was obvious that Mie would return soon with backup. Although it would cost her, the terrible woman had to abandon her base. It was not much of a problem for her, but for her men, left to themselves, without a means of transport, in the middle of an area teeming with the forces of order, it was another story altogether…

But Madame Atomos was not sentimental. On the contrary, she hoped that the flight of 100 men would force Smith Beffort's people to give her more leeway. Still, she would not be absolutely safe. After taking the underground tunnel, she would come out in a town located inside the danger zone. Naturally she could wait there until the storm blew over, but waiting was not recommended at such a time. Plus, after Armstrong's death, as well as the others, she had no idea where the cold generator was stashed!

Mie escaped, Armstrong dead, the camp unusable. It was enough for one day and Madame Atomos would not allow the loss of the one and only sample of her new weapon. She had already forced herself to forget about the loss of Bells & Lustig and of her apartment on 15th Avenue…

"Should I give the order, Madame?" Tom asked, nervously counting the seconds tick off.

Madame Atomos looked at him without seeing him. "Do it."

"How are the men going to get out of here?"

Madame Atomos sneered. "Let them figure it out! If they didn't let Mrs. Beffort get away, we wouldn't be in this situation!"

She controlled her boiling rage, put her hand on the black's shoulder and whispered, "I have nothing against you, Tom, and I'll prove it by giving you the helicopter. Tell the pilot in secret and take whoever you want on your team. Try to get to the New Africa headquarters."

Tom was trembling with gratitude and had to hold himself back from bending down and kissing his boss' hand. An ironic spark flashed in Madame Atomos' eyes as she went back to the building. With 100 men running around the countryside and a helicopter trying to fly away, Smith Beffort would have plenty to keep him busy!

Madame Atomos went down into her own headquarters, sat in front of the radio and called the New Africa headquarters. New Africa was not too badly organized because from Louisiana they answered almost immediately.

"Madame Atomos here. Give me Colonel Roberts."

The "colonel" must not have been sleeping because he was on the line right away.

"Here," Madame Atomos said, "nothing is working out. We're evacuating camp 124 before blowing it up. Armstrong's dead. Before he died he hid the cold generator with one of your partners, but I don't know who. Find it!"

"Understood, Madame," the self-promoted Colonel Roberts said. "Can I ask if you can still count on the ten million dollars?" Quite casually he was stirring things up.

"You'll have it, Roberts, if I get my cold generator back."

"But our agreement."

"Be quiet! If your men had been better trained, better equipped and better armed, this wouldn't have happened! A Colonel Sanders, that's what you are, Roberts! And you're in charge of a bunch of chickens! Do what I say and everything will be all right. I'll call back in an hour. That should give you plenty of time to contact whoever's got the cold generator. Do you understand?"

"I understand, Madame, I understand. I was just thinking that…"

He was about to make excuses, but Madame Atomos turned him off. She swiped up the two paralyzing pistols that were her sole prize for the dark day, and set the detonator at 10. This meant that everything would blow in ten minutes, including the stragglers.

Madame Atomos locked up, lifted the trapdoor, grabbed a flashlight kept there for emergencies and climbed down into the three-foot hole to where the three tunnels met. She pressed a button that automatically closed the trapdoor and took the tunnel heading south, double time. After a half-mile she heard a quiet rumbling and knew that camp 124 was in ruins. Then the earth was shaken by a shockwave and the tunnel collapsed far behind her. Satisfied now, Madame Atomos got back on her way, covered another half-mile in ten minutes, climbed up a simple ladder and came out in the basement of her house through a trapdoor.

She stayed out of the light as she climbed up to the second floor and opened a window. Behind the hill, the fire in camp 124 was lighting up the sky. In the south shined the lights of Umbarger, a small town on Highway

60, which led directly to New Mexico through Herefort, Friona and Farwell.

But without the cold generator Madame Atomos could not take this route without turning the New Africa Organization and the A.O.F.M.A. against her. She was not totally independent anymore! This was something she had to admit with bitterness. Mie told the truth when she said that her prestige was not what it used to be. Every time she attacked the United States, it ended in failure. And after so many defeats, she was unable to rebuild the fantastic power that had once made the world tremble.

Moreover, she was alone again, almost as poor as after the destruction of Atomia Island, as if everything that had been accomplished since then was for nothing. Rejuvenated, in excellent health, Madame Atomos saw herself cornered, able to do nothing, and was almost thinking that a hostile wheel of fortune was making her pay for the offense that science had committed against mother nature by changing her into a young woman.

For a full thirty minutes Madame Atomos was buried in dark thoughts, staring into the night, questioning herself in vain about the meaning of her future life. She had fought for years to avenge the deaths in Hiroshima and Nagasaki, killed boatloads of Americans, but this did not stop the United States from prospering, as if Madame Atomos did not exist.

During this half-hour Madame Atomos understood that she had become a petty criminal and that her ultimate goal would remain a dream if she did not get her power back. Smith Beffort and his wife, the FBI and the Green Dragon Force were an iron wall that she would eventually crash into by continuing on this absurd path. She had to cross out New Africa and the A.O.F.M.A.

and step back in order to move forward, retreat in order to attack!

Madame Atomos had made her decision and breathed more calmly. She would abandon everything and start by no longer calling the New Africa HQ in Louisiana. At 1 am on December 20, Madame Atomos climbed into her speedy Javelin and headed for New Mexico.

Hiroshima! Nagasaki!

If she escaped the forces searching for her, she would become the Empress of Evil!

Chapter Twelve

After Umbarger Madame Atomos knew that getting to New Mexico would be no walk in the park. It looked like Smith Beffort had done what was necessary to block the roads leading into neighboring states because Highway 60 had a police roadblock right after the little town. Madame Atomos pulled her Javelin over to the side of the road, turned off the lights and took some time to think about it. The police were not moving. Their role was to keep people from getting through, but they did not have to work inside the perimeter where Madame Atomos and her gang were surrounded.

Madame Atomos could clear the way with her paralyzing pistols, except that would mean giving Beffort's men a trail to follow. Presently no one knew where she was and logically she should have taken off in the helicopter, which must already have been spotted by the radars. Very soon the air force would take action, the helicopter would go down in flames and the search parties would find a pile of burnt bodies. With a little luck they might believe that one of the unidentifiable corpses was hers.

But aside from this, Madame Atomos had no reason to stay here. She had to keep moving at any price, even at the risk of being stopped and recognized by a patrol, which would start a fight and eventually result in something she had no desire to do. Then, in a few hours, the sun would rise...

Madame Atomos checked her weapons. The pistol taken off Lucky Simms was almost empty, but the one from Mie Azusa-Beffort was full. Since the dreadful woman's goal was to reach Mexico and she knew that Smith Beffort would get on her back and start fighting, the sooner the better.

Madame Atomos started the engine, turned on the lights and shot off like a cannon. The blockade was nothing like a wall, just two reflective barriers with a sign that read, *Stop! Police!* But there were a dozen well-armed policemen guarding it with a number of patrol cars and the classic motorcycle duo. It was impressive and more so when the rifles started pointing at the Javelin, which was driving too fast for a law-abiding citizen. Madame Atomos giggled involuntarily when she shot her ray and cruised between the barriers, saluting the paralyzed cops as she passed by.

This first round had only been a formality, but the fight was bound to get nasty before the final bell. Madame Atomos put the pedal to the metal and sped through Dawn without seeing a living soul, and continued onto Hereford, located around 50 miles from New Mexico. She drove straight as an arrow, took a turn, and found herself less than 300 yards from a second roadblock, wisely stuck on a narrow part of the road. Madame Atomos grinded her teeth at the same time as she put on the brakes. She had to squint in the bright spotlight signaling her to stop. Then the spotlight went out and only the blinking lights of the *Stop! Police!* illuminated a barrier pole and a swarm of police and behind the checkpoint another barrier!

This time Madame Atomos had run into a far more serious obstacle. She knew that she would not get through and that a U-turn, even lightning fast, would sic the dogs of hell on her. With nothing else to do, she instinctively yanked the wheel to the right, jumped over a small ditch, and started climbing up a steep hill. A siren wailed, machine guns fired and the spotlight swept over the land.

The Javelin flew over the peak and plunged down the other side, kicking up clumps of dirt. It was all happening so fast that Madame Atomos could not control anything. She was reacting purely by reflex to steer clear of obstacles, but she could not avoid the barbed wire fence that the Javelin ran over, making an awful noise and ripping out the posts that dragged behind it like a ball and chain. Then all of a sudden the barbed wire broke, freeing the Javelin to continue its mad race across the fields and woods, avoiding trees, ditches and hedges until it chanced upon a narrow, winding, paved road that went nowhere. Madame Atomos was traumatized, but still thought of turning off her lights. The moon was bright enough for her to see the ditches, but not for her to read the road signs. In fact, she had no idea whether she was heading back east or continuing on to New Mexico!

After driving straight through a sleepy town whose name she did not recognize, she saw a light bouncing around in her rear-view mirror. Given the circumstances, it could only be a police motorcycle, shrewder or luckier than his colleagues. Madame Atomos sped up, taking risks, and missed a hairpin turn that landed her in the countryside. A treeless countryside with muddy ground where the wheels of the Javelin spun around, revving the engine. Curtains! Lights out!

Madame Atomos got out, pistols aimed and ready, fully aware that she was not dressed to play the guerrilla warrior. A fur coat, high heels and a miniskirt! Awful! Through woods and bushes, she would soon be torn to shreds…

But the over-eager motorcycle cop solved her problem by taking the turn at a reasonable speed. The paralyzing ray petrified him on his bike, which continued rolling straight ahead before it toppled over near the Javelin with its engine screaming. Madame Atomos turned it off, shed her fur coat, not without a twinge of regret, and started undressing the policeman. She was familiar with motorcycles…

20 minutes later a motorcycle cop entered Friona. Unless you took a really close look, it was impossible to imagine that the helmet, the sunglasses and leather clothes were disguising the greatest criminal of all time. Madame Atomos got her bearings and headed for Bovina on the two-wheeled beast. Now in addition to the paralyzing pistols, she had the 38 special that she had christened by killing the policeman before throwing his body into a deep hole. Even if they found the Javelin, since dead men don't talk, it would take a while before Beffort and his men suspected the truth.

Now Madame Atomos was on her way, but not as much as she figured because the gas was starting to splash around between her thighs, a clear sign that the tank was emptying fast. Of course, Madame Atomos knew she could not fill up at a pump! A motorcycle cop with a high-pitched voice—there was no way!

The bike got her into Wilsey, coughed and died on a small, deserted, silent street. Madame Atomos hid it under a porch and wandered around, dragging her feet because of the big boots that had replaced her heels. Someone was sure to notice her like this. It was infuriating to be on foot and only ten miles from New Mexico! It was 3:30 am and the alarm must have been given a long time ago to Smith Beffort, the Green Dragon Force and company. If they did not know that Madame

Atomos was on a bike, they at least knew that she was somewhere within a small area.

A blinking light appeared and Madame Atomos jumped behind an embankment and watched the police car cruise slowly by, shining its spotlight on the shadow zones now and again. Apparently they were searching inside an ever-shrinking circle.

Madame Atomos ran to another street when the taillights had disappeared and spotted a drab sign: Hotel Serena. At this time of night it was a godsend! Madame Atomos went into the lobby where she saw a receptionist napping behind the counter. Without waking him up she paralyzed him, closed the front door and walked up to the rooms. In front of room 26 were two pairs of shoes, one of which was a woman's. Madame Atomos tried them on and smiled because they fit. Then she knocked hard on the door. They must have been sleeping well because she had to keep knocking before a sleepy voice asked what she wanted.

"Police!" Madame Atomos grunted. "ID check!"

It was bad acting, but at this hour the guest was not listening closely. He groaned, got up and went to open the door. Before he even had time to be surprised, he was paralyzed. Madame Atomos snuck in through the door and closed it behind her.

"What is it, John?"

Sitting in bed, the young woman's scream was caught in her throat by the paralyzing ray. She sat there with her mouth gaping and a stupid look on her face. Madame Atomos turned on the lights before searching the dresser and suitcase. She found a very pretty beige outfit that fit like a glove, complete with a mink coat, a very elegant hat with a veil and fur-lined half-boots. The veil did not go with the rest, but it would serve well to obscure her face.

She grabbed Isa Tucson's ID and the car keys and since she did not want to wake up the hotel by killing them, she bound and gagged them. Once this was done, she turned off the lights, locked the door behind her and went down the stairs carrying the suitcase, like any other traveler. Downstairs the receptionist was still sleeping. Since he was sleeping when Madame Atomos had arrived, he would remember nothing.

Madame Atomos opened the door, looked around the street and quickly spotted the Tucsons' car. It was a new Oldsmobile Cutlass Supreme that started up right away and glided onto Highway 60. Six miles down the road Madame Atomos saw a third roadblock appear in her headlights. She was pretty much expecting it but still felt butterflies in her stomach. She pulled up to the *Stop! Police!* sign where she veered off into the control lane, one hand on the butt of her paralyzing pistol, ready for anything, especially the unexpected.

A police officer came up waving his hand. Madame Atomos lowered her window, "What's happening, officer?"

The cop tried to pierce the secret of the veil, but his gaze was diverted by the generous offer of a bare thigh. He was young and susceptible to such sights and so forgot that a veil at four in the morning was suspicious… "Your ID, please."

Madame Atomos' left hand dug into her bag and brought out the ID. The officer took it, asked for the car registration and received it right away. Then he checked the license plates, front and back, opened the trunk and inspected it for a long time. Madame Atomos saw another policeman come up, but the others remained at their post, fingers on their triggers. She knew that her freedom was hanging by a thread.

"Could you get out, Madame? We'd like to search your car."

The other policeman was a lieutenant with gray hair, a sharp eye and extremely wary. Madame Atomos was holding the 38 special and had a pistol under her fur coat. She did not have time to slip the other into her bag because the lieutenant was opening the door, forcing her to step out. Standing between the two barriers in the cold light of the lanterns, she felt naked.

At a sign from the lieutenant two policemen started searching the car carefully, like customs officers. Madame Atomos turned up the collar of her coat and hunched her shoulders, as anyone would do in the bitter cold and icy wind. The first officer walked by and gave her papers to the lieutenant without saying a word. After scrutinizing them he looked at Madame Atomos and asked, "Where are you coming from?"

"From Wilsey."

The lieutenant put a lazy finger on the butt of his 38 in the holster. "How come the other roadblocks didn't register you? You live in Abilene. To get to Wilsey, you'd have to…"

"Who said I came directly from Abilene?" Madame Atomos interrupted coldly, despite her growing anxiety. "I just came from the Serena Hotel where I spent the night. Call them, lieutenant. The receptionist was sleeping when I left, but he'll confirm that I was there, as well as my husband."

"Why isn't your husband with you?"

"It's because he's sick that we stopped at the Serena. I'm going to a funeral at 10 o'clock in Bernardo. Since it's my father, you'll understand why I'm traveling at night, won't you?" This seemed innocent enough, but it explained the hat and veil.

"Nothing in the car, lieutenant."

The lieutenant gave her back her papers. "You can get back on your way, Mrs. Tucson. I'll inform the checkpoint at Farwell so you won't have to explain so much."

"Thank you," Madame Atomos mumbled. She got back in the car, closed the door, drove around the barrier and sped up as she watched the roadblock vanish in her rear-view mirror. She was terribly, fantastically lucky and this put her in a good mood.

Hiroshima! Nagasaki! She could start singing...

The helicopter had been brought down by a fighter jet over Palo Duro Canyon and the rescue squad had, in fact, found nothing but charred bodies. But no one had thought for a second that Madame Atomos was among the victims. They knew she was too smart to trust her precious life to a machine bound for destruction.

Madame Atomos' guards, a motley crew, was scampering through the countryside trying to throw off the dogs on their heels. The men had nothing more urgent to do than throw away their arms and Owen Bernitz, who had arrested a dozen of them, said, "The poor guys, just stupid enough to find Papa Mao's book intelligent."

Nevertheless, Madame Atomos was not out of the woods yet because the teleprinters were typing like crazy between Amarillo and Lubbock, from Sante Fe to Albuquerque. By radio and telephone they were following up on the countless traces of Madame Atomos.

In the Malibu Smith Beffort, Akamatsu and Witter had just left the Serena Hotel and were heading for New

Mexico. They got to the Farwell roadblock, stopped the car and got out. "Smith Beffort," he introduced himself.

The lieutenant straightened up.

"So tell me about this Mrs. Tucson," Smith spoke a little menacingly.

The lieutenant could see that he was going to have bitter pill to swallow. "She passed by around 4 am. Her ID and appears were all in order."

"Naturally you saw her face?"

"She was in mourning and a veil…"

"That was Madame Atomos, lieutenant! Madame Atomos in the flesh and blood! She was driving an Olds Supreme, wearing a beige outfit, a fur coat and half-boots! Thanks to you she's an hour and a half ahead of us! This may seem like only 90 minutes to you, but for a woman like her, it's like a whole day!"

He was furious and would have bawled him out longer if Mie had not brought him back down to earth. "Smith! They just found the Oldsmobile in Elida, New Mexico, 125 miles from the border!"

Beffort left the poor lieutenant standing there and got back behind the wheel where he heard Stutton at 555-6289 saying, "The engine was still warm and then some guy named Owen reported his car stolen, a white Ford Fairlane. The whole sector is under surveillance and they're checking all the cars driving on 70. Do you read me, Yellow Mask?"

"Loud and clear, Ralph," Smith responded. "Where are you?"

"Just left Hereford."

"Keep on going and round up the Green Dragon Force! If Madame Atomos gets into Mexico, we'll lose her for sure!"

He signed out and turned the Malibu loose. The speedometer was quickly pushing 150. No, Madame Atomos was not out of the woods yet!

Chapter Thirteen

Madame Atomos entered Roswell at eight in the morning. Instead of abandoning the white Ford Fairlane in a parking lot, she took it to a garage for a tune-up. Like that the car would be hidden from the search parties for a few hours. She was feeling good, but she still did not have eyes in the back of her head. The police were pretty much everywhere and to tell the truth she was rather surprised to have come so far so easily. However, she would have bet that it would not last. They were going to give her description on the police band, if they had not already done it, and what had been her great disguise would stick out like a sore thumb. It was not every day, especially during the week, that a young woman walked around with a veil hanging from her hat. This veil was the first thing she threw in the gutter. Next came the hat at the corner and then Madame Atomos hid out in a dark corner of the bus station until 9 o'clock.

No one paid any special attention to her, which meant that the public at large was not yet informed by the newspapers or radio. It was obviously a ploy by Beffort who knew that she was not listening in on him and so he was hiding the trap he was preparing. It was fair game, too fair, because Madame Atomos was terribly hampered by the lack of information.

At 9 o'clock Roswell woke up. The offices and shops opened and a few buses took off from the station. Madame Atomos did the same and mingled with the crowd to stay incognito until she found a shop to buy new clothes and change her look with a sweat suit and sport shoes and a good solid coat. She stuffed Mrs. Tucson's fur and clothes into a box and went back out to the street. Later, she emptied the box into a locker, went to a shopping mall and dropped a few more bills on a stage makeup kit, a tennis racket with a cover and small suitcase with the initials P.A.A.

Madame Atomos, hunted but with a pocket full of cash, epitomized the Japanese proverb that said *jigoku no sata mo kané shidaï*.[8]

At 10 o'clock Madame Atomos got lost in the crowd at the train station, went down to the bathrooms, rented a private room for two hours for 4.20 dollars and shut herself in. Alone in the air-conditioned, sound-proofed room she treated herself to a very hot bath, thoroughly dried herself off and opened the makeup kit to start transforming herself into a young black woman. This was nothing new—she was just redoing what had worked so well in her flight from Santa Cruz[9]. It took her a full hour before the mirror reflected a completely black body. Satisfied, Madame Atomos got dressed, tucked her long hair into a cute beret and set a pair of lightly tinted sunglasses on her nose.

At 11:45 she left the station. Her clothes, tennis racket and little suitcase made her look like an athlete on a trip. Except that if they checked her Madame Atomos could not present any ID. So, she had to work cautiously, not take risks, but without going overboard with it either. He who doesn't move forward, moves backward. Even if bad luck was waiting by the side of the road, Madame Atomos had to keep going to Mexico.

The street hawkers were running around outside waving the special Atomos edition. Public enemy No. 1

---

[8] Even Hell takes money to get through.
[9] See *The Mark of Madame Atomos*.

had her face all over the front page, as well as her complete description on page 2, followed by pages 3 and 4 detailing her exploits since she left camp 124. This time Smith Beffort was letting the dogs loose.

Madame Atomos walked along reading the newspaper and went into a drugstore to listen to the radio, which was informing the public that the roads going south were closed and the US-Mexico border would not be easy to get through, etc. Then a last minute bulletin announced that the white Ford Fairlane had just been found in a garage in Roswell... Madame Atomos gulped down her Coke, but stayed glued to her stool. Things were happening fast, too fast, and Beffort's people were not putting all their eggs in one basket.

The radio broadcast a soppy little tune before a nervous reporter started questioning the mechanic who had reported the Ford. "Mr. Prewitt, tell our listeners how Madame Atomos came into your garage."

"Lickety-split. And I knew right away that something was fishy. But I had no idea that..."

"And yet you just said that there was something troubling about this woman?"

"Yeah, her eyes!"

Madame Atomos felt sickened and left without listening to the rest. She grabbed her racket and suitcase, but hesitated a minute on the sidewalk before deciding to take immediate action. She hailed a cab and got taken to the airport. As soon as she got there, she knew that she would not be able to get a ticket on a regular flight. The airport was teeming with policemen and G-men, checking everyone's ID regardless of their age, sex or race. Madame Atomos did not go in. Instead, she bought a map of the city and studied it for a long time. After that the fugitive got on a bus going south, to the end of the line, which was not far from the private airstrip of the flying club that she had noted.

Madame Atomos went on foot, feeling like she had never been so vulnerable with only her paralyzing pistols and none of her deadly gadgets that had until now got her out of sticky situations. For a woman of her caliber, it was tough.

At 12:55 she entered the parking lot of the airstrip where only two cars sat. It was calm. It was quiet. A heavy serenity like in the suburbs at dinnertime. Madame Atomos walked to the office, rang the bell and opened the door as she was told to do. Inside was a sturdy, tanned fellow with sky-blue eyes. "What can I do for you?"

Madame Atomos put down her suitcase, slipped her hand into her pocket and around the butt of the 38. Of course, she did not forget to smile or stick out her chest while doing this. Since the guy did not seem turned off by the color of her skin, she figured there was no reason to play the little black girl who loved southern Whites. "I've got a championship match in Los Alamos and the first round starts at 3 pm. Can I charter a plane?"

The guy looked surprised. "It's always possible, but you'd get there on time with a regular airline and it'd cost less."

"I just came from the airport. No seats available."

The guy looked up at the clock and combed his hand through his hair. "I see…"

"What do you see?" Madame Atomos snapped. "I can pay. Do you want to work or not?"

Blacks had changed over the past few years, but they still remained well behaved, with a kind of atavistic humility that the next generation would not be able to wipe out completely. This girl must have been somebody in the tennis world to sneer at him like this. But then again, she was a real looker.

The guy smiled, "It's not that, Miss. Let's just say you came at a bad time. I'm alone here and the pilots won't be back until two. To get to Los Alamos in time would be cutting it mighty thin."

Madame Atomos managed to keep her smile and nodded toward the parking lot. "Do you always drive two cars?"

"The other belongs to the mechanic."

"It's because I'm black, isn't it?"

"Don't be stupid! I swear there's no one here but the mechanic and me. Wait for the pilots to get back and we'll get you wherever you want to go."

The single eye of the 38 stared at the man. "I won't wait, young man," Madame Atomos assured him. "Get your mechanic on the horn. Get him over here right away and don't say anything stupid. I've got an itchy trigger finger."

The guy shook his head in disbelief. "All this to play tennis! You're a little crazy, aren't you?"

Madame Atomos took off her beret and sunglasses. She showed her slanted eyes and straight hair. "Have you seen me anywhere before?"

He guy stood up slowly. He was not smiling anymore and even lost a little of his tan. Her skin color was all off, but all the rest fit perfectly with the description of Madame Atomos. "You're Madame Atomos."

"I am. The mechanic. Anytime now."

The man picked up the phone, dialed a two-digit number keeping his eye on the 38 aimed at him, and said very slowly and clearly, "Joe? Can you come over for a minute... No, just something you have to sign... Yes, right now." He hung up and stood frozen.

"Sit down," Madame Atomos ordered. "And don't be a hero when your pal gets here. You married?"

"Yes."

"Children?"

"Three."

"Well, think about them before doing anything stupid. A good life insurance policy is no substitute for a father or husband."

Footsteps came hurrying along the gravel outside. Madame Atomos slipped over to the wall next to the door and hid her weapon under her coat.

Joe entered without knocking, still wiping his hands with a rag. He kicked the door shut while saying, "You're starting to piss me off with all your papers, Jack."

He saw the expression on his friend's face and turned around to find Madame Atomos and her 38. Jack said, "Stay calm, Joe. It's Madame Atomos."

She was happy to see the effect that her name made and said, "Okay, I want to go to Mexico on the shortest, fastest route. We're going to leave now and don't tell me you don't have a plane ready to take off. Move it!"

She stepped away to let the two men pass by and followed a safe distance behind as they rounded the hangar. She had left her tennis racket and suitcase, but she had put back on the beret and sunglasses. At the start of the runway there were a dozen tourist planes lined up. The two men headed straight for one of them and stopped. The plane was a brand new Wrach 1006 five-seater, twin-engine.

The mechanic looked at Madame Atomos. "It almost flies by itself. I checked it this morning and filled it up. With this you'll be in Mexico in less than two hours."

Madame Atomos had an unpleasant, wry smile. "*We'll* be in Mexico in less than two hours," she corrected. "And you're going to fly it almost by itself. Come on, get in!"

They looked at each other and scrambled on board. With Madame Atomos it was better not to argue because she turned out corpses faster than a sewing machine made stitches.

Madame Atomos made them back up to the cockpit before climbing on herself and shutting the door. She had just succeeded in the first part of her plan without any trouble and this was a good omen. It would probably go as smooth as ice until the Mexican border. Airplanes had not been grounded in New Mexico, which had surprised Madame Atomos a little, but there was no reason why an order would be given anytime soon.

Madame Atomos took a map and traced a flight plan with her fingernail for Jack, who was sitting in the pilot's seat. She explained, "You'll follow this route to Nogales, then we'll hop over to Mexico and you'll head for the coast. Start the engines."

The engines roared. Madame Atomos had 600 miles and two hours before she could find shelter.

At 1:38 pm, or a dozen minutes after the Wrach 1006 took off, the centralizing station in Socorro was informed that an unidentified airplane had just flown over the north of Las Cruces. With no radio response, no flight plan and no authorization, the plane was breaking the law. Therefore, it was reported as such and because of the exceptional circumstances created by the presence of Madame Atomos, Smith Beffort was notified immediately. He reacted in the blink of an eye.

"It's her! Witter, ask for precise details from Socorro! Yosho, contact the US air force. I need a supersonic jet right now!"

The FBI bureau in Roswell went into a frenzy, but it still took 20 minutes before they knew exactly what was happening. Beffort finally learned that it belonged to the city's air club and was heading to Mexico at almost 300 miles per hour. The club's director and mechanic were missing, so they figured that Madame Atomos had taken them hostage to guarantee her safety. Killing Madame Atomos was one thing. Sacrificing two innocent people to achieve this goal was something else altogether...

The Malibu raced to the runway and pulled up to the fighter-bomber that the US air force had made available to Beffort. Then Stutton's voice came over the speaker: "The 1006's last location seems to put it heading southwest, which would bring it into Mexico through Douglas and Nogales. Got that, Yellow Mask?"

Beffort confirmed, "Okay, Stutton! Are they sure that those two guys are on the plane?"

"9 out 10 chances they are," Stutton replied. "They were still at the airstrip around 12:30 and didn't go anywhere. A taxi driver remembers a pretty young black woman going there. He remembers her because she was carrying a tennis racket. Well, a tennis racket and a suitcase with the initials P.A.A. were found in the office."

"What's that got to do with Madame Atomos?"

"In the suitcase they found a makeup kit with a pot of black cream that was almost empty."

Beffort and Mie glanced at each other. The girl in question could be Madame Atomos, but she could also be an accomplice belonging to New Africa or the A.O.F.M.A., trying to throw them off track with the

Wrach 1006. With Madame Atomos it was always very hard to know what was the truth. As it happened, Stutton's latest communication created more doubt than certainty about the presence of Madame Atomos in the twin-engine plane.

Smith told Stutton that he was getting on the bomber and so Yellow Mask would not be answering.

"What about the Green Dragon?" Stutton asked.

"Let Bernitz and his boys keep searching. When we get up to the Wrach, we'll see if it's really Madame Atomos on board. If so, Bernitz can give up. Wait for my instructions. Over and out."

He got out of the Malibu and walked up to the bomber with Mie, Akamatsu and Witter right behind him. Mie hurried up to him. "Smith, I hope you're not forgetting about the weapons she's got?"

"Paralyzing pistols, I know."

"Up to 500 yards. If our plane gets inside that range and Madame Atomos is on the Wrach…" She left the sentence unfinished, but everyone knew that the bomber would crash to the ground if Madame Atomos paralyzed its occupants.

Smith opened his arms and shrugged. "It's a risk, but we have to take it. We're not going to let Madame Atomos get away, are we?"

It was a rhetorical question and he did not wait for an answer before climbing onto the plane. From now on, whatever happened, the dice were cast.

Chapter Fourteen

Madame Atomos took her bearings and smiled. The 1006 was going to fly over the border in two minutes. As far as the eye could see the sky was empty, but the alert would be given when the plane flew into Mexican air space. This was expected, inevitable, but Madame Atomos figured it was the lesser of evils. She was already nearing her goal.

She changed seats, sat behind Joe and said, "Get your radio working. No need to identify yourself. Call M.W.0.99 for M.A.66."

She had exchanged the 38 for a paralyzing pistol, but was sitting far enough behind the two men to keep them from trying to surprise her. Moreover, her attitude discouraged such boldness. Joe turned on the radio, sent the message a few times and signaled that his call was not being answered.

Madame Atomos tensed up. "Try again!"

The mechanic began again, kept it up for two minutes, then shook his head. He leaned forward, keeping his headphones away from the sinister woman, hoping that she would not hear the calls that M.W.O.99 was yelling out. But his hopes were dashed.

"Let me sit there and you go sit in the second row."

Joe stood up and dropped the headphones, ready to try something, but changed his mind when he saw the pistol staring at him and Madame Atomos just out of reach.

She burst out laughing at him. "Well, stay calm. I really don't want to kill you, but if you give me good reason… When I've gotten off your plane, you'll be free to go home. Go and sit down like a good boy."

Joe went to the second row and sat down. Madame Atomos pressed the trigger. There was a flash of light and a soft sizzling sound.

Jack swung around, very pale. "You killed him!"

"No. He'll be paralyzed for an hour. I can't deal with the radio and watch both of you at the same time, can I?"

She brushed by the pilot, sat in the other seat and slipped on the headphones. Jack got raging mad and started a nosedive. Madame Atomos threatened him with her weapon.

"Go ahead! Like that we'll crash nice and easy!" He pulled up at the mountaintop and banked away. He had just discovered the power he held. "You can't fly and you don't have a parachute to jump out of this plane! What's to stop me from landing in Nogales?"

"You're starting to annoy me," Madame Atomos said calmly.

"Could be, but you've got to admit I've made a point."

Madame Atomos shrugged, grabbed her 38 and put a bullet in his head. Jack slowly slumped over and she helped him fall by pulling him toward her. Then she took the commands, gained a little altitude and got back on her way. Where did this idiot come up with the idea that she could not fly? Her last escape from the trap in Oakland had been related in all the papers. And now she had a parachute.

Madame Atomos turned on the automatic pilot, dragged the corpse to the back of the plane and went to sit back down. Now the plane was over New Mexico and strange as it seemed, no US air force jet fighter had shown up to intercept her. It was not normal. A gnawing concern arose in her. She scrutinized the sky, saw nothing, and this worried her more than reassured her. Smith Beffort was not the kind of man to be fooled by such rudimentary tactics as she had used to get out of Roswell. Madame Atomos was certain that the 1006 was being closely watched.

They had not attacked because of the two men on board, so they were waiting for her to touch down. Now, Madame Atomos had no intention of doing this. She concentrated, watched the skies again and ended up making out a tiny spot shining behind her. Of course she knew that this plane was looking for her but had not yet spotted her. The 1006 was camouflaged by the mountains and forests, which were very thick in the area. Moreover, the nosedive that the 1006 had taken at Jack's whim must have slipped it under the radars. By keeping a low altitude, Madame Atomos would increase her chances.

She started playing leapfrog with the ragged mountaintops, then put back on her headset and sent out her message: M.A.66 here! Calling M.W.0.99!"

The response came back in a flash: "M.W.0.99 here! Why'd you stop your messages, M.A.66?"

"Technical problems," Madame Atomos said. "Are you ready to pick me up?"

"We've been waiting for you since yesterday. Everything's ready, but you're flying too far from point X.35 where we thought we had to get you. You can see on your map that you've strayed off to Santa Ana. Head back to X.35."

"Will do. Description?"

"800-yard grassy runway bordered by trees on all sides. You have to come in from the east to use the slope to slow down."

The man had a Japanese accent, but spoke in English out of habit. Madame Atomos resorted to their native tongue for the rest of the conversation.

High up in the sky on board the fighter-bomber Smith Beffort had cancelled the order to approach when he heard the all too familiar voice of Madame Atomos echo through his headphones. He waved to his partners that the 1006 was indeed carrying their fearsome enemy and tried to listen to the rest of the conversation, but because of Madame Atomos' initiative to speak Japanese he did not understand a word. He ripped off the headphones and gave them to Akamatsu.

"Silence," Yosho said with a furrowed brow.

"She was speaking Japanese!"

"Maybe, but she's not talking now..."

Smith slammed his fist into the palm of his hand. "Damn! I'm sure her last words gave some crucial information that we desperately need right now! All I understood was that she had to land at some mysterious point X.35 and that it wouldn't be easy because the runway's only 800 yards long."

The pilot turned around. "She might be able to land, but not us. We've got to strike before it's too late, Sir!"

"And kill two innocent people at the same time!"

The pilot turned back. Far away, skimming the mountains, he saw the Wrach 1006 that was soaring calmly toward the southwest. Compared to the fighter the 1006 was a tortoise. The pilot knew that he could bring her down on the first flyby.

Smith saw what he saw. "Don't get excited, major. Madame Atomos can't escape us. She'll run out of fuel before us and if she lands, she'll be surrounded by the Mexican police."

"It's a big forest," the pilot complained.

"Sure, but if she can't get out of it, I'll be satisfied. The main thing is to keep her from doing more damage, which we've done. Then, even if we have to mobilize the entire Mexican army, we'll find her."

Akamatsu grimaced. "She has accomplices, Smith. And it looks like they must be organized. They have a radio, secret land, probably a way to hide Madame Atomos as long as necessary. Maybe you should get the advice of James Edward Evans…"

"About what?"

Akamatsu watched the skies. "Madame Atomos' two hostages will be executed when the 1006 touches down. Considering that, maybe we'd do better to preempt it by killing two birds…"

"No!" Smith cut him off. "My mission is to defend Americans, not to use them to further my own plans against Madame Atomos! As long as I'm in charge, no one's going to touch that airplane!"

He leaned over and examined the land through his binoculars. Highway 15 snaked narrowly through the bush and the Rio Sonora unwound farther south. To the west, but still pretty far away, was the Gulf of California, a region where Madame Atomos had sown fear and death a few years earlier when she was master of Atomos City and a thousand servants with motor-brains.

The dreadful woman must have kept a refuge from that time, maintained by people devoted to her cause, and her return to the shores of the Gulf of California owed nothing to chance. It was a return to her origins in a way because it was clear that the A.O.F.M.A. did not know about other small, independent groups. Nevertheless, it also proved that Madame Atomos had an escape route in reserve and that she was abandoning two of her organizations—New Africa and the A.O.F.M.A.—that could no longer rely on her destructive power.

A movement behind him shook Beffort out of his thoughts. He turned around and saw that the radio operator was waving a message at him. "Direct from Washington," he said.

Beffort took the message and clenched his jaws as he read: *Order from the White House in agreement with the Mexican government authorizing the mission over its territory: Shoot down the Wrach 1006 without delay. Stop. Take no account of hostages. Stop. Report immediately. Stop. Washington, 15.30 GMT. Stop.*

Without saying a word, Smith gave the message to the commanding officer and everyone went to battle stations.

Madame Atomos spotted point X.35, finished buckling up her parachute and almost screamed when she saw the bright silver flash of a military plane closing in on her like an eagle on its prey. She banked, dove, saw the missiles and felt the 1006 shake on impact. She had the feeling that the world was keeling over. This lasted a fraction of a second, then Madame Atomos' vision cleared. The 1006 was still in the air, by the side of a mountain, the fighter was already starting to turn for a second pass. Madame Atomos looked down at the X.35 terrain, which was like a clearing, and saw a man waving his arms. He heard the fighter coming back and jumped into the trees. Madame Atomos forced herself to stay calm as she watched the fighter return like she was watching death approach. Maybe she could not avoid the attack, but one thing was for sure, the fighter could not turn on a dime!

Madame Atomos counted 40 seconds and pushed the stick when the fighter lit up with orange flashes. A din of smashed metal and the 1006 nosed up as its left engine exploded in flames. The altimeter read 1300 feet. The fighter raced by.

Madame Atomos opened the door and jumped, dropping like a stone. She counted again up to ten, pulled the handle and her parachute shot open as the landscape leveled off. She was falling into the clearing, but the fighter would be turning around by now. Down below, the man was waving more frantically and she could hear him yelling. At the same time the fighter made a big circle and 1006 listed to the side, toward the mountain, in a trail of fire and black smoke that the wind blew into her parachute. Madame Atomos continued falling between walls of smoke and hearing the super-sonic engines scream in the distance, but the sound of its gunfire was lost in the wind.

Astonished, Madame Atomos could not believe her luck until her feet touched the ground. She tucked and rolled merrily in the dry grass before she was seized by two powerful hands and a voice said in Japanese, "Let me do it, Madame!"

She was out of the straps in no time. Then she was picked up and held tightly against a stout chest. The man ran into the forest, panting, growling like a fantastically strong animal. Madame Atomos was slapped by the low branches, but she heard the incredible explosion as she was thrown to the ground with her bearer by the blast from the bomb. Debris rained down around them and another bomb exploded farther away.

"Follow me!"

The smoke cleared. Madame Atomos ran behind her savior, crossed a stream, a path, and then a road. All of a sudden the man stopped and threw himself to the ground, covering her, while hell ravaged the forest, smashing trees and ripping off the high branches that hissed down on them. In a daze, Madame Atomos pushed the man who was suffocating her, tried to speak, but remained speechless on seeing everything catch fire.

"Napalm!"

Lifted up with one arm, Madame Atomos pulled herself together in time to realize that she was on the move again, literally being dragged behind the man, who was swearing up a storm. He lifted her to jump over a bank and set off again, bellowing and howling. Madame Atomos was lost, tried to keep up, but her legs started buckling under her. Her clothes were in shreds; she had no more shoes; no more weapons; and tears were running down her cheeks.

She gathered her strength and shouted, "Stop!"

Miraculously, the whole infernal hullaballoo ceased.

Madame Atomos stared into the night, the calm, and squinted when a little, dancing light pierced the dark. Then the circle of light grew bigger, wider, filled the cave, revealing a cot, shelves full of provisions, guns lined up against the wall. In one corner was a two-way radio. In another corner were a table and three chairs. And finally there was the man.

A Japanese man, huge, knotted with muscles…

Madame Atomos flopped onto the cot, stretched out, closed her eyes and asked, "Who are you?"

"Isadori, Madame. I was the one on the radio with you."

"Shh. Where are we?"

"At post X.35, Madame."

The giant was polite and his way of speaking belied a certain culture. Madame Atomos opened an inquisitive eye. She was half-naked and Isadori's clothes were badly affected by the mad race through the forest. Still full of emotion, Madame Atomos examined her savior more closely.

"Thank you, Isadori. I owe you my life."

The giant leaned over, his hands cupped together, and said, "Thanks to God. He allowed a poor gardener to save the most beautiful flower in his garden."

It was spoken sweetly. Madame Atomos giggled. A small spark lit up behind her dark eyes. She waved to the man to come closer. "When do we have to leave here?"

"Later tonight, Madame. The fighter-bomber will keep pounding the forest and the army and Mexican police will start searching through it. And I know that a few helicopters are waiting in Santa Ana and Hermosillo. They'll be joining the hunt and maybe some dogs will be sniffing out our trail. If you don't want to die, we have to stay here for now. If you're hungry, I can get you something to eat. If you're thirsty, I can prepare some tea. In short, Madame, I'm at your service."

Madame Atomos was swimming in it. She raised herself on one elbow, put her long-nailed hand on the giant's chest and whispered, "I'm hungry and thirsty, Isadori, but first I very much want to show you my appreciation. Come here."

There was no mistake about it. Madame Atomos knew how to say the right things in the right way. The man leaned over again. "Madame, you're making me the happiest of all your servants."

Madame Atomos smiled. She loved it.

Isadori leaned over and caressed Madame Atomos with stunning gentleness, taking off her rags one by one, careful of the sensitive parts of the magnificent body offered to him. Then he lay down next to her...

Madame Atomos moaned with pleasure, kissed the Japanese man and, in a word, surrendered to him. A delight.

Chapter Fifteen

In the wreckage of the 1006 that had crashed into the side of the mountain, they had found two half-burnt corpses. With the preliminary examination they knew that one of them had been shot in the head. The other had no wounds, but let himself burn without reacting. The parachute that Madame Atomos had used was lying like a wilted flower on the X.35 runway. Its straps had been cut with a razor. They found nothing around it but bomb craters, uprooted trees and piles of earth. A lunar landscape.

With his hands in his pocket Smith Beffort contemplated all this with a jaded eye. The forest was teeming with soldiers and helicopters were ceaselessly patrolling the skies. In the distance, dogs were barking at nothing. Because of the napalm, the craters and the ravaged ground, they could not find a trace. They went round and round the clearing, chasing things that had nothing to do with Madame Atomos.

Mie took her husband's arm. "We're losing, aren't we, Smith?"

"Washington lost," Smith corrected. "The guys in the White House are going to whoop it up and call it a victory. In reality, no one can say with certainty whether Madame Atomos is dead or alive."

Witter spit. He was furious. "She's alive!" he declared. "She intended to jump all along, not land the plane, and everything was set up for her on the ground."

Akamatsu lit a cigarette. "If it weren't for all the smoke, she'd be at our mercy. But you have to admit that she always gets unbelievably lucky."

His discouragement came through in every word and he did not try to hide it. Time was passing. Hundreds of searchers were checking the forest, but nothing had been found to confirm or deny the death of Madame Atomos.

Finally at 5:10 pm a captain leading a group of policemen came into the clearing. He dropped a bag at Beffort's feet and said, "Look what we picked up."

Smith opened the bag and saw a pair of shoes, two paralyzing pistols, a 38 special and pieces of muddy, burnt clothing. Mie squatted down and put together almost an entire suit and half a coat.

"Not one drop of blood!" she said with astonishment.

Beffort snickered. "She lost her clothes, shoes and weapons, but the machine guns and napalm didn't touch her. Now I'd bet my life she's hiding somewhere around here. But night's falling…"

Mie stood up holding strips of clothes that obviously did not belong to Madame Atomos. The fabric was rougher. Between two fingers she held out a shirt sleeve ripped off at the shoulder.

Akamatsu whistled. "The guy wearing this shirt is a big boy. Look, Smith, it's almost as long as my two arms."

"A giant, eh?" Witter grumbled. "That's all we need. Maybe Madame Atomos is going to attack the USA with an army of giants. Not that a fellow that big could go unnoticed."

Akamatsu furrowed his brow and guessed, "He's probably over six and a half feet tall. Smith, don't you think this guy might be a lead?"

Beffort shrugged. "We knew about Ida Brown, Costello and Armstrong and we were counting on them to lead us to Madame Atomos. Now, they're all dead and Madame Atomos is still running around."

Mie looked hard at her husband. "You don't know that, Smith. Maybe her corpse is lying at the bottom of a crater covered with debris. Maybe you're just imagining her alive and far away, resting up on the edge of the forest."

Smith smiled. "That's a lot of maybes, Mie. In fact, we've got an unsolvable problem: Is Madame Atomos dead or alive? Personally, considering our past experience in the matter, I believe she survived." He looked up at the darkening sky. "Whatever the case, the night's going to stop our search. Let's go back to Santa Ana. We're doing nothing here."

They got into the helicopter that the Mexican authorities had left to Beffort and it took off. In Santa Ana, Smith called the main FBI bureau and was quickly on the line with J.E.E., who asked, "Where are you, Smith?"

"Santa Ana, the Magdalena Hotel," Beffort answered curtly.

"Madame Atomos?"

"Flew the coop."

Evans grinded his teeth. He had tried in vain to oppose Washington's decision, but was stonewalled by the President's secretary. He was seriously thinking of quitting and almost jumped out of his chair when Smith said, "When I get back, I'm handing in my resignation."

J.E.E.'s laugh got his hackles up. "Why are you laughing, Evans? What's so funny? To see years of hard work thrown down the drain by a bunch of deadbeats who…"

"Stop! I'm quitting too!" Evans barked.

The line went silent all of a sudden. Finally, Beffort said, "Well, if we both give up, that'll leave Madame Atomos practically unopposed. By the time our replacements learn the ropes, it'll be water under the bridge."

"That's exactly what I told myself after I calmed down, Smith. When I left the White House I was ready to chuck everything. I saw myself on a lake, fishing for pike or trout. It was really nice and it lasted right up until I pictured an Atomos horde armed with disintegrators…"

"Okay! Give it a rest!" Beffort shouted.

"You started it. Listen, Smith, I think the White House got mixed up in our business for the first time since Madame Atomos showed up because the President's only got a month to go and he wanted to put on a little show before leaving.[10] When the new President is busy with the country's affairs, he won't have time to think about us. He'll be trying to avoid a heart attack first of all, unless it's an attack on his life… So, are you staying?"

"Yes."

Evans let out a sigh of relief. "Great. Stay in Mexico with your team and find Madame Atomos for me. She can't get far. The roads are being watched and since there's not a lot of people in the area, your job should be easier."

"So you say!"

---

[10] Even though the presidential elections take place the first Tuesday in November, the new term does not start officially until January 20 the following year. This story took place in December 1968, so Richard Nixon had just been elected, but Lyndon B. Johnson was still in the White House.

"They're not empty words, Smith. The Mexican government is taking this seriously, organizing it like the Olympics[11] and we know that our neighbors to the south can be really efficient when they want. The army is centered in Sonora and they'll soon have thousands of men going after Madame Atomos. In my opinion, you've never had as many aces in the hole. Madame Atomos can't get lost in the crowd or the streets or the buildings down there. No sports cars or airplanes for her. She's left with buses and trains. But if she tries that, her life won't be worth a plug nickel."

"You ate your breakfast today, eh?"

"And you missed lunch, my friend. Get to work, Smith. I'm sure you'll get results. Goodbye."

He hung up to make sure he had the last word, but this did not stop Smith Beffort from shrugging his shoulders. With all his heart and soul he knew that Madame Atomos would escape again despite all their efforts.

Evans had not lied in claiming that the Mexican government was going all out. From Santa Ana to Hermosillo, from Bahia Kino to Desemboque, thousands of soldiers were combing the region, sector by sector, combing the highways and roads, pouring into the forests and climbing the mountains.

The towns were in a state of siege and the civilians were told over the radio to stay home. The army had received orders to shoot on sight every individual not wearing a uniform and unfortunately they had just killed some farmers coming back from the fields.

---

[11] The Olympic games had just been held in Mexico from October 12 to 27, 1968.

In the cave, Madame Atomos and Isadori were finishing their dinner in peace. The lovemaking had been only an interlude and the Japanese man went right back to being her bodyguard. Madame Atomos like his style more and more, but because time was running out, she naturally started to bare her claws.

"It's almost midnight, Isadori, and you said we were going to leave tonight."

The giant bowed. "Be patient, Madame. We'll get ready when the island station gives us the signal. If I'm not mistaken, it shouldn't be long."

Madame Atomos nibbled on a cracker, poured her fifth cup of tea and looked up when a red light started blinking on the radio. Isadori glided over, surprisingly agile for a man of his size, and flipped a switch. There was silence, then a short hiss and Isadori cut off the reception.

"What happened?" Madame Atomos asked.

"Sped up message," The Japanese said flatly. "In San Esteban they must know that the police are listening in." He fiddled with the device and started the recorder. "Now the message will playback normally."

The tape recorder made a triple beep that corresponded with the blinking lights before a voice spoke clearly in Japanese: "Island station of San Esteban to post X.35. Prepare yourselves in field dress No. 14. A car will pick you up at 0:15 hours. It can only stay at the post for a few seconds or risk serious trouble. I repeat: field dress 14 at 0:15. Out."

Isadori went to a huge closet, which Madame Atomos had not noticed because it was built into the stone wall, and slid open a heavy door. In 30 seconds two Mexican army uniforms were thrown on the ground.

"I think it should fit you, Madame. Do you want to try it on? If you tuck your hair into the helmet, you'll look perfect."

While speaking he got dressed himself and pulled out two army regulation rifles. Madame Atomos got dressed. The uniform was a little big, but it could work. She tied her big boots, tucked her hair into the helmet and stood up.

"How I look, Isadori?"

"Like a young soldier, Madame." He handed her a rifle. "It's loaded. In case you need to…"

"Don't worry, I know how to use it."

They waited until 12:12 and Isadori turned off the oil lamp, took Madame Atomos by the arm and guided her through the darkness. Madame Atomos heard a click, something slid open softly, and they were outside under the starry sky. The night was full of engines humming, dogs barking and spotlights sweeping through the forest.

Isadori flattened Madame Atomos against the rock, worked the bolt of his rifle and whispered, "A car is coming this way. Be on your guard, it might not be ours."

Madame Atomos narrowed her eyes to scrutinize the invisible strip of road. Then she was almost blinded by a pair of headlights. Isadori raised his rifle.

"Stop! San Esteban!" a Japanese voice shouted. The Jeep bounded up to them and stopped. "Get in the back!"

Madame Atomos was lifted like a feather by Isadori, who set her down in an uncomfortable seat. Isadori jumped in and the Jeep took off immediately. Madame Atomos saw two men in the front seats. The driver was disguised as a simple soldier, but the passenger was wearing the uniform and stripes of a captain. The Jeep looked like it belonged to the army, equipped with a swiveling .50 caliber machine gun and a radio whose curved antenna bobbed on every bump.

Madame Atomos mentally tipped her hat to Dr. Miwa whom she had put in charge of the San Esteban station three years earlier. He had done a remarkable job under difficult conditions and knew how to adapt to circumstances in the shortest possible time. Like the Jeep and uniforms! In the middle of the Mexican army, it was the best way to go unnoticed.

The Jeep drove for a good hour without meeting anyone before leaving the forest and heading down Highway 15, which stretched along practically the whole western coast of Mexico from Nogales to Mexico City. In Hermosillo there were nothing but troops and military vehicles. The Jeep drove through town, turned south, and got on Highway 16 that linked Hermosillo to Bahia Kino.

The 16 ended at the ocean, but before that they still had to cross the small town of Costa Rica where military checkpoints might be set up. Madame Atomos wondered what would happen if a patrol asked for their papers and when the Jeep entered the town, she wondered again.

No barriers, no checkpoints. Bottlenecks of men and machines. A huge chaos… The Jeep got through with relatively ease, left the city limits of Costa Rica, and once again headed for Bahia Kino. Madame Atomos breathed a little more freely as she snuck a peek at Isadori, who was clutching his rifle, watching in front and back, determined to defend his master to the death. Since they had left the cave, he had not uttered a word. Extraordinary!

In the front seats, the two other men were not talkative either. They just kept their eyes wide open. Madame Atomos had the feeling that Dr. Miwa knew how to keep the old Atomos structure in his organization. She had neglected Miwa. She was wrong to have done so.

15 minutes later the Jeep entered Bahia Kino and turned south before the ocean onto a rough, winding road. Isadori relaxed and leaned over, "We're there, Madame. The boat's at the end of this road."

The Jeep, all lights off, barreled down a slope, rolled onto a beach and stopped at the edge of the waves. Madame Atomos followed Isadori, who lifted her up to keep her feet dry, and stepped onto the deck of a speed-boat. A Japanese man bowed to her and led her down to a small but comfortable cabin. Madame Atomos watched the Jeep leave.

Isadori came into the room. "The Jeep," he explained, "should get back to its unit without raising any suspicions. There should be no clues for our enemies to follow."

The speedboat started its engines, shot over the waves and raced out to sea. It veered around the southern tip of Tiburon Island and headed straight for San Esteban Island, which it reached in less than ten minutes. When they landed, Isadori helped Madame Atomos step onto the pier and led her to a car that was parked close by. He opened the door and Madame Atomos got in to discover Dr. Miwa, old Japan as ever with his white moustache and lacquered skin.

She sat, smiled and held out her hand. "How are you, Miwa?"

The old man bowed his head and kissed her hand. "Better now that you're here, Madame Atomos. I've been worrying about you for a long time. But no harm can come to you now."

The car headed for the center of the island. Madame Atomos lit a cigarette offered to her by Miwa, blew out the smoke and asked, "Your work?"

The old man smiled weakly. "I'm happy to tell you that I have built a new motor-brain, microscopic, no bigger than the head of a pin. Truthfully, it can work in the brain of a small bird."

Madame Atomos started dreaming. With this new weapon she would have the United States on its knees...

Pete Rawlik: *Before the War, Five Dragons Roar*

*The Pacific Ocean, West of the Territory of Hawaii,
December 1939*

It was an hour before dawn, and the flagship of the
Oceanic Steamship Company, the *SS Claridon*, crashed
through the waves, sending a spray of dark water over
the bow. The five figures that had arranged themselves
on the deck flinched as the cold wind and water whipped
around them. There were a Japanese couple, a man and a
woman, and two Chinese men. Several yards away stood
another man, also of Japanese descent.

The Japanese man with his back to the ocean was
suave and well-groomed, with hair cut in the Prussian
manner that framed a pair of round wire-rimmed glasses.
His black suit blended into the wicked-looking pistol he
held in his right hand. Moonlight reflected off his teeth,
which some time ago had been replaced with gold dupli-
cates. His smile widened as his partner, a stern and seri-
ous-looking young Japanese woman in a conservative
black dress, spoke:

"A very clever trap, Mister Chan," there were tones
of both respect and sarcasm in the woman's voice. "Tell
me if you would, in the interest of science, what mistake
did I make?"

Lieutenant Chan shifted his considerable weight
and grinned slyly. It was as much a communication to
the two foreign agents facing him as it was to the former
FBI agent to his left and the other Japanese.

"Your attempts to divert our attention to other suspects were expertly executed, Dr. Yoshimuta," he said. "Unfortunately, both the people you attempted to frame, Mr. Gottfried Venger and Mrs. Nora Charles, had alibis for the night in question. They were engaged in a rather loud and somewhat vicious argument concerning the recent invasion of Poland by Germany. Mrs. Charles was quite enraged by Mr. Venger's support of the German Chancellor. Her husband spent the rest of the evening calming her down with several dozen martinis. Mr. Venger ended the night in the ship's lounge playing cards with Mr. Cranston and Mr. Reid."

"Those men could be lying," she proffered.

Chan's partner, James Wong, waved his gun menacingly. "They could be, Doctor, but we have our reasons for taking them at their word." He was taller than his compatriots, with graying hair and a thin haggard look that made him look older than he was. His voice was cultured and betrayed a cosmopolitan upbringing. "Only you and your friend Mr. Aratomoto—Ichirou Aratomoto that is—had both the means and opportunity to murder the aging Mr. Jak Kim back in Honolulu. Though we are still puzzled as to the motive."

The man standing to the side, nearly equidistant from the opposing factions, cautiously raised his arm. A careful observer would have noticed that he bore a striking resemblance to the man standing next to Dr. Yoshimuta, whom Wong had identified as "Ichirou Aratamoto." The glasses and haircut were the same, as were the general shape of the face and shoulders. Indeed, the differences between the two were only superficial. Kentarou Aratamoto wore a white suit, and was slightly heavier than Ichirou, and he seemed to have all his own teeth.

"Perhaps James, if you please, I can offer an explanation," he said. "Mr. Kim was not as he claimed from Korea, but was in actuality Japan's master spy, Oka Yuma."

His black-suited double, Ichirou, shook his head, though he was careful to keep the gun steady. "You will forgive me, brother," he said, "but I think you would agree that Oka Yuma's days as Japan's master spy were over long ago. He was a relic of a less sophisticated time, the memory of which the Empire would like to erase. It was most unfortunate that he had to be... liquidated."

"Lovely people you are thinking of working for, Kentarou," the prematurely aged Wong sneered. "Killing a man just because he was old."

Doctor Yoshimuta laughed sinisterly. "No, Mr. Wong, I suppose you wouldn't think of us as very nice people. We don't have that luxury. The European powers that have for so long held sway in Asia are failing, falling, fleeing. There is a void and Japan intends to fill it, first in China and then... well, we shall see, won't we? For this, we need the best. We need men who are capable, daring, unafraid, loyal. It has been many years since Kentarou has been to Japan, but he is still a child of the Rising Sun. His mother was a princess, imperial blood flows through his veins. He will come with us and, together, the Aratamoto brothers will help lead the Empire to its rightful place."

Chan lowered his gun. "Kentarou, is this what you want?" he asked. "Who was it that tried to kill you in Port Said? And when you were sick and I took your place in Panama, who was it that tried to kill me? Do you think it would have made a difference if it had been you?"

Wong chimed in, "We're your friends Kentarou. I got you that job at Berkford University, teaching Criminalistics remember? We've worked together. You've just moved to Hawaii, bought a house on Punch Bowl Hill. Charlie got you a job training the state militia. Are you going to throw that all away because this man says he's your brother?"

Kentarou Aratamoto turned to face both Chan and Wong. "You misunderstand, James" he said. "This man, Ichirou, he is my brother, my older twin, born as I was in 1894 in San Francisco. Family honor requires that I owe him some measure of fidelity."

"I am not sure that Mr. Wong understands the concept of fidelity, Kentarou san," cautioned Dr. Yoshimuta. "After all, it was Fu Wong that terrorized the city of San Francisco during the summer of 1935. How many men did your brother kill, Mr. Wong?"

Unable to control himself Chan quoted a long forgotten aphorism, "Families sometimes like large trees, can bear bitter fruit."

Dr. Yoshimuta laughed sinisterly. "That applies to you as well, Mr. Chan. Tell me, before your mother died, did she tell you who your father was?"

Chan tried to stifle his response, but she caught the moment of doubt on his face.

"I see; she didn't, but you've discovered that little secret on your own? Michael Croft is really such a transparent alias, and so easily checked. All the Manchurian had to do was to review the British peerage."

Wong straightened up. "What has the Manchurian to do with this?" he asked. "Is he involved?"

Now it was Ichirou Aratamoto's turn to be sly. "You will find, Mr. Wong, that when it comes to Asia, there is little that the Manchurian does not involve himself in, sometimes to our detriment, sometimes to our benefit. In this case, our recent campaign in Nanking gained us access to one of his strongholds. There, we found references to many things, including the lineage of Mister Chan, and of course your own plans to return to China as the Devil Doctor's ally. We assume that you have achieved what your brother could not, that you have all twelve of the Confucian coins; that you shall travel to Keelat and take up the mantle of Fen Chu? Will you seek to avenge the death of your wife Win Lee on the whole of the Empire of Japan?"

Wong's face turned to stone. "You should not have killed her, Ichirou. She would have given you the map."

Ichirou looked puzzled for a moment. "Oh, I see, it is very funny. I should tell you sometime the story of that map, and the trouble it caused. Many people died trying to find that oil. But you misunderstand; I did not kill Win Lee. Her own father did that, when he learned that she had married you, a man of low standing, a half-breed who freely served foreign masters."

Suddenly Kentarou was in motion, "*James! No!*" he shouted.

But it was too late. Enraged by Ichirou's words, James Lee Wong's gun fired a barrage of bullets at the Japanese agent who dove to the side, grabbing Dr. Yoshimuta and whisking her over the side of the boat into the darkness beyond.

Chan ran to the railing, moving at a speed one would not have thought possible for his size. As he reached the edge of the boat, he led with his gun, usually reluctant to engage in battle, but for once eager to use a weapon other than his mind. He peered over and quickly turned away. Then, like a roaring freight train, he was suddenly on top of Wong and Kentarou, whisking them back in the other direction.

Two minutes later, the deck erupted in fire, twisted metal and wooden splinters that showered down on the three men like an avalanche of destruction.

As the crew dealt with the flames and damage, the three detectives licked their wounds.

"They escaped?" queried Wong.

Chan nodded. "It was waiting for them, a small submarine with a very large gun."

Kentarou Aratamoto was attempting to brush the larger pieces of debris off of his suit. "Please, did you really think I was going to go with them?" he asked.

Wong found that a rather large metal splinter had pierced the skin between his forefinger and thumb. "It was a definite possibility," he replied. "As they said, my own family isn't exactly without its bad seeds. My nephew Richard is following in my footsteps, but my niece is making quite a reputation as San Francisco's Dragon Queen. So when you ask me whether or not I thought you would go with them, I have to say that I thought it was a definite possibility."

Chan found his hat and emptied it of debris. "I think we should perhaps discuss a more serious issue. Must explain to Oceanic Steamship Company and the captain about the hole in the bow of ship, and then tell the passengers that we must go back to Honolulu."

Kentarou smiled, "You are not concerned over what Oka Yuma, Yoshimuta and my brother were doing in Pearl Harbor?"

Chan smiled that sly smile. "Sixty-five summers has taught me much, mostly that knowledge like hole in trousers; will be revealed when time least convenient.

Am more concerned with thought that James will be leaving us for dubious venture."

James Wong hung his head. "Sadly, my path is not yet clear. I have all twelve coins, but not yet the will to wield the power they bestow. Right now, though, I could use some breakfast."

Chan nodded. "Captain tells me that ship's cook, Egg Shen, has an excellent supply of Chinese delicacies."

As the Sun rose over the stern, the three men staggered down the deck in search of a warm cup of oolong tea.

SF & FANTASY

Alphonse Allais. *The Adventures of Captain Cap*
Henri Allorge. *The Great Cataclysm*
Guy d'Armen. *Doc Ardan: The City of Gold and Lepers*
G.-J. Arnaud. *The Ice Company*
Charles Asselineau. *The Double Life*
Cyprien Bérard. *The Vampire Lord Ruthwen*
S. Henry Berthoud. *Martyrs of Science*
Aloysius Bertrand. *Gaspard de la Nuit*
Richard Bessière. *The Gardens of the Apocalypse*
Albert Bleunard. *Ever Smaller*
Félix Bodin. *The Novel of the Future*
Louis Boussenard. *Monsieur Synthesis*
Alphonse Brown. *City of Glass; The Conquest of the Air*
Emile Calvet. *In a Thousand Years*
André Caroff. *The Terror of Madame Atomos; Miss Atomos; The Return of Madame Atomos; The Mistake of Madame Atomos; The Monsters of Madame Atomos; The Revenge of Madame Atomos; The Resurrection of Madame Atomos; The Mark of Madame Atomos*
Félicien Champsaur. *The Human Arrow; Ouha, King of the Apes; Pharaoh's Wife*
Didier de Chousy. *Ignis*
Jules Clarétie. *Obsession*
Michel Corday. *The Eternal Flame*
Captain Danrit. *Undersea Odyssey*
C. I. Defontenay. *Star (Psi Cassiopeia)*
Charles Derennes. *The People of the Pole*
Georges Dodds (anthologist). *The Missing Link*
Harry Dickson. *The Heir of Dracula*
Jules Dornay. *Lord Ruthven Begins*
Alfred Driou. *The Adventures of a Parisian Aeronaut*
Sâr Dubnotal *vs. Jack the Ripper*
Alexandre Dumas. *The Return of Lord Ruthven*
Renée Dunan. *Baal*
J.-C. Dunyach. *The Night Orchid; The Thieves of Silence*
Henri Duvernois. *The Man Who Found Himself*
Achille Eyraud. *Voyage to Venus*
Henri Falk. *The Age of Lead*

Paul Féval. *Anne of the Isles; Knightshade; Revenants; Vampire City; The Vampire Countess; The Wandering Jew's Daughter*
Paul Féval, *fils. Felifax, the Tiger-Man*
Charles de Fieux. *Lamékis*
Arnould Galopin. *Doctor Omega; Doctor Omega and the Shadowmen* (anthology)
Judith Gautier. *Isoline and the Serpent-Flower*
Léon Gozlan. *The Vampire of the Val-de-Grâce*
G.L. Gick. *Harry Dickson and the Werewolf of Rutherford Grange*
Edmond Haraucourt. *Illusions of Immortality*
Nathalie Henneberg. *The Green Gods*
V. Hugo, P. Foucher & P. Meurice. *The Hunchback of Notre-Dame*
Romain d'Huissier. *Hexagon: Dark Matter*
Michel Jeury. *Chronolysis*
Gustave Kahn. *The Tale of Gold and Silence*
Gérard Klein. *The Mote in Time's Eye*
Fernand Kolney. *Love in 5000 Years*
Paul Lacroix. *Danse Macabre*
Louis-Guillaume de La Follie. *The Unpretentious Philosopher*
Jean de La Hire. *Enter the Nyctalope; The Nyctalope on Mars; The Nyctalope vs. Lucifer; The Nyctalope Steps In; Night of the Nyctalope; Return of the Nyctalope; The Fiery Wheel*
Etienne-Léon de Lamothe-Langon. *The Virgin Vampire*
André Laurie. *Spiridon*
Gabriel de Lautrec. *The Vengeance of the Oval Portrait*
Alain le Drimeur. *The Future City*
Georges Le Faure & Henri de Graffigny. *The Extraordinary Adventures of a Russian Scientist Across the Solar System* (2 vols.)
Gustave Le Rouge. *The Vampires of Mars; The Dominion of the World* (w/Gustave Guitton) (4 vols.)
Jules Lermina. *Mysteryville; Panic in Paris; To-Ho and the Gold Destroyers; The Secret of Zippelius*
André Lichtenberger. *The Centaurs; The Children of the Crab*
Jean-Marc & Randy Lofficier. *Edgar Allan Poe on Mars; The Katrina Protocol; Pacifica; Robonocchio; Return of the Nyctalope;* (anthologists) *Tales of the Shadowmen 1-9*
Xavier Mauméjean. *The League of Heroes*
Joseph Méry. *The Tower of Destiny*
Hippolyte Mettais. *The Year 5865*
Louise Michel. *The Human Microbes; The New World*
Tony Moilin. *Paris in the Year 2000*

José Moselli. *Illa's End*
John-Antoine Nau. *Enemy Force*
Marie Nizet. *Captain Vampire*
C. Nodier, A. Beraud & Toussaint-Merle. *Frankenstein*
Henri de Parville. *An Inhabitant of the Planet Mars*
Gaston de Pawlowski. *Journey to the Land of the 4th Dimension*
Georges Pellerin. *The World in 2000 Years*
Ernest Pérochon. *The Frenetic People*
Pierre Pelot. *The Child Who Walked on the Sky*
J. Polidori, C. Nodier, E. Scribe. *Lord Ruthven the Vampire*
P.-A. Ponson du Terrail. *The Vampire and the Devil's Son; The Immortal Woman*
Edgar Quinet. *Ahasuerus*
Henri de Régnier. *A Surfeit of Mirrors*
Maurice Renard. *The Blue Peril; Doctor Lerne; The Doctored Man; A Man Among the Microbes; The Master of Light*
Jean Richepin. *The Wing; The Crazy Corner*
Albert Robida. *The Adventures of Saturnin Farandoul; The Clock of the Centuries; Chalet in the Sky; The Electric Life*
J.-H. Rosny Aîné. *Helgvor of the Blue River; The Givreuse Enigma; The Mysterious Force; The Navigators of Space; Vamireh; The World of the Variants; The Young Vampire*
Marcel Rouff. *Journey to the Inverted World*
Han Ryner. *The Superhumans*
Brian Stableford. *The New Faust at the Tragicomique;The Empire of the Necromancers (The Shadow of Frankenstein; Frankenstein and the Vampire Countess; Frankenstein in London); Sherlock Holmes & The Vampires of Eternity; The Stones of Camelot; The Wayward Muse.* (anthologist) *The Germans on Venus; News from the Moon; The Supreme Progress; The World Above the World; Nemoville; Investigations of the Future*
Jacques Spitz. *The Eye of Purgatory*
Kurt Steiner. *Ortog*
Eugène Thébault. *Radio-Terror*
C.-F. Tiphaigne de La Roche. *Amilec*
Louis Ulbach. *Prince Bonifacio*
Théo Varlet. *The Golden Rock. The Xenobiotic Invasion; The Castaways of Eros; Timeslip Troopers* (w/André Blandin); *The Martian Epic* (w/Octave Joncquel)
Paul Vibert. *The Mysterious Fluid*
Villiers de l'Isle-Adam. *The Scaffold; The Vampire Soul*

Philippe Ward. *Artahe*
Philippe Ward & Sylvie Miller. *The Song of Montségur*

MYSTERIES & THRILLERS

M. Allain & P. Souvestre. *The Daughter of Fantômas*
A. Anicet-Bourgeois, Lucien Dabril. *Rocambole*
A. Bernède. *Belphegor*; *Judex* (w/Louis Feuillade); *The Return of Judex* (w/Louis Feuillade); *The Shadow of Judex*
A. Bisson & G. Livet. *Nick Carter vs. Fantômas*
V. Darlay & H. de Gorsse. *Arsène Lupin vs. Sherlock Holmes: The Stage Play*
Séamas Duffy. *Sherlock Holmes in Paris*
Paul Féval. *Gentlemen of the Night; John Devil; The Black Coats ('Salem Street; The Invisible Weapon; The Parisian Jungle; The Companions of the Treasure; Heart of Steel; The Cadet Gang; The Sword-Swallower)*
Emile Gaboriau. *Monsieur Lecoq*
Goron & Emile Gautier. *Spawn of the Penitentiary*
Rick Lai. *Shadows of the Opera: Retribution in Blood; Sisters of the Shadows: The Curse of Cagliostro*
Steve Leadley. *Sherlock Holmes: The Circle of Blood*
Maurice Leblanc. *Arsène Lupin vs. Countess Cagliostro; Arsène Lupin vs. Sherlock Holmes (The Blonde Phantom; The Hollow Needle); The Many Faces of Arsène Lupin*
Gaston Leroux. *Chéri-Bibi; The Phantom of the Opera; Rouletabille & the Mystery of the Yellow Room; Rouletabille at Krupp's*
Richard Marsh. *The Complete Adventures of Judith Lee*
William Patrick Maynard. *The Terror of Fu Manchu; The Destiny of Fu Manchu*
Frank J. Morlock. *Sherlock Holmes: The Grand Horizontals; Sherlock Holmes vs Jack the Ripper*
Antonin Reschal. *The Adventures of Miss Boston*
P. de Wattyne & Y. Walter. *Sherlock Holmes vs. Fantômas*
David White. *Fantômas in America*
Pierre Yrondy. *The Adventures of Thérèse Arnaud*

SCREENPLAYS

Mike Baron. *The Iron Triangle*

Emma Bull & Will Shetterly. *Nightspeeder; War for the Oaks*
Gerry Conway & Roy Thomas. *Doc Dynamo*
Steve Englehart. *Majorca*
James Hudnall. *The Devastator*
Jean-Marc & Randy Lofficier. *Royal Flush*
J.-M. & R. Lofficier & Marc Agapit. *Despair*
J.-M. & R. Lofficier & Joël Houssin. *City*
Andrew Paquette. *Peripheral Vision*
Robert L. Robinson, Jr. *Judex*
R. Thomas, J. Hendler & L. Sprague de Camp. *Rivers of Time*

NON-FICTION

Stephen R. Bissette. *Blur 1-5. Green Mountain Cinema 1; Teen Angels*
Win Scott Eckert. *Crossovers* (2 vols.)
Jean-Marc & Randy Lofficier. *Shadowmen* (2 vols.)
Randy Lofficier. *Over Here*

ART BOOKS

J.-M. Lofficier & D. Taylor. *Tongue*Lash*
Jean-Pierre Normand. *Science Fiction Illustrations*
Raven Okeefe. *Raven's L'il Critters; Rave's Faves*
Randy Lofficier & Raven Okeefe. *If Your Possum Go Daylight...*
Daniele Serra. *Illusions*

HEXAGON COMICS

Franco Frescura & Luciano Bernasconi. *Wampus*
Franco Frescura & Giorgio Trevisan. *CLASH*
L. Bernasconi, J.-M. Lofficier & Juan Roncagliolo Berger. *Phenix*
Claude Legrand, J.-M. Lofficier & L. Bernasconi. *Kabur*
Franco Oneta. *Zembla*
L. Buffolente, Lofficier & J.-J. Dzialowski. *Strangers: Homicron*
Danilo Grossi. *Strangers: Jaydee*
Claude Legrand & Luciano Bernasconi. *Strangers: Starlock*